The
Pinnacle Club
by
Drew Thorn

Book 1 of The Sandy Powell Trilogy

THORNEBROOK
LLC

THE PINNACLE CLUB

Paperback ISBN: 978-1-7352612-2-5

Hard Cover ISBN: 978-1-7352612-3-2

Library of Congress Control Number: 2020911379

Paperback 1st Edition June 2020

Paperback 2nd Edition February 2021

Cover Art by Steve Bassett

Published by Thornebrook, LLC

Springfield, Missouri

Amazing Partner

Many thanks to my partner in life, Judy for making this journey through life so amazing. Special thanks for your editing, smoothing, and additions which made this a much, much, better novel.

Special Thanks

First, I must thank my amazing editor who patiently fixed so many grammatical errors. She also provided valuable input to speed up or better explain sections in the book. While she chooses to remain anonymous, she is not forgotten.

I would also like to thank the Springfield Writers Guild which inspires hundreds of writers here in the Ozarks. A special shout-out to the members of our Thriller group. They've all taught me so much and all have become close friends.

A very special group are fellow authors who have become a critique group. Your thoughts and feedback have been a tremendous help to my writing. They are outstanding authors check out their books.

Steve Bassett   Penname: Eli Pope

Bill Rogers   Penname: Malcolm Tanner

Tim Straus   Penname: Antim Straus

Yummmmmm

I would like to offer special thanks to the restaurants I know and love for permission to use their names in this book. Please go and enjoy their incredible meals and mention the book.

L'Auberge Chez François

332 Springvale Rd, Great Falls, VA 22066

Jimmy's Old Town Tavern

697 Spring St, Herndon, VA 20170

Charlie Gitto's

5226 Shaw Ave, St. Louis, MO 63110

Please note the author has visited and enjoyed dining at virtually all the restaurants and pubs mentioned in the book.

Prologue

Beaumont, TX

For millions of years, the sun beat down upon the oceans and diatoms flourished, grew, and died. They drifted down to the seafloor like greasy snowflakes. Over the millennia, they built up hundreds of feet deep. At some point, the oceans dried up and were covered with salt from the evaporating seawater. Time and pressure converted these decayed diatoms into oil, representing millions of years of solar energy. The real power today in oil is in the people that control it, and that power burns hotter than the sun that created it.

****

Malcolm Holden was obsessed with the breakup of his oil company by the Sherman Antitrust legislation. Today he had an illegal plan to put things back together.

It was a cool spring day in 1916 in Beaumont, Texas, the weather almost as rare as the dinner about to be served. Malcolm Holden was a close friend of Robert McKinley and while an unusual request, Robert and his family were all too happy to oblige and vacate their home for the day. The McKinleys' Beaux-Arts Colonial-style house was elegantly appointed. The interior was as stunning as the outside, with attention to every detail, ornate woodworking, Persian rugs, and graceful furnishings.

Malcolm had become friends with Robert during the Spindletop oil discovery. Robert and Malcolm both owned land at Spindletop, and they had prospered drilling for oil in the salt dome. Malcolm at 45, while wealthy beyond imagination, was everything people picture of a wild cat oilman. At six foot one, he had broad shoulders and a narrow waist; his big hands could easily grab a four-foot wrench or a person's neck. His dark nearly black eyes gave the clear impression of a man who won battles – not always fairly.

The dinner meeting was held in secret. Malcolm had brought his longtime butler, Cyrus, and personal chef, Rene Petit as well as his sous chef. Petit, a world-class French chef, was busy in the kitchen pulling together another festive dinner. A constant stream of French expletives emanated from the kitchen.

Malcolm, sipping a cup of strong rich coffee on the porch, was only mildly aware of the cool gentle breeze and the view of McKinley's gardens. His only thoughts were of propelling his company to even greater prominence.

Over the past five years, the government had worked hard both through legislation and the courts to decimate the monopoly he and a few others held over the oil business. Unfortunately, the government succeeded. The virtually complete control Malcolm and his business associates held had been gutted like a fish, and their power to drive profitable prices was nearly gone.

No doubt about it, Malcolm thought, a frown on his face, recreating the monopoly is key.

Malcolm expected Heinrick Schroder and Edward Walker to arrive shortly. He had confirmed that both had arrived in town, Heinrick earlier this week and Edward only yesterday. It had been a few years since they had seen each other, and today's meeting was risky due to the potential antitrust lawsuits of the government.

Malcolm was immersed in his thoughts when he was interrupted by his butler, Cyrus, advising him of Mr. Schroder's arrival. Malcolm met Heinrick at the front door. Short and a bit stout, Heinrick always had a twinkle in his bright blue eyes. People often read him wrong, believing he was a nice warm guy – he was not. Heinrick won his battles with his head.

"Heinrick, how was your trip?"

Heinrick looked Malcolm in the eye. "Great, I've got a Pullman car so the journey, while long, was smooth and productive. I now have an office in Denver, so I stopped to check-in; it was good to escape from Los Angeles. It's been over a year since I visited my wells here at 'Swindletop', so your meeting was not only an interesting idea - but it was also timely as well."

Malcolm thought, how appropriate to use the nickname 'Swindletop' since so many deals, wells, and profits here were the result of honest men being swindled or fooled by men like themselves.

Heinrick and Malcolm had just settled into comfortable caned high back chairs when Cyrus appeared. "May I prepare you a snack or perhaps something to drink?" he offered.

Malcolm told Heinrick, "My chef Rene is preparing something for an early dinner so make certain you leave space."

Heinrick said to Cyrus, "I would like a muddled Bourbon Old Fashioned with a touch of mint."

Malcolm thought for a moment. "Cyrus, make that two, the mint sounds like an interesting touch and will fit well with this bright weather."

Twenty minutes later, Cyrus appeared on the porch. "Excuse me, gentlemen, Mr. Walker has arrived."

Malcolm and Heinrick stood and moved through the house following Cyrus who opened the door just as Edward was walking up the front steps. The three old friends greeted each other warmly, as Edward moved into the front foyer. Nearly six-foot-tall of slight build with piercing grey eyes, no one would guess he was only 58.

"Let's retire to the porch, shall we? Dinner will be served shortly," Malcolm said.

Malcolm, Heinrick, and Edward moved through the house to the side porch and found that Cyrus had rearranged the chairs in a triangle. After the men had taken their seats, Cyrus took another drink order.

"Gentlemen, I've brought an absolutely stunning Scotch Whiskey I believe you'll enjoy," Malcolm said. Both agreed and Cyrus was off to prepare fresh drinks.

Cyrus returned with drinks and a box of cigars. He advised Malcolm that dinner would be ready in about an hour and then left the men to their business.

Malcolm began, "Edward, Heinrick, I want to thank

you for each taking a long journey to meet. The past few years, ever since the breakup of our company by the Sherman Antitrust Act, I have felt we needed to find a way around the laws so we could work together again."

Heinrick said, "I agree, I find it totally incredible that after all the money we paid those lousy politicians in Washington they still turned on us and ripped our industry apart."

Edward nodded, adding, "Those worthless bums, they're like leeches taking our money and not following through on their commitments to us. We need to find more trustworthy politicians to advance our agenda."

Malcolm continued, "The stark reality is you can never trust a politician, and we will never get them to repeal the antitrust laws. I believe we have to focus on three things, supply, demand, and competition. If we control all three, we can demand our price and reap the profits we deserve."

Heinrick interjected, "That's a great idea Malcolm, but our hands are tied with the antitrust legislation. What's your plan to work around it?"

Malcolm replied, "Heinrick, you're right getting around the legislation is key. I've thought about it a lot over the past several months, and I think I've come up with the solution."

Henrick and Edward leaned in toward Malcolm as if to close ranks.

"Let's hear it," Henrick said.

"First, I've chosen the two of you because I trust you. We're all wealthy, ambitious and we have worked together in the past. We could all retire now but that's not who we are. I believe we need to create a new company, an equally divided, joint, private company outside the United States that can protect the interests of our public companies. This company will focus on the three things I mentioned. Together we control about fifty-five percent of the oil business today, and I believe we can once again dominate the business. However, if we truly compete with each other, we will never dominate and reap the profits that are possible."

Edward said, "Malcolm, I agree with your outcome, your goals, but we're prohibited by the new laws from working together. We know Justice and now the FTC is watching to see if we try to bypass the law. They have too many investigators and the power of the courts to take us down. How do you suggest we avoid the Justice Department?"

Malcolm replied, "Obviously, this new company needs to be invisible, completely covert."

Heinrick interrupted, nodding slowly, "The new company has to be very small, too many tongues and one will leak. We can only hire people we can trust."

"Or ultimately control," added Edward, his eyes and tone making it clear what was meant by 'ultimately.'

Malcolm sat back in his chair, "I firmly believe if we keep competing with each other it will be our downfall. As I said when we started this conversation, we can only win if we trust and share with each other in secret. Together we will truly become rich beyond our imaginations, and we will control our destinies."

Edward added, "I agree, this is a good plan. We'll reap fortunes. But to really expand and keep things flowing we must find other sources."

Heinrick replied, "My friends, we're beginning to pull significant oil out of our wells near Los Angeles and I think we have discovered another Spindletop in Wyoming near Casper."

"Great news," Edward said, "Let's buy up the property and capture the supply before we get a bunch of wildcatters sucking off the easy money and pushing the price down."

"Of course," Heinrick said, "But there's a hitch in Wyoming. The government owns the land and the mineral rights. In fact, the Navy controls it and says it's essential for national defense."

"When I'm back east, I'll push the Secretary of the Interior to take control over the Navy; it's their land. I'm sure some money spread around Interior will grease the skids because traditionally that's a very sleazy organization."

Malcolm added a thought to the conversation, "Gentlemen, we also must consider foreign opportunities for supply."

"Agreed," Heinrick said, "In fact, I've been pursuing a few ventures in Germany, and Baku near the Caspian Sea. They have some interesting new developments we should pursue."

Edward piped in, "We have been having good fortune with wells in Persia, I will get both of you some information on those wells."

Malcolm put his hands up. "My friends, I believe we have covered the big issues on supply. We will come back to all of this later but let's discuss demand."

Heinrick raised his hands. "As I was about to say, one of the interesting developments from Europe is the distillation of crude oil. We know the light sweet in Pennsylvania can be used almost out of the ground but the oil in Europe isn't of the same quality. They call the process refining and essentially build large stills similar to what's used for whiskey. They separate the oil into various components but with much more control than we have here. The result is they have many different products to sell, increasing the value of each barrel of crude."

Edward, always patient, but on-point said, "I stopped on my way here and met with Henry Ford. His model T and similar horseless carriages are beginning to sell, and they run on gasoline. I remember when we used to dump it in the river in Pennsylvania back when we made kerosene for lamps. We discussed his plans in some detail, and he certainly has a passion for success. I invested $100,000 with Ford in exchange for stock to help prop up his growing company. If he can continue to build cars as cheap as he suggests everyone will need gasoline."

Malcolm added, "I've been very pleased with my horseless carriage, simple, easy, and at least as comfortable as a horse-drawn coach. I agree if he can build them as cheap as he says everyone will want one and will be able to afford it."

Edward thought for a moment. "Several other fledgling companies are trying to build autos. Why don't each of you support a company? You know how we believe in competition." They all laughed.

Cyrus approached the men on the porch. "My apologies gentlemen for the interruption but dinner is served."

"I knew you had a good reason, as always," Edward said, nodding his approval and understanding.

"Now the most important leg of the table," Malcolm continued, "My biggest concern is competition. I see it in two ways. First is, of course, other oil companies, and second is other forms of energy. I think we have a compelling case against coal for transport, such as rail, ships, and of course autos. But electricity and city lights are still using coal and coal gas. There's talk about building more dams to create electricity. All of these threaten demand."

Heinrick said, "Some of this we can overcome with a steady supply and a solid business proposition. Oil is so much cleaner. We can assure our markets of supply and at the same time create problems in what others supply. In the end, we benefit."

Edward nodded and spoke thoughtfully, "Agreed, my concern is the unknown sources of energy. There are bound to be new inventions. If we can disrupt them early, it will be much less expensive than competing with them after they're established."

"Ok, I think we agree on the competitive nature," Malcolm began, "And we will disrupt where we can and be ever watchful."

The conversation slowed a bit as the men enjoyed a delicious dinner of parsnip soup, duck a l'orange, imported cheeses, and classic vanilla crème brûlée with a touch of mint. Fine wines were paired with each course.

After dinner, they continued their discussion with brandy and cigars on the porch. They talked at length about the division of tasks, funding, and forming the new company. Just as they were planning how they'd divide the country between their public companies for sales and marketing, they were interrupted by Richard, Edward's security guard.

"Excuse me, sir," Richard said, "We caught a reporter from the Beaumont Enterprise sneaking up on the house. We took him down, and he is bound and gagged."

Edward asked, "How much does he know?"

"It would appear, nothing sir, he never got close enough to the house to see or hear anything."

Malcolm interrupted, "Edward, obviously he was on to something by the fact he was here." Then turning and looking straight into Richard's eyes he said sternly, "I suggest you gents dispose of him but make it look like an accident, perhaps a broken neck from a fall from his horse. We will all be ready to leave shortly so you can bring him and his horse and dump the body close to town – far away from here."

Edward added, "Tell the others we will be ready to leave shortly."

Richard nodded and disappeared as quickly as he had arrived.

"Well, gents it has been wonderful. I believe a very profitable afternoon and evening," Malcolm said, "Again, I want to thank you for traveling so far. What do you suggest we name our new venture?"

Edward replied, "How about the Pinnacle Club? We're at the top of the game, and it's a very private club."

"Perfect," Heinrick said. They all clicked their brandy snifters and said: "To the Pinnacle Club."

The gentlemen stood up, shook hands, and agreed to stay in touch through secret channels.

Part One

Dick Powell was a natural inventor. His inquisitive mind constantly got him into trouble growing up on a small hill farm outside of Manchester, Vermont. From the time he was ten years old Dick had worked odd jobs on neighboring farms and at the sawmill in Shaftsbury a few miles from home.

At dinner, Dick's dad said, "Dick you received a letter today."

"Wow, thanks." Dick opened the letter and read quietly. "You won't believe it. I won that state-wide scholarship contest, and I'll get $400 a year for all four years of college. I could go to college this fall."

"You make us so proud, son. I can give you a hundred dollars a year, but you'll have to come up with the rest. Where do you want to go?"

"I have always dreamed of going to Rensselaer Polytechnic Institute in Troy, New York. The tuition at RPI is $600. Then add in books, fees, along with room and board, it'll be about $1000 a year. Between the scholarship, Dad's money, and what I've saved I can cover the first year."

Chapter 2   Houston, TX   1949

A warm muggy evening, three old friends gathered for dinner in a small Italian restaurant. They'd rented out the restaurant for the evening. Strategically placed around the perimeter were security guards dressed in plain clothes. Personal bodyguards were inside. This dinner, like so many in the past, was held in secret.

John Whitney, Cordell Holden, and Buck Weekes were now in control of the three largest oil companies in the world. Their reach was global, their power immense. Each company was a household name and publicly appeared to be fierce competitors. While in secret, they continued to plan and operate as one large firm.

John looked every bit the corporate executive he was. Running the global operations of American Petroleum demanded his constant attention as the new property, mineral rights, and companies were acquired by the company. The company had expanded operations by licensing dealers throughout the US heartland and had subsidiaries beginning to form in the rubble of Europe. "Cordell and Buck, it's always too long since I saw you last. It's a shame we can't get together more often, more openly. Roughly 35 years ago our founders started what we've come to know as the Pinnacle Club, and here we are again celebrating success, telling war stories, and planning the future."

Buck was every bit a Texas oilman as his father-in-law Heinrick Schroder was German. Buck had met Heidrick's daughter, Heidi, at a party in Beaumont, near Spindletop, and they lived in Los Angeles. While Weekes appeared as if he worked on an oil rig, he was actually a brilliant strategist, who'd a nose for finding oil. Like American Petroleum, Sunco Power was global and very profitable for its stockholders. Sunco marketed gasoline and oil products both through franchises and company-owned stations. Weekes liked the fact that he controlled his retail chain. His operations ran on the West Coast from Canada to Mexico. He also had operations covering half of Canada. In some states, he and Whitney's company competed fiercely though, in reality, it was all a ruse to keep the Justice Department out of their hair. Buck leaned forward and said, "John you're right we've done very well."

Cordell Holden ran TXO out of New York City. Like the others, operations were global and TXO's marketing focused on the East Coast and South America. Cordell was a numbers guy like his predecessor Malcolm Holden. Everything about Cordell was average, and he didn't stand out in a crowd except his hawkish nose and his near coal-black eyes. "Buck, how's Heinrich these days? "

"Thanks for asking, he's well, enjoying retirement. He spends a lot of time at the beach with his grand kids, but he still comes to the office once or twice a week, and he is always thinking. I still think his most brilliant idea was the Hindenburg. Getting a dirigible to blow up was almost easy but getting the newspapers to focus on the hydrogen gas as the cause of the explosion was absolutely brilliant."

"Well, my favorite is the Teapot Dome scandal. First, The Pinnacle Club got control of the oil switched from the Navy to the Interior Department then they got President Harding and Albert Fall, Secretary of the Interior, to take the blame for the leases which ultimately, our companies won. The whole thing was so well-planned from start to finish," Cordell said.

"Agreed, gentlemen, we've weathered the Great Depression, profited from the war, and emerged controlling the oil business in the US and much of the world, but I'm as concerned as ever that our business is threatened," John said. "Our business is selling energy to the world, powering industry and cars. The nuclear bombs dropped in Japan represent almost unlimited energy and could threaten to take away our business."

"John, I concur with your assessment, but I've a strategy for this," Buck said. "Just like the Hindenburg scared people about hydrogen, we need to create the same panic about nuclear energy. I think we've several years before scientists figure out how to harness the atom. We need to build our defenses now, so we're ready for this new competition."

Cordell said with a grin, "Buck, are you suggesting we influence people on nuclear?"

"I believe we create two lasting images in the public's mind. First is the nuclear blast, this huge ball of fire. In addition, the images of people near the blast that survived but were burned or poisoned by the bomb. We have to make this form of power very scary to people," Buck said. John and Cordell nodded their heads in agreement.

John said, "I've one other item of business we need to discuss. As our reach has extended globally, it has become increasingly difficult to keep track of all that's going on around the world. I would like to recommend that we have our joint shell company retain the services of Paragon Research. Paragon has a global reach; it's a small tight company that does both investigative research and has a paramilitary arm that can be quite effective in challenging situations. I discovered them when we had a dispute in Baku, Azerbaijan a few years ago. They pulled together information that pointed to several key politicians who were influencing against our interests. Based on this information, Paragon sent in a very small paramilitary group and eliminated the problem."

"John," Buck responded, "It sounds interesting, but how do we know they'll keep our joint interest quiet, and how do you plan to use them?"

"First, they're a virtually invisible organization based in New York City. They use small offices around the world that they call cells. Only the top few people know about the cell details. Each cell is isolated and doesn't know about the assets of the other cells. So, any information breaches are contained. My plans are to have them keep an active watch on our mutual interests globally and watch for any competitive companies or energy sources."

Cordell nodded and replied, "If you feel this is a good investment then I'll support it. We all know that we always need more information and occasionally we have issues that need elimination. In fact, I know someone in mind in the Middle East right now for whom it would be helpful if he had an accident. How much do they cost?"

"The cost is manageable; they'd work under our shell company of course. A $500,000 per year retainer gives us an exclusive. As they do work for us, they bill us time and materials, so we just keep funding the retainer. They estimate about $1 million per year from each of our companies unless we have a major action."

Buck said, "Let's do it." And Cordell nodded his head in agreement.

Over dinner, they discussed at length developments in the Middle East, including opportunities to support political leaders, and the realignment of Middle East countries by the British and French.

Chapter 3   Washington, D.C.   1957

Jerry Weathering couldn't believe his luck. He'd joined the Patent Office in 1936 and had been there for 20 years. Shortly after joining the Patent Office, he was transferred to a new division to examine energy patents. He still recalled the evening many years ago when he'd been approached by a man in a bar.

Paul had offered to buy him a drink and as they conversed over many topics, they moved to a booth and ordered dinner. Their conversation turned to life and money. Paul said he would pay $300 per copy of any patent filings Jerry discovered that posed a threat to current forms of energy. If Paul's boss determined a patent never needed to be issued, Jerry would be paid an additional $700. How Jerry derailed the patent was up to him.

Jerry couldn't believe his ears and repeated back to him, "Let me get this straight. If I come across a patent related to a new form of energy, and I derail it, I get a total of $1,000."

Paul replied, "That's right".

"Paul, I see ten to twenty new patents a week all related to energy. You don't want to see all of them, do you?"

"No obviously not," Paul frowned. "I only want to

see patents that relate to new ways to create energy. You need to determine if you think it's of value and don't send me a lot of bullshit or this deal is off," he said in a firm tone.

"So how do we meet?"

Paul looked at Jerry and said, "We don't. Do you have an outside windowed office?"

"Yes."

"Well, when you've got something. I want you to put a bright red coffee mug in your office window and then you can drop the document at an agreed-upon location. I'll leave the money for you in the same spot. Where do you live?" Paul already knew the answer but needed to bring Jerry along.

"I live in Alexandria right across the river at 263 West Linden Street just off Russell Road."

"Check your mailbox on Friday, and I'll give you full details. Just to show you how sincere we are, here is a little something." Paul palmed $500 to Jerry as they shook hands. Paul slipped out of the booth and was gone.

Jerry shook his head in disbelief. He couldn't believe his luck but a part of him wondered what he just got himself into. But, for the money... and he knew he was in.

Jerry had never seen Paul again. He never even learned his full name and he guessed other people did the drop because the handwriting changed from time to time.

Chapter 4   Great Falls, VA 1959

Dick Powell fondly recalled the first time he met Admiral Keyes several years ago. The Admiral had been transferred from the Naval Base in San Diego to Washington to manage the engineering efforts.

"Commander Powell, a pleasure to meet you. I hear great things, and I would like to know your back story. Please have a seat and tell me about yourself."

"Thank you, sir. Well, I grew up on a small dairy farm on the hills of Vermont. I was lucky enough to win a scholarship and went to Rensselaer Polytechnic Institute, RPI, for chemical engineering."

"Great school, world-renowned."

"Two of the best things in my life happened my freshmen year. I met my wife-to-be, Mary; she was attending nearby Russell Sage College. The second thing was I met Captain Scott. Captain Scott was teaching the chemistry of munitions. He introduced me to the Navy, and I've been here ever since."

"Tell me a little bit about your Navy career."

"I was fortunate to be fluent in German, so spent a few months at the end of World War II in Peenemünde, Germany recruiting rocket scientists to move to the US. These days I work mostly at home in a lab built by the Navy to look like a barn. I'm close enough that if needed I can drive into the Navy Yard or Annapolis."

"Thank you, Commander. I look forward to reading your reports on new kinds of electroplating that will prevent ordinary steel from rusting."

Back home, Dick was at work in the 'The Barn' as he called it, but in reality, it was a full working laboratory. While the ground level and loft looked like a barn, beneath was a full 12-foot-high basement with secret stairs behind a cupboard. Being the consummate engineer, Dick had his notebook close at hand as he recorded his concoction of basic metal salts and catalysts. Dick had placed four steel plates in the water bath hung from a metal frame, each metal plate about one inch apart. At each end of the tank were large copper electrodes. Dick had added precisely measured quantities of various salts.

As Dick walked to another table to get more chemicals, he accidentally hit the power switch turning on the DC transformer. The transformer had been giving him fits for the past week, and he'd a new one on order. While he was at the other workbench measuring out more chemicals the transformer hummed away. Walking back to the tank with his chemicals he noticed the water boiling away and heard the distinct low hum of the transformer.

Dick always had a curved briar pipe hanging from his mouth, a habit acquired from his years with Captain Scott. Often unlit, it was an appendage of his face. Dick thought the water boiling this is strange. He cautiously felt the side of the tank and it was cool to the touch. He pulled a wooden match from a box on the table and struck it to light his pipe. BOOM, a large flash of blue light erupted from the top of the tank, and Dick was knocked ten feet across the barn floor, his head hitting the shelf on a bench anchored to the wall.

Several minutes later he came to. His head ached and it took him a moment to get his bearings. He noticed the ceiling above the tank had been scorched by the explosion, and he felt a knot rising on the back of his head. Slowly he gathered himself together and approached the workbench. Everything was in disarray, but the water was still boiling away. Dick turned off the transformer and the boiling stopped.

He thought to himself; best not light another match here. He turned on the basement exhaust fan and air poured in from hidden vents in the ceiling. The fan pulled air out of the basement, and it exhausted out through what appeared to be an old stone well about twenty feet from the barn.

Upstairs, he walked out the back door. His shoes crunched on the frosty grass as he approached the barnyard fence where three Guernsey cows were eating hay enjoying the warming morning sun. All three ambled over to the fence to see Dick.

Dick scratched Krista the oldest. She enjoyed being scratched behind her topknot right between her ears. Carol, the two-year-old, butted Krista out of the way, impatient to have the attention and her face rubbed. Robin, the third Guernsey and by far the most patient, stood alongside waiting until Dick rubbed her neck. A gesture that she enjoyed. "Well, girls I was just knocked ass over teacups." Dick rubbed the back of his head and felt the bump had grown to a significant egg.

He lit his pipe and contemplated what had happened.

Dick recalled his college days and how they'd burned various gases in the laboratory, gasoline, propane, butane, and hydrogen among others. Each had different characteristics. What was coming out of the tank? He lit his pipe and began to think. The cows realized they'd received all the attention they were going to get and wandered back to the hay rack, except for Robin who stood close by watching Dick and patiently chewing her cud. Dick thought about the chemicals in the tank and his only conclusion was it had to be hydrogen. There were no carbon compounds in the tank and carbon was the basic building block for most burning gases like gasoline and propane.

Dick returned to the lab. Once downstairs, he started straightening up the items that had been knocked about by the explosion. He made a few notes about what had just happened when his stomach told him it was lunchtime and the clock confirmed it.

Dick walked the 100 yards between the barn and the house. Having warmed up just enough, the grass was now damp, making a squishing sound beneath his feet. As he entered the house through the rear boot room, he removed his wet shoes and heavy coat before entering the kitchen.

Dick's wife Mary was at the stove warming up some homemade ham and split pea soup. Mary turned just in time to receive a warm peck on the cheek from her still very amorous husband of many years.

"Hi, honey. How was your morning?"

"Well, interesting! I managed to set off a small,

unexpected explosion but only my noggin was seriously damaged."

"Are you okay?"

"Yes, fine. Just an ostrich egg on my head."

Mary said with a chuckle, "Well maybe that bump knocked some common sense into that hard Navy head of yours. Oh, can you call the kids down to lunch?"

"Sure, dear. Josh and Beth, time for lunch" Dick blared. Feet could be heard heading down the stairs.

Beth was the first to emerge in the kitchen. "Hi, Dad." Beth was a beautiful 17-year-old just beginning to discover the world and, Dick feared, perhaps boys too.

Shortly behind her was Josh. Tall and lean he slid into his chair at the kitchen table. Josh was 12 years old with close-cropped light brown hair and an obvious bundle of energy.

Beth helped her mother by setting the table and getting milk out of the refrigerator. With everyone seated, Dick said a brief grace. The kids were home from school this week and enjoying the early Easter break.

Dick said, "Josh, I want you to clean out the cow stalls, put fresh bedding down and clean out the empty calf pen." Josh just nodded.

Mary said, "Your dad had a small explosion in the shop and bumped his head."

Dick kind of grumbled, "I want you kids to please stay out of the shop for the next few days while I work on this experiment."

Beth inquired, "Dad, what's it you're working on? "

Dick looked up from his soup. "Well, I'm not really sure. This one has me guessing. I'll share it with you when I understand it better."

After that, the talk turned to activities involving the kids – school, 4-H activities, and the like. Dick realized he'd made had the right decision bringing his family up in a farm lifestyle.

After lunch, Dick spent the afternoon documenting everything he could about what transpired that morning including information about the chemicals, the plates, and the transformer. It seemed pretty obvious that he was generating hydrogen gas out of the watery solution. When he replaced the solution with plain water no gas was generated. It's clearly a unique combination of electricity and the solution.

It was Friday afternoon, and Dick had long ago promised Mary he wouldn't work on the weekend, if possible. Being a bit anal, Dick spent the last hour cleaning up the shop. This always gave him a fresh start Monday morning.

He headed back to the house for a brief cup of afternoon tea before he went to the barn to milk and make certain all the animals were bedded down for the evening. Beth was in the kitchen and put on the kettle as she saw her dad walking to the house. When he entered the kitchen she asked, "Dad how are you feeling?"

"Oh, fine honey, just a that nasty bump on my head."

Beth was always fascinated by her father's projects and eager to learn all she could. "So, what happened?"

As he drank his tea, Dick told his daughter about his experiment.

Beth went into the parlor where her Mom was mending clothes and said, "Mom, I'm going to go out and help Dad with chores."

"Okay honey, just make sure you put your boots on and a warm coat - it feels chilly out."

Beth and her dad headed off for the barn together. Beth always loved being with him. He was so smart. She always learned new and exciting things when they talked. Her dad's confidence also created an aura of security and she always felt so safe when she was near him.

When they were in the milk house, Dick turned to Beth and said, "While you feed the cows, I'll start the milking. Just remember their grain and that Carol gets three scoops while the other two get two scoops." With that, he grabbed the stainless-steel milk pail and the short three-legged stool.

When Beth returned from feeding the cows, her dad was milking Carol. The Surge milking machine was gently pulsing away. Dick knew about how long each cow took to milk out. He leaned his head forward against her side just in front of her rear leg and above the udder. This natural indent gave him advance warning if the cow decided to raise her leg, although they rarely kicked, and he knew they liked being milked. Knowing she was nearly done; he felt each quarter to make sure it had milked out. He turned off the suction and carried the milking machine out to the alley behind the cows where he removed the lid and poured the warm milk into the stainless-steel pail.

Krista, knowing, she was next, had leaned over tight to Carol. It was almost a game as Dick pushed her back over to create the opening where he could sit between the two. Dick was always fascinated at how cows knew just how to position themselves so that they could maximize contact with him. It was almost like a cat rubbing against your leg.

Beth sat on a bale of hay behind the cows. "So, Dad, what happened in the shop today."

"I think I may have come up with a new way to produce hydrogen gas."

Beth knew that hydrogen was the first element on the periodic table and that hydrogen and oxygen made up water and she shook her head, perplexed. "OK," she responded. "That sounds like a big deal, but I don't understand, why did it blow up?"

Dick was still sitting on a stool and leaned into Krista. Without looking up he smiled and nodded slowly. "You're correct. It's or could be, a very big deal. And it blew up because hydrogen is very flammable. It burns like gasoline but doesn't make any fumes. When it burns basically it creates water."

"So, then why don't we use hydrogen instead of gasoline?" Beth asked, a puzzled look on her face.

"Well, I guess a couple of reasons; the first is that hydrogen is a gas and gasoline is a liquid which makes gasoline easier to handle. The other thing is it takes more energy to create hydrogen than you get from burning it."

"Where did the hydrogen you created come from?"

"Had to come from the water in the tank."

"Do you think it took more energy to create it than you produced?"

"Beth," this time Dick looked up and smiled at his daughter, "That's the million-dollar question I'll have to figure out next week, but my guess is perhaps not." And he chuckled, shook his head, and said, "You do ask great questions that make me think."

Beth just smiled as she carried the last pail full of the rich golden milk to the milk house. She poured the milk through a strainer and into glass bottles. A small old refrigerator in the milk house kept the bottles cold. When she returned to her bale, she said, "Looks like enough for Mom to make some butter and cheese tomorrow."

"Yes, dear. We will bring one bottle with us tonight, so we have milk in the house for the morning."

As he walked back to the house, Dick thanked Beth for all her help and he thought, did it take more energy?

Dick couldn't help but think about his discovery all weekend. Monday morning, right after chores and breakfast, he eagerly went to the lab. Starting with a clean table he reassembled everything just as he had it on Friday. He poured the solution he saved from Friday into the tank and positioned the plates and the transformer. When he turned on the switch, sure enough, the solution bubbled, and gas was produced.

Dick then replicated the entire setup on another table. He fabricated a sealed top to the tank that had a short pipe for attaching a hose. The hose looped down and attached to the bottom of another container half-full of water. Dick knew from his college days as the gas was produced, it would go out through the hose and bubble up through the water. The water would prevent a flashback like what had happened on Friday. Dick mixed a new batch of the solution, set up the system, and borrowed the transformer from the original setup. Powered up, the solution bubbled away and generated copious amounts of gas.

Later that morning the new transformer arrived. Dick tried it out and could tell right away gas production was insignificant with the new transformer. What was the difference? Why didn't it work with the new transformer? He would have to figure out the difference quickly before the old transformer simply stopped working.

Over the next few days, Dick documented everything. According to his calculations, he was generating substantially more energy in the form of hydrogen gas than the electricity required to run the system. If this held true it was a massive breakthrough.

Dick was now faced with a true dilemma, was this a Navy invention or his own? He could justify it in his mind as his own invention. First, he was trying to develop a means to improve corrosion resistance, and this certainly had nothing to do with that. Second, if this really was a new form of energy production, then in the Navy's hands it might never see the light of day and could spend the rest of its useful life sitting on someone's desk.

Dick knew he had to talk to his superior, Admiral Keyes, about his discovery and get his blessing on how to proceed. Dick contacted the Admiral's office at the Navy Yard and got on his calendar.

Friday morning Dick sat stiffly in front of the admiral. He briefed him on his current project for a new steel coating and his discovery of hydrogen gas production. After considerable thought and discussions, the Admiral agreed with Dick that he would retain ownership of his discovery. The Admiral asked Dick to keep him fully apprised of any new developments. The Admiral said he would send Dick a letter authorizing him to spend his free time on the gas experiment and that he was the inventor.

Several weeks later Dick completed writing the patent for his invention. He enjoyed visiting the Patent and Trademark Office in the Commerce Building on

Constitution Avenue and E Street to check out and understand existing patents. In his research at the PTO's library on existing hydrogen gas generators, he was surprised to find only a handful. He completed the patent and hand-delivered it to the PTO, received a receipt for the filing, and watched as the clerk stamped it with the receipt date. The clerk took the patent and slipped it into a letter sorter in the slot marked Energy. Dick sighed knowing that he had his patent was filed.

Arriving home, Dick packed up the experiment in several boxes and put them on a shelf in the lab. He continued his work on corrosion-resistant electroplating.

Chapter 6   Washington, DC

It was June 1957 when Jerry finally read Dick Powell's patent for producing hydrogen. He recognized this was likely $2,000 in his pocket. Over the years the price had gone up, but one thing never changed - he could use the money.

Jerry once again placed the old red coffee mug in his office window and a copy of the patent in a plain brown envelope. Tonight, he would put the envelope in the drop spot, and tomorrow he would pick up the initial $800.

Carla Sanner took her daily stroll up 14th Street past the Patent Office in the Commerce building as she checked two windows with a quick glance. Each window was a different informer. Carla was a petite blonde, her cropped hair and lack of flash made her look the part of a tourist or local housewife, perfect in her role. She immediately noticed the red coffee mug in the window on the third floor, second from the left of the last wing. She didn't know or want to know who the source was, but she immediately knew the drop spot for this source, an old fake fallen tree in the woods in Alexandria. This one was paid $800 for first spotting the patent and another $1,200 when it disappeared. The amounts varied depending on the person and, even though she had a coded note in her purse with the amounts, she knew them all by heart. Carla checked four more buildings in downtown DC, stopped at the bank for the cash, and went home.

Carla left a note for her husband, Aaron, who was still at work patrolling his beat along Constitution Avenue. Aaron was a DC cop and had been a close friend of Ray Lewis, the president of Paragon Research when they were in the service together. When Ray took over Paragon, he arranged the job for Carla. She loved it, for the most part, because it was so easy. She walked around DC to see if various people had information for the firm and was well paid for her efforts.

Carla took the bus from their apartment near Capitol Hill across the Potomac. She changed buses in Rosslyn and went south to Alexandria. She knew she would be early and went to a favorite coffee shop to wait. Carla went to the drop a little after 7 p.m., reached under the fake log, and removed the envelope from the shelf in the log. She then replaced it with the envelope that held the cash. Putting the unopened envelope in her bag, she made a return bus trip home.

After reading Carla's note, Aaron had fixed a light dinner of ham sandwiches and canned peas. When Carla walked in the door, Aaron got off the couch and gave her a warm embrace and a brief kiss on the lips. "How was your day?"

"Good," she replied. Carla was slipping out of her overcoat. "I had one pick up and all went well. Let me change into something more comfortable," she said with a wink.

"You got it with pizzazz dear," the husky tone of anticipation in his voice. "Let's go to the range this weekend. With you carrying all that cash you need to practice."

The next morning Carla went to the Paragon office at 11th and F Street. She'd become close friends with Max, the latest district manager. Max Silverman was a small man who looked like a bookish accountant, but Max's cold grey eyes left little doubt he would cut your heart out if crossed. Max knew of Aaron and Carla's relationship with Ray and her many years with the firm. While he'd only been with the firm a few years, he ran the office smoothly, and it was an important office for Paragon. In the Paragon tradition, Max was compartmentalized and didn't know the full nature of the firm's projects. Max took the envelope from Carla and added it to the stack to review.

Even in his short period with the firm he'd successfully led many assignments. Some were really easy. A word to the wise, and many lobbyists would drop an idea or a legislative push. For the more difficult lobbyists, cash was generally all it took. In Max's mind, lobbyists had no morals, their only interest was in the almighty dollar.

The inventors were a bit different. Most of them seemed to be nervous ninnies. Pressure could come by threatening to tell their bosses or share photos of an indiscreet evening with significant people. Once you understood what made them tick, you could generally push them over. Some would take a bribe and walk away from an idea. Unfortunately, there were some, the truly hardcore inventors, that could never let go of an idea and required more direct persuasion.

Later that morning, Max reviewed the copy of the patent in the envelope that Carla had brought in. The patent looked very solid and well written. The process described certainly led the reader to believe it could create hydrogen gas in abundant amounts and that the net energy produced far exceeded the energy required to operate the system. Clearly, this patent required attention.

With the patent information in hand, Max called in Doris Adams. Doris, a bit overweight, middle-aged mother of four was his best researcher. Given a few days, Doris could find dirt on a heavenly angel. Max asked Doris to investigate Richard Powell of Great Falls. She began to dig.

A week later Doris had a slim report she presented to Max. "Wow! A whole week and that's all you got?" Max exclaimed incredulously.

"Yup, the man is an honest-to-goodness-angel. Faithfully married, two kids in school, college-educated, small farm, a few cows, and works for the Navy doing research. No mistress, no debt that I could find, and Episcopalian."

"What makes him tick?"

Doris replied, "As far as I can tell, family and his work. Based on some of his filed patents, the guy is brilliant and works with explosives and metals for the Navy."

Max kind of huffed and said, "Ok, well, I'll take it from here, thanks."

Wasting no time, he went straight to the phone.

"Ray, this is Max in DC. I've got a challenging inventor. Can you send one of your specialists?"

"No problem," the man on the other end of the phone replied. "I'll have Tony meet with you at your office in a few days."

Several days later, Tony Ammasso knocked on Max's door.

"Hi, you must be Tony. Welcome to Washington."

He replied, "Glad to be here. How can I help?"

"Well," Max began, "I've got an inventor that's as clean as a whistle, and I think perhaps an unusual approach could get him to stop his new invention."

Max continued to brief Tony on what Doris had learned and provided him with individual photos of the Powell family.

Tony said, as he was leaving Max's office, "This sure is uncommon. I'll let you know how it goes down. See you in a few days."

Chapter 7   Washington, DC

Tony Ammasso slept in, which was easy to do under the plush, down comforter in the upscale hotel. It was a misty, dreary day in DC, and he was in no rush to drive out to Great Falls. After all, he didn't need to be there till 2 p.m.

When he finally did rise, Tony showered, got dressed, and put on a light raincoat and an old baseball cap. Over breakfast in a nearby coffee shop, he reviewed the plan and was pleased with the weather for the day ahead. With the rain, his attire was appropriate and, even more importantly, non descript.

Tony walked the mile from his hotel to the Key Bridge. Crossing over the Potomac, he enjoyed watching the river lazily flowing through DC headed for the Chesapeake Bay. Looking upstream, he could see the Georgetown boathouse and the beginning of the Potomac Gorge. He finally arrived in Rosslyn at the Virginia end of the bridge where he was looking for a diner with a parking lot in the back.

People were starting to break for lunch and Tony leaned against a building watching the parking lot in the rear of Billy's Diner. After ten minutes, the truck he'd been hoping for pulled in and parked. Two men got out and walked around the side of the diner and entered from the front. Tony knew they'd be in the diner for at least 30 minutes, so he waited a few minutes to make sure one of them didn't return for a forgotten item. He walked over to the green 1950 F-series Ford pickup truck. The truck with its classic snub nose had a six-and-a-half-foot bed. Tony easily popped the door lock and jumped onto the bench seat reaching under the steering wheel and hotwired the car.

Tony drove out George Washington Memorial Parkway towards Great Falls. The views from the ridgetop route over the Potomac gorge were beautiful, and he even stopped at one of the scenic pull-offs to admire the view. Then, taking Georgetown Pike, he motored past magnificent horse farms and country houses. The countryside was a mixture of rural America and occasional opulence.

Tony continued his drive west and passed near the Nike missile battery. It was part of 13 Nike missile batteries that surrounded Washington to protect against Russian bombers during the cold war. It was the world's first surface-to-air missile system. He drove into Herndon, Virginia, and parked on Locust Street a few blocks from the high school. It was 3:00 so he had a short wait until school let out at 3:30. He really appreciated all the research that Doris had completed, even knowing what bus the Powell kids would take. He looked again at the photos of Beth and Joshua.

Fifteen minutes later he ambled down the street toward the high school. He would look like any other parent waiting for the kids to be released. A few minutes later he spotted Beth and Joshua.

Tony walked up to Beth and Josh well before they

got to the bus. He reached into his breast pocket and pulled out a thick sealed letter-size envelope. Tony said to Beth, "Excuse me, Beth, would you give this to your father."

Beth had a surprised look. "Sure," not knowing what else to say. Tony continued in the same direction walking away from them.

****

On the bus, Beth asked Josh, "Do you know who that was?"

"No idea. Must be a friend of Dad's."

They rode the bus home to their drop-off on Georgetown Pike at the end of their road. Beth and Josh walked down the gravel road enjoying the now clear sky with the abundant smell of the wildflowers enhanced by today's light rain. The envelope in Beth's book bag was forgotten as they entered the kitchen, and each grabbed a sandwich Mary had made for them. After eating and changing clothes they ran outside to see the cows.

After dinner, Beth started to work on her homework and came across the envelope. She went to her father and said, "Dad, a man gave me this when we left school today."

Taking the thick envelope Dick asked, "What man?"

"I don't know, he knew my name, so I guess it's some friend of yours."

"Ok, thanks."

****

Mary was in the kitchen as Dick opened the envelope in the parlor. He almost spit out his pipe as a pile of one-hundred-dollar bills and a letter fell out. He set the cash aside, unfolded the typed letter, and began to read.

Dear Mr. Powell, We have come to understand that you have created a method to produce gas. We strongly demand that you stop your efforts. The enclosed cash is to offset any future potential gains. Destroy all equipment, notes and stop pursuing this avenue. If you do not stop, you will be putting yourself and your family in extreme danger. This is your only warning.

Dick sat back in his old oak Morris chair, took a long pull on his pipe, and then another and another. Dick counted the money. $5,000. As much as his year's pay as a Lieutenant Commander.

Dick put the letter and cash back in the envelope. He went over to the walnut Davenport desk and opened the top. Pulling out one of the inside drawers, he reached inside and flipped the hidden latch, releasing the secret spring-loaded letter compartment. He added the envelope to the small pile in the compartment. He closed it and returned the top to its resting place. Dick walked into the kitchen and gave Mary a hug and said, "I'm going out to check on the cows. I will be back in a bit."

Mary said, "Everything all right?"

To which he replied, "Oh fine, just need to think for a bit."

Dick walked over to the fence. The cows were laying down and chewing their cud. Carol, the two-year-old rolled onto her front knees and then rocked forward and stood up with her rear legs and finally put her front feet under her. She arched her back getting a kink out and moseyed over to Dick at the fence.

He rubbed her head and neck while he pondered what was going on. His first thought was how did this person know about his hydrogen gas discovery? Only he and Admiral Keyes knew, and he trusted the admiral implicitly. Maybe it was someone else like the admiral's assistant in the Navy office, but he didn't think that could be the source. As he thought more it occurred to him that the patent office also knew about his discovery.

The more important questions, he thought, were who and why. Who'd threaten and pay that much money to stop his discovery?

And he realized it had to be someone who saw hydrogen either as a potential moneymaker or who felt it would be competition.

Of course, his patent filing didn't provide enough detail on his solution for someone to replicate the discovery but perhaps they'd already discovered the same thing and didn't want the competition. Thinking back to his days at RPI, Dick could think of several multiple independent discoveries like Isaac Newton and others discovering calculus as well as Darwin and Wallace both postulating evolution independently.

The flip side was someone who saw his discovery as a competitive source of energy. Inexpensive creation of hydrogen gas would compete with nuclear, hydro, and coal as well as oil and gas companies. He knew that inexpensive hydrogen would provide a pollution-free form of new energy at a low, almost free cost.

There was a long list of potential people or companies that his discovery threatened. The list was far too long to solve this way. Being an engineer at heart, Dick flipped the equation in his head; he had to work backward to solve the problem.

The bottom line, he was not going to let someone threaten his family, himself, or this world-changing discovery.

He began to formulate a plan to reverse the gears on this dilemma. First, tomorrow he had to eliminate the threat to his family.

Chapter 8   Great Falls, VA

Dick knew he couldn't make any drastic changes to his routine since someone might be watching him. He went about his normal routine and did his milking and a few chores before seeing the kids off to school. In the kitchen, he told Mary that something was going on and that he couldn't get into detail. But he wanted her and the kids to go to Grandpa's farm in Vermont for a few weeks.

"I don't understand why I need to leave. Are you in trouble?"

"I can't say but it's important for you and the kids to be safe. I'm going to go over to the Schmidt farm to ask if we can borrow his spare car, so you can drive up to Vermont tonight. I want you to pack some bags for you and the kids and stay in the house today."

"Dick, what's going on?"

He calmly replied, "As I said, there's a potential threat I'm aware of, and I want you to go tonight. I will be fine."

He walked through the barn and out the back door and then through the fields to the Schmidt farm. Kurt Schmidt was in the barnyard steering his dozen Holsteins out to pasture. Dick leaned up against the barnyard fence and patiently waited until Kurt closed the gate and walked over. With his slight German accent, Kurt said, "Dick how are you, haven't seen you since the fair last month."

"I'm good, Kurt. But I'm here because I need a favor."

"Of course, anything, how can I help?"

Slowly Dick said, "I would like to rent your old Nash for a few weeks. Mary and the kids need to go visit my grandfather in Vermont and I don't have a spare car. I'll pay you $25 per week and of course, return it full of gas."

Kurt looked at him and said, "You don't need to pay me, it just sits in the shed. Just take it."

"No, I insist on paying and will be very grateful to you for letting me use it."

Kurt climbed over the fence, and they began walking to the shed. He opened the car door and turned the key. The flathead straight 6-cylinder engine purred to life. The lime green Nash Rambler station wagon was not a huge car but given the sleek lines of the car with its rounded nose, it was easy to see how it got great mileage and was very dependable.

"There's a spare tire in the back along with the jack and wrenches. We just changed the oil before putting it away this summer."

Kurt climbed out and said, "I hope Mary and the kids have a safe trip and say hello to the family for me. There's no rush to get it back."

"I can't thank you enough." He handed Kurt fifty dollars and said, "I insist".

Dick drove home, parked the car in the barn, and

closed the doors. Inside, Dick went down to the basement and carried several boxes of stuff upstairs. He assembled the electroplating set up on a table. If someone came snooping around, he wanted them to think this was the discovery and not search for the hidden entrance to the basement. Confident that his first part of the plan was in place, Dick walked over to the house for lunch.

Mary had packed the suitcases. Dick told her that she and the kids would leave after dark and drive a few hours before stopping for the night. They'd made the journey many times from Virginia to Vermont, so she knew the way. The 450-mile trip would take a few days, but it was all main roads until they got to Bennington, Vermont, and then only another 30 miles on gravel roads to Manchester.

They ate a quiet lunch with an undercurrent of tension in the air. After lunch, Dick drove to Great Falls and called his father from a payphone in town. "Dad, something is going on here in Virginia. I'm sending Mary and the kids up to visit you and mom for a few weeks."

"Something going on?"

"Possibly, I can't go into details."

"I totally understand, and we will look for them to arrive in a few days."

"Thanks, Dad."

After dinner and under the cover of darkness, Dick, Mary, and the kids took the bags out to the Schmidt's car. Everyone had big hugs and Dick reminded the kids to be good. Mary shed a few tears when she kissed Dick. "You be careful and stay in touch."

Dick kissed her back, "Of course and I will be fine."

Mary drove down the road with the lights off till they reached Georgetown Pike and then headed east to cross the Potomac.

After they left, Dick went into the house and took his Winchester Model 70 wrapped in a blanket out to his truck and tucked it in behind the seat. Turning in for the night he took his prized Ithaca 'Colt Government' out of the bedside table drawer, pulled the slide back, put a shell in the chamber, and laid it on top of the table.

Tony had spent the day uncomfortably nestled in the woods just north of the Powell farm. He had observed Dick walk off and return with the Nash but guessed incorrectly that he'd gone to get one of Powell's cars back from a neighbor. He returned to the city at dusk and didn't see Mary and the kids drive off.

The next morning Dick was off to the barn a bit earlier than usual. He had slept well knowing Mary and the kids were safe, and there was nothing he could do yet. After finishing chores, he turned the cows out and went in for breakfast. He tucked his pistol into the back of his trousers and walked over to the truck. Not knowing if his phone line was tapped, he drove to town and called Admiral Keyes.

"Admiral, I received a letter yesterday demanding I drop the gas project I briefed you on a few months ago. Somebody found out about it and clearly doesn't want me to proceed. I'm unclear if it's a competitor with a similar concept or an energy company that wants it to go away. Any remote chance my discovery was disclosed by someone in your office?"

"Absolutely not from here. I didn't share our discussion with anyone and filed my notes on our conversation in my personal office safe."

Dick sighed. "As I expected but had to ask. Then it had to come from the patent office. I'll check that out."

"Dick," the admiral's tone was somber and a bit worried, "Would you like me to send a few Marines out to watch over you and the family?"

"No sir, I'm fine. I sent Mary and the kids to my father's place in Vermont for a few weeks while I sort this out. I need to do a little reconnoitering so no need to send in the marines yet. But thank you and I will keep you in the loop. I don't expect to be in the office for the next few days."

Keyes replied, "Take the time you need, but be safe and don't hesitate to call if you need support."

Dick drove back towards the farm but took a different approach so he could park a mile away from the farm on the north side. It was the only direction someone could hide since there were a pastures on the east, south, and west. Dick put the sidearm in his holster and slung the rifle on his back. He walked carefully toward the farm keeping his eyes open for someone spying on the farm. A few hundred yards down the road he spotted the guy sitting with his back to a tree watching the farm from the woods. Dick knew if he kept watching, the guy would instinctively sense he was being watched. Dick knew what he needed to know for now and carefully returned to his truck.

Circling back around he drove up to the farm from Georgetown Pike and acted as if all was normal.

The next day, after chores, Dick dressed in his best suit and drove into DC. He parked, then walked in the side door of the U.S. Patent Office. In the Greek-style rotunda, he approached the same person who'd received his patent many months ago.

"Hi, my name is Richard Powell, and I registered a patent application with you in April regarding an invention for energy production. I'd like to meet briefly with the energy examiner."

The pleasant gal behind the counter replied, "This is unusual sir, but I'll try to reach him to see if he is available for a brief chat. Please have a seat."

Dick sat on a nearby bench and patiently waited. About fifteen minutes later a short middle-aged bookish man with thick coke-bottle glasses appeared from a door across the lobby.

Dick stood and walked toward the man.

"Hello, are you Richard Powell?"

"I'm and I wanted to inquire about the status of a patent I applied for regarding a new method for producing hydrogen gas."

"I'm Jerry Weathering. I'm sorry Mr. Powell but we have no record of a recent patent filed by you. I've got over 500 patents waiting for review, and I quickly reviewed our log of incoming patents, and there's nothing in the log under your name for this year. Are you the inventor?"

Dick noticed the man was beginning to sweat and fidget like a child caught doing something wrong. "Yes, I'm, and I registered it with the lady at the counter in

April of this year."

"Well, again I'm sorry, but it must have been lost. Perhaps you could resubmit it."

Dick squared his shoulders and replied, "I will, but I've got another issue. It would appear that someone, perhaps you, Jerry, shared the patent information with someone else that's resulted in an unfortunate situation. Did you share my patent information with someone outside this office?"

Now sweating profusely, Jerry replied, "Mr. Powell, I don't care for your tone or your accusation. I wish you would leave this office before I call security."

Dick looked down on him straight through Jerry's thick glasses. "I will go now but you haven't heard the end of this from me and I've got powerful resources at my disposal." Dick turned, with ingrained military precision and left the man shaking in his polished black shoes.

When Weathering returned to his office, he wiped his brow and immediately placed his red coffee cup in the window.

Dick now knew something he didn't know this morning. He knew who leaked his discovery, but he still didn't know whom he shared it with.

Chapter 9 Great Falls, VA

Jerry Weathering's frantic note was in Max's hand the next day. He called Ray in New York and updated him on the situation.

Ray Lewis leaned back in his chair at the Paragon Research office in Manhattan and thought about what brought him to this moment. Nearly twenty years ago his father, Bob, had been a cop and then became a private investigator. Through hard work, luck, and fortune he'd grown and transformed Paragon into a global clandestine organization.

Bob had met John Whitney in 1939 and been retained to help him solve a problem in the oil fields in Baku. A few years later John again approached Bob with a project that transformed Paragon into the company it was now. Paragon was retained by a small company based in the Cayman Islands with virtually unlimited money to research competitive sources of energy and maintain information on competitive oil and energy companies. Paragon also influenced government officials and others to get lucrative arrangements for companies recommended by the office in the Caymans. Bob knew nothing about the company in the Caymans. Only that cash flowed freely.

Ray pondered the problem in DC and decided the cleanest thing was to see that Richard Powell had an accident. He put in a call to the Pinnacle Club to get approval to take this action. Several hours later he had the green light. His contact's final words were, "It seems the best solution, just make sure it's an accident." He put a call into one of his best, Chris, and soon he was on his way to DC to meet up with Tony.

****

Dick woke up very early and went out to the barn. He grabbed three halters off a hook and went to the pasture to awaken the cows. In the darkness, each slowly arose, and he put the halters on them. Having been to the county fair since they were calves, all were comfortable with the halters. Taking the three leads in hand, he started to walk across the fields and through the gates leading the cows to the Schmidt farm.

Kurt was in the barn just beginning to start milking when Dick arrived. Knocking on the barn door Dick said good morning.

"I need another favor. I may also be gone for a few days, and I was hoping you could add my girls to your herd. I'd be pleased if you'd keep the milk in exchange for their care."

Sitting on his three-legged stool putting the milker on the first cow, "Absolutely, happy to add your cows but probably won't want to let them go. They always look terrific."

"Well, once you taste that rich Golden Guernsey milk you probably will want more. Again, many thanks, Kurt. I will see you in a few days."

Dick walked back through the fields as dawn was

beginning to brighten his walk. He jumped in the truck and drove to Herndon. It was still too early to make phone calls, so he enjoyed breakfast at a diner. Afterwards, he called Mary, "Good morning, dear. How was the drive?"

"Uneventful. The Nash was a pleasure to drive, and we arrived yesterday afternoon. The kids were great and played in the backseat all the way. Your dad is a treasure, and all is well."

"Things remain complex here, but I'm starting to sort them out and plan to meet with the Admiral later today. I left a note in the secret spot in the pantry and there's an envelope in the secret compartment in the desk."

Mary asked, "What's going on?"

"Some people want to steal my discovery, but I'm getting to the bottom of it. Don't worry. I'll have it all sorted out in a few days. I'll keep you posted."

Dick next called Admiral Keyes's office to learn that he had to go to Norfolk and would return later that night. He made an appointment to meet the admiral at the Navy Yard the following day at 2 p.m. Dick then returned to the farm.

He went into the barn and discovered someone had torn apart his false setup on the table and left a note.

Mr. Powell this is your last and final warning. Cease and desist.

He went down in the secret basement carefully closing the entrance behind him. Dick worked in the basement straightening things up and making sure his hydrogen project was well packed away.

Carefully closing the secret door, Dick Powell exited

the barn through the backdoor, circled around, and walked to the house. He now was certain that his life was at risk, so he continued his plans. In the parlor he selected his favorite poem from a shelf, 'The Road Not Taken' by Robert Frost, and also took the book, 'The Autobiography of Benjamin Franklin' to the kitchen table. Just in case things went poorly, he wanted to create clues to help someone discover his secret, but he also wanted to make it difficult for someone to simply find it. First, he wrote a brief note.

Begin with my favorite. Remove all the spaces and punctuation.

1.6,1.1,1.22,1.3,2.10,4.19,1.10,1.18,1.7,

1.1,2.27,1.12,1.2,1.6,1.1,1.12,1.4,1.14,

1.6,1.8,2.24,1.20,1.4,1.10,2.10,2.27,1.6,

1.4,1.7,2.24,1.12,2.10,4.7,1.2,1.10,1.1,2.17

1.6,1.7,1.7,20

Then he took 'The Autobiography of Benjamin Franklin' and carefully covered the book with heavy white paper yielding a new white cover. He carefully labeled it 'The Water Gas' by Richard Beckwith. Having read the autobiography multiple times, he began to write on various pages in the book. He put the book in his bag that he took when going to the Navy Yard.

Dick then wrote a note to Mary. He opened the secret compartment in the pantry and left two envelopes. One simply addressed 'Mary,' the other labeled 'For the Future.' He added these to the other envelope already in the secret cupboard.

Dick went upstairs. Using binoculars, he spotted the watcher who was well-camouflaged on the edge of the woods. He was impressed, this guy was good. If he hadn't known where to look for him, he wouldn't have seen him from the house or the barn.

Now for Phase Two.

Dick walked out of the house straight to the truck without looking towards the woods. He jumped in the truck and spun the tires as he left the yard. He hoped this would give the watcher something to consider. As before, he drove back around and approached the farm from the north. Again, he crept up on the watcher. Taking his Winchester, he carefully sighted on the tree about a foot above the watcher's head and fired.

Bark flew everywhere, Dick pulled the bolt back ejecting the shell and fed another round into the chamber. The watcher hit the dirt and scrambled behind the tree. Dick yelled out, "This is MY last and final warning. Go away and leave me alone or next time I won't shoot the tree. Are we CLEAR!"

The watcher yelled back, "CRYSTAL!"

Dick walked backward the half-mile to his truck. He drove to Herndon to get an early dinner then returned to the farm. He hoped he was now safe but remained on guard. With the pistol back on the side table, he turned in.

****

Tony arrived back at the hotel in DC well after dark. There was an envelope waiting for him at the front desk. Tony read the note and called Chris's room. Together they walked quietly a few blocks and entered a steakhouse for dinner. In a quiet booth, Tony updated Chris on the events so far, finishing with today's details. It was agreed they'd drive out near the farm and see how things unfolded and look for an opportunity for an accident.

They drove past the farm and saw Dick's truck parked. Past the farm, they turned around and parked out of sight of the house. About an hour later, they heard the truck start and drive out of the yard. At a discreet distance, they followed the truck to Georgetown Pike and saw it head toward DC. Still maintaining a safe distance, they followed the truck to downtown Washington. They speculated along the drive that Dick was headed for his office at the Navy Yard.

****

Dick had a feeling he was being followed but couldn't be certain. At this time of day, many cars were driving into DC. He had an appointment with the Admiral at 2 p.m., but he had a stop to make before going to the Naval Yard. Dick drove east on Independence Avenue past the Tidal Basin and its famed Cherry Trees and the magnificent obelisk, the Washington Monument. Driving up the hill and past the Capitol, he turned left on First Street SE and was incredibly lucky to find someone pulling out, creating an open parking spot right in front of the Library of Congress.

Tony yelled out, "Watch it he just turned left."

"Not to worry, I got it, Chris said. They made the

turn and drove past Powell as he exited the truck. They circled around the Capitol and parked on Independence with a view of his truck.

Dick passed the beautiful Neptune Fountain and walked up the stairs to the right. He entered the building and walked through the Great Hall with its incredible marble floor and on through to the Main Reading Room. He walked up to the massive circular desk at the heart of the reading room. A librarian greeted him. Pulling his hand-labeled book wrapped in simple string out of his satchel. "I would like to add this book to the permanent collection for future generations."

The librarian replied, "Of course, we'd be honored Are you the author?"

"No, my father created this modification of Benjamin Franklin's autobiography with his notes."

"Again, an honor. Is there anything else I may assist you with, sir?"

"No, I've got to keep going. I've got a meeting at the Navy Yard, many thanks." Dick turned and walked back to the truck.

After climbing into the truck, he looked at his watch. It was nearing noon and his stomach told him he should grab a bite before what could be a long afternoon. Dick turned right on East Capitol and right again on 2nd Street and then took a quick left on Independence. After a block, he spotted a small restaurant on the left on the ground floor of a brownstone. With luck, he found a parking spot within a hundred feet of the restaurant. Dick crossed the street and entered the restaurant. While he ate lunch, he pondered the past few days determining what he would discuss with the Admiral to seek his advice.

Tony and Chris had to scramble to keep up with Powell but were lucky as they watched him enter the restaurant. Chris said to Tony, "I have an idea that could solve our challenge, clean and simple. Circle around the block." Before reaching the front of the restaurant they parked and waited.

Twenty minutes later, Dick walked out of the restaurant. What a delicious lunch, he thought and, confident in his plans for meeting with the Admiral, proceeded to walk back to his truck. He walked down the block and across the street to the truck. As he reached the vehicle and opened the door, a car shot down the street. Dick thought this isn't how I saw this ending and there was no time to get out of the way. The car struck him, and the door ripped off the truck. He was driven to the pavement, the car passing over his body. The impact killed him instantly.

Tony and Chris drove off, a simple hit and run with a stolen car. They drove several miles away from the accident and parked the car in an alley, leaving the keys in the car, then walked away, back to the hotel.

****

The Admiral was surprised that Dick hadn't turned up for his meeting. Since it was completely out of character, he felt concerned. The next morning as two DC policemen entered his office, he dreaded what they'd say, and he stood as they entered.

"Excuse us, Admiral, we were informed that Commander Richard Powell worked for you. Is that correct?"

"Yes, he does. May I inquire what this is about?"

Commander Powell was killed by an apparent hit and run driver yesterday. We're still looking for the car. We sent someone to his home in Great Falls, but there was no one home so we came here."

"Thank you, gentlemen, I know the family and will reach out to them from our office. Where's the body, and who do I need to talk to about the next steps?"

"You can contact the DC morgue, and they'll work with you. We will inform them to expect your call."

Admiral Keyes had the emergency contact details for Dick's father, but he didn't want to deliver this news over the phone. He contacted the Naval Reserve office in Albany, New York, and spoke with the commanding officer. He explained the situation and requested that a chaplain, a senior officer, and two fully armed Marines be sent to Dick's parent's house. He told them that they should escort Mary and the kids back to DC, adding they should do whatever it took to keep them safe.

The entire family was shocked, and all returned to Washington. The Admiral made arrangements for Dick to be buried at Arlington if Mary wished. When they finally arrived in DC the Admiral met with Mary in his office at the Navy Yard. They shared what each knew, which was not a lot. The Admiral said he would have two Marines stationed at their house 24-7 until they all felt safe. Mary decided she would prefer to have Dick buried at the Episcopal Church cemetery in Great Falls so his grave would be nearby. The following weekend a memorial service was held, and over a hundred neighbors and naval personnel attended. Admiral Keyes was honored to provide the eulogy.

About a week later when things had settled down and the kids were back in school, Mary recalled what Dick had said on their last call. She went to the pantry and opened the hidden compartment and found the two letters. She opened the one addressed to her.

Dearest Mary, if you are reading this, something terrible happened. I think it best you simply forget about my discovery and never discuss it again. I have left another note for someone in the future, someone strong and of good character, to consider taking this forward, but this is not for you or the kids. There is too much danger.

I love you with all my heart and want you to know that I am looking down on you and the kids from heaven. Please move forward with your life, and I look forward to seeing you in heaven, I pray, many years from now.

Love, Dick

Mary simply wept for an hour. She closed the compartment and didn't open the other envelope. Later in the afternoon, she opened the secret drawer in the Davenport and discovered the envelope with the warning letter and the cash. She put the letter and the cash back in the hidden drawer.

Part Two

Present Day

Chapter 11   Fairfax, VA

Sandy Powell woke up a few minutes before 5:30 a.m. like every other morning. A crisp spring breeze was wafting through the open windows. He swung out of bed, though some might describe it as a lurch, only to almost step on Copper, his golden retriever.

"Copper," he said in an exasperated tone, shaking his head but smiling at his faithful companion, "You've got to find a better spot. What's wrong with your dog bed?"

He leaned his handsome, strong six-foot-one frame over to rub Copper's ears. A former Navy SEAL turned high school biology teacher. Sandy loved his life. Great house and location, fun and interesting job that was stimulating, and of course, his wonderful companion, Copper. He smiled at these thoughts, and his blue eyes twinkled as he was off to the kitchen to make a strong pot of coffee and his routine morning call.

"Good morning mate," Sandy said over his Skype phone. "How are you tonight."

Sandy's best friend Jackson replied, "Well you know, just another fall day here in Australia. To translate to Fahrenheit for you Yanks, a cool 75 degrees, a bit of moon, and sitting on the back deck by the pool."

"Nice here too, cool light breeze, almost fell over Copper when I got up."

"Any other exciting plans for today?" Jackson chuckled at his best friend's recanting of the familiar morning routine.

"Well, I'm off to see Aunt Beth today. She called this week and asked me to stop by. I may go downtown tonight."

"From Aunt Beth to downtown in one day..." Jackson teased. "You know I'll expect a full report when you call tomorrow – especially about the downtown adventures."

"You got it," Sandy said smiling at his old buddy's interest in his social life – or maybe lack of... he thought a bit ruefully. "How about you?"

"Well today, I went into Sydney, down to the Rocks. You'll remember that old small pub on George Street, the oldest Pub in Sydney? I met up there with some old mates from the service. Plan to do a bit of surfing tomorrow over at Merewether Beach. There's a nice right to left break, and the swells have been good this week. Plenty of cute gals as well."

"I swear that's all you Aussie boys do is surf. Well, I've got to get my morning run in and then off to Aunt Beth's. Have a great sleep, my friend."

"Thanks, mate, you have a great day too. Say hi to Aunt Beth for me," and Jackson signed off.

Sandy lived in a traditional split-level home in

Fairfax, Virginia, a Washington, D.C. suburb. As normal, he and Copper started their day with a morning run in Mantua Park that was immediately behind his house. Then, after a shower for Sandy and breakfast for both, they were ready to hit the road.

"Copper are you ready for a road trip to see Aunt Beth?" Sandy asked. "Let's take the convertible." The 2014 Mazda RX-8 convertible technically didn't exist, but Sandy had pulled a few strings through a friend in Hiroshima who acquired parts from a prototype. Last winter Sandy did the conversion, and now he had a one-of-a-kind. When he completed the conversion, he completely repainted the car with a deep metallic blue with sporty yellow pinstriping. It was fast, sleek but not gaudy. He loved this car.

They jumped in the car and were soon off to Aunt Beth's home in Great Falls about 15 miles away. The Mazda purred down the road and snaked through the rolling corners on Trap Road. "Copper," Sandy sighed contentedly, "This car is so much fun to drive. It's like it's on rails." But Copper didn't reply, not even with his soft, 'woof' sound of agreement. Instead, he was standing on the seat with his head out the side window smelling a million scents and loving the rushing air. Sandy glanced at his dog, smiled, and thought how lucky he was to have such a great life.

Aunt Beth's turn-of-the-century farmhouse was on the right side of a long gravel lane. The white two-story house had black shutters and a full-size porch that ran the entire width of the front of the house. Several red barns and outbuildings were behind the house. Sandy pulled onto the gravel drive and spotted Aunt Beth tending one of the flowerbeds alongside the house. As soon as the car slowed, Copper leaped over the door and rushed over to Aunt Beth. Sandy ambled over while Copper, having already exchanged greetings, was off to discover rabbits and squirrels and any other potential playmates around the barns.

Sandy greeted Aunt Beth with a warm but gentle hug. Aunt Beth had the family's blue-green eyes, a slight frame, and at 72 was quite spry. "Aunt Beth you're looking well." He noticed the lawn always neat as pin, needed to be seriously mowed.

"Sandy, how about a cup of coffee while I enjoy a cup of tea? Let's go into the house and sit for a while, it feels a bit chilly."

Sandy thought this odd as the day was warming, but he nodded and whistled as Copper joined them on their way to the back door. The kitchen had been remodeled several years ago, so it was modern and airy with a small table.

"Sandy," Aunt Beth smiled a bit sadly as she looked into his face, "Why don't you take a seat while I put on the kettle."

Sandy nodded and thought as much as he loved his aunt, he had to prepare his mind for her instant coffee. It reminded him of his days in the service eating MREs, although they weren't his idea of a meal, and he was rarely ready to eat them. You did what you had to do.

As he looked down, Sandy saw Robert Frost's, "The Road Not Taken" on the table. He picked it up and began to read.

Aunt Beth noticed and said, "That was Papa's absolute favorite poem. When we were little, he used to read it to us at least once a week when we went to bed."

Sandy nodded as she put the mug of coffee down in front of him. "I always liked this piece too," he said, smiling a bit stiffly as he prepared to take his first sip of the brew.

Aunt Beth nodded "How about some cookies? homemade snickerdoodles."

Copper rested on the floor close to Sandy's feet eagerly watching Aunt Beth prepare the plate of cookies.

Sandy laughed. "My favorites and..."

"And if one happens to break up and fall on the floor for Copper," Aunt Beth grinned.

"That would be just fine," Sandy completed the thought.

After that, Aunt Beth sat down with her tea. Sandy started giving her updates about his students and activities at the school where he taught.

Aunt Beth, normally full of interest in her nephew's activities, seemed distant.

"Aunt Beth are you ok; you seem a bit tired."

"Well, to be honest," she looked him in the eye and said as calmly as possible, "My doctor discovered I've got cancer and it seems to explain why I've been a bit tired and peaked of late."

"My goodness, Aunt Beth!" Sandy exclaimed, concerned and shocked.

"Well, you know me with doctors, I don't follow

much of what they say and try to avoid them, but it's some kind of bone cancer. Unfortunately, it seems to have spread throughout my body, and my doctor felt it was untreatable. He said I've got a few months."

Sandy was moved, almost to tears. It seemed hard to believe his Aunt Beth, with whom he had always been close, might not be around much longer. She'd been there for him, had provided great advice when he transferred to the Pentagon, and then followed her footsteps into teaching. "How can I help?"

"You're too sweet," she smiled weakly, "If you could mow the lawn and do a few odd chores about the farm today, that would be a huge help."

Sandy spent the rest of the day working around the farm, mowing, trimming, and pulling some weeds. Aunt Beth stopped early, but Sandy and Copper kept going, and it was past five when they said goodbye to Aunt Beth, giving her a long hug and promising to come back very soon.

Sandy put the top up on the Mazda before he left as the day had turned a bit cooler.

He thought a bit about how he missed his dad, who'd died in an auto accident about five years ago, now Aunt Beth would be gone soon too. Then it would be just his mom. Since he had no siblings. He sighed and decided he needed to get out to St. Louis more often to visit his mother, to spend more time with her while he could.

Over the next few months, Aunt Beth's health continued to deteriorate. True to his word, Sandy spent more and more time helping her. During their visits, she told him stories about when she and her brother grew up. Many of her stories focused on his grandfather and his inventions. She also told Sandy that Papa had secrets, but she never would say anything further.

Finally, the pain and the tiredness became too much, and Aunt Beth had to be put in a hospice in Reston. In the last few weeks, she mostly slept. One day in July, Sandy received the call he knew would come but dreaded.

Aunt Beth was gone.

The memorial was a beautiful service with many of Aunt Beth's friends and former students attending. Aunt Beth was interred with her parents in the Episcopal Cemetery in Great Falls. The one bright note in all of this was that Sandy got to spend some time with his mom who made the trip from St. Louis to honor and remember her sister-in-law. He also got to see many other relatives, some of whom he hadn't seen for years.

After everyone left, life settled back to a sense of normality for Sandy with a new routine. On the weekend he and Copper would drive to the farm, mow, weed, and check on the house and barns, generally keeping things up as Aunt Beth had for so many years. About three weeks after the funeral, Sandy got a call from an attorney informing him that Aunt Beth had included him in her will and asked if he would like to attend a reading of the will on Friday.

"Of course," Sandy responded.

Friday dawned and Sandy joined several people in the conference room of Waldon & Sutter's office in

Reston. Aunt Beth's lawyer, Gary Sutter, entered the conference room and advised the others of their portion of the estate. She'd left generous amounts to the Great Falls Garden Club, two close friends, and the Great Falls High School where she'd taught for forty years. He then informed them that those who already received the information on their bequests would have to leave as the balance of the will was intended only for Sandy. Thanks and condolences were offered to Sandy for Aunt Beth's life and generosity.

Gary and Sandy took their seats again. Gary advised Sandy that Aunt Beth had left the balance of the estate solely to him. Sandy was beginning to think of her old furnishings and things about the barn and realized that the extent of her holdings was unknown to him.

"Mr. Powell you'll receive the farm, about 60 acres, house, and all the contents. There's no mortgage. After the distribution of the funds to the others, you'll receive approximately $270,000 in cash, stock, and insurance benefits. Your Aunt Beth further instructed us to provide complete assistance to you with the transfers and any tax issues."

Sandy was floored; he couldn't believe what was happening.

"Sandy, Aunt Beth also left you an envelope with clear instructions that you're to read this in private; I can step out of the room if you wish."

"No, no, I can read this when I get home." Sandy took the envelope and thanked Sutter for his assistance.

The Pinnacle Club formed in 1916 by three tycoons of the oil industry was now over 100 years old. The tiny office located in the Cayman Islands had a staff of five and two full-time security people. It was not on anyone's radar and planned to remain that way. Over many years, the leadership of the three parent companies had been passed down from one generation to another.

Jacob Holden, great-grandson of Malcolm Holden and CEO of Texas Oil and Gas, simply known as TXO was handing over the reins. Harold Watson, or as everybody knew him HW was now the new CEO. HW grew up in a tiny prairie town of Vega, Oklahoma on old Route 66. He went to Baylor for business and entered Texas Oil straight out of college. Eventually he was transferred to headquarters in Westchester, NY. HW had worked his way up the ladder and grown the company both vertically and horizontally. Last evening the board had approved HW becoming CEO and asked Jacob Holden to stay on as Chairman, recognizing that he would be semi-retired.

In Jacob's former and now HW's new CEO's office, Jacob turned over the reins to HW. "Well, HW,

THE PINNACLE CLUB | 61

welcome to the top, you earned it, and I've every confidence you'll grow and expand the company as the family has over the years. As you know, since I had no children, you're the first CEO of the company that isn't a Holden, which tells you how much respect we have for you. I'm here for you and welcome your thoughts on how to continue to grow the company. And understand that I will only provide advice at your request. However, there are things you need to become aware of that only the CEO knows."

"Jacob, thank you for your support, over the years you've been a guiding light and I will work hard to do justice to the family and the company."

"I know you will, HW. And now, more importantly, you must continue to work smart, as you always have. So only a few people on the planet know what I'm about to share with you. Over a hundred years ago, after the breakup of the oil barons by the politicians, a secret pact was created between my great-grandfather, Malcolm Holden, Heinrick Schroder, and Edward Walker. They created the Pinnacle Club, a secret club to control the oil, gas, and energy industries. As CEO, you'll replace me on an exclusive board which also includes Bryce Carrington, CEO of American Petroleum, and Reginald Clark at Sunco. Each of the companies secretly funds the Pinnacle Club which has a small office in Grand Cayman. Currently, the Club has about $300 million collectively in numbered accounts."

HW was surprised to say the least, about the revelation. "Jacob, what does the Club do?"

"The Club has stayed true to the vision of the founders. The three companies have worked together to control the supply, demand, and distribution of our crude and products. To the public and politicians, we're fierce competitors, but in reality, we're working together. The other area that we address is competitive forms of energy. We have a global clandestine research and paramilitary group, Paragon Research, that we pay millions a year to watch for new forms of energy or to influence governments to support our efforts."

Jacob continued, "For example, many years ago, an inventor discovered a method of inexpensively creating hydrogen gas from water. Fortunately, that inventor was killed by a hit-and-run driver, and the discovery never made the light of day. Another example is the oil fields in Ukraine. Our three companies have shared in 30% of the oil and gas production for decades because we control the politicians in Ukraine and Russia. Totally off the books and we don't touch the politicians; our research group does it. The Hindenburg was our group's effort to scare people about hydrogen. Three Mile Island was us; I could go on and on."

HW was stunned. "So, the group kills people."

"Sometimes but not often, usually cash or a threat of a scandal does the job."

"Wow, where does all the money go?"

"You now completely control hundreds of millions of dollars growing in offshore numbered accounts that you can use any way you see fit to invest in other growth areas and all off the books of Texas Oil. Today, you personally now have complete control of all of that. There's much more I will share with you over the weeks to come. Right now, I need to show you something."

Jacob walked over to a large painting of an old oil rig hanging on the wall. He reached up and pressed hidden buttons on the top and bottom of the frame. Then he swung the frame away from the wall, but the wall looked like the rest of the wall. Pressing again on hidden buttons, he swung the wall away, revealing a large safe with a digital keypad. First, he scanned his fingerprint and then entered a ten-digit code opening the safe. Inside were stock certificates, bonds, and a huge pile of cash. "There's a million in cash here in case for any reason you need it. In addition, tens of millions in stock certificates and bonds. All off the books. I will get your fingerprint and code registered next week. Again, it's completely up to you how to use and invest these funds and securities."

HW sat in a chair near the desk and pressed his fingers together, almost like he was praying. "Jacob, this is all amazing. Who'd have thought a cowboy from Oklahoma would be in a position like this. I don't have the words to thank you enough for this windfall and opportunity. I give you my sacred honor to treat your trust with confidence and integrity."

Jacob looked HW straight in the eye. "I know; otherwise, you wouldn't be in that seat. Let's go have a big steak dinner and celebrate."

Chapter 13   Fairfax, VA

Sandy arrived home after the reading of the will. He was amazed at his good fortune, and at the same time, missed wonderful Aunt Beth. He poured a generous glass of scotch on the rocks and sat in his favorite chair in the family room. Copper lay on his comfy rug near Sandy. He opened the letter from Aunt Beth.

My dearest nephew Sandy,

Knowing that you are reading this means I have moved on to a new and exciting place. Having lost so many friends over the years, I know your sense of loss. Please, rest easy I am in a happy place.

Just before your grandmother died, she told me of a family secret, and now I pass it on to you. A hit-and-run driver killed your grandfather, but it was not an accident. It was murder. He had made a discovery, and someone killed him to keep that discovery a secret.

She told me never to open the hidden envelope or speak of it to anyone. She told me to leave it to someone in the next generation after I died. That person must be strong, smart, and capable, and that you are. I was to warn you that the envelope could put you in danger and that you must be very cautious.

In the pantry next to my kitchen is a secret hiding spot. Go in the pantry and remove everything on the shelves in the cupboard on the right, including the shelves. You will discover the back of the cupboard can be removed and will reveal the letter left by my father to a future generation. I believe you are the person to discover what he left.

Whatever you learn, be careful and do not risk your life because neither my dad, your grandfather, nor I would wish that.

With all my love, Aunt Beth

"Well, Copper," Sandy said to his companion who looked up at him upon hearing his name. "This is an unexpected twist to the day. Let's have a nice dinner, turn in early, and drive out to the farm in the morning. There's no telling what we're in for."

The next morning after breakfast, Sandy and Copper jumped in the Mazda and were off to Great Falls. On the drive, Sandy thought about his good fortune. Great Falls, while appearing rural, was full of mansions. Football and basketball stars, lobbyists, and corporate executives lived in Great Falls. Sixty acres was worth millions of dollars, but he also loved the farm. Perhaps he should sell the house in Fairfax and move out here. A great idea he would have to consider. He rolled down the gravel road and turned into the yard, parking near the house.

Sandy unlocked the front door and turned off the alarm. Copper lay down on the floor in the kitchen and almost instantly was fast asleep. Sandy chuckled, *Oh a dog's life... I swear all you do is sleep.*

He went into the pantry and began removing all the cans, jars, and boxes from the cupboard, moving them to the kitchen table. Then he removed the shelves. Behind the middle shelf were two half-inch holes. Using his fingers, he pulled the panel out of the back of the cupboard. There were two envelopes on a small shelf in the space behind the cupboard. Sandy took them and sat at the kitchen table.

One envelope had no markings, and he opened it first. Inside he found three stock certificates. One was an old IBM stock certificate for 1,000 shares dated 1950. The second was 500 shares of John Deere dated 1953 and the third was 500 shares of Kellogg dated 1954. Well, this would take some work to figure out if there was much value, but very interesting.

The second envelope was addressed 'For the Future.' He opened it to find a strange carefully handwritten letter.

Begin with my favorite. Remove all the spaces and punctuation.

1.6,1.1,1.22,1.3,2.10,4.19,1.10,1.18,1.7,

1.1,2.27,1.12,1.2,1.6,1.1,1.12,1.4,1.14,

1.6,1.8,2.24,1.20,1.4,1.10,2.10,2.27,1.6,

1.4,1.7,2.24,1.12,2.10,4.7,1.2,1.10,1.1,2.17

1.6,1.7,1.7,20

Well, he thought, I do have a puzzle of sorts to solve. This will require some serious thinking.

Sandy returned the back to the cupboard, restored the shelves, and put everything back in place. Going outside he did some chores around the house and mowed the lawn. With everything put away in the barn, he went back to the house, reset the alarm, and locked up.

Driving home, he thought about the reading of the will and Aunt Beth's request that the following be engraved on her headstone, "I took the one less traveled by." It was from the Robert Frost poem, and she'd told him that it was Papa's favorite. Shaking his head in disbelief, he wondered "Could it be that simple?"

When he got home, Sandy went to the bookcase and pulled out a collection of Frost's poems. Turning to the most famous, he read it through.

Remembering that Papa was an engineer, Ok, just follow the steps. He turned on his laptop and got a copy of "The Road Not Taken" from the web and pasted it into a blank word document. Using the replace function he removed all the spaces and punctuation. It looked kind of goofy.

tworoadsdivergedinayellowwood
andsorryicouldnottravelboth
andbeonetravelerlongistood
andlookeddownoneasfarasicould
towhereitbentintheundergrowth
thentooktheotherasjustasfair
andhavingperhapsthebetterclaim,
becauseitwasgrassyandwantedwear
thoughasforthatthepassingthere
hadwornthemreallyaboutthesame
andboththatmorningequallylay
inleavesnostephadtroddenblack
ohikeptthefirstforanotherday
yetknowinghowwayleadsontoway
idoubtedifishouldevercomeback
ishallbetellingthiswithasigh
somewhereagesandageshence
tworoadsdivergedinawoodandi
itooktheonelesstraveledby
andthathasmadeallthedifference

Sandy thought for a moment. Ok next step, what do the numbers mean?

He started with the first pair of numbers. Perhaps they were the line and position. 1.6 Line 1 sixth letter equals 'a' 1.1 Line 1 first letter is 't.' It was tedious. He decided a better way was to paste it into Excel and write a simple formula to find each letter. Soon he had

decoded   the   note   and   it   read
'atlocfindthewatergasbyrichardbeckwithadd20'   by
adding spaces he had.

at loc find the water gas by richard beckwith add 20

Sandy thought how much harder it must have been for his grandfather who didn't have a computer. He grabbed a short glass of scotch and went out on the deck with Copper. The weather was classic Washington, hot and muggy. So, what was 'loc?' He set the glass down He went back to his laptop and Googled 'books at loc.' and the first answer was "Book/Printed Material, Available Online | Library of Congress." Of course, the Library of Congress – cool. He wasn't sure about the 'add 20' part but figured it would reveal itself in time.

Chapter 14 Fairfax, VA

The next morning after a five-mile run and a light breakfast, Sandy drove to the Vienna Metro station near Nutley Street and parked in the garage. At nine in the morning, he had to circle around and around up four floors to find a parking spot on the roof. Grabbing his backpack, he took the bridge over to the station, which was situated between the inbound and outbound lanes of I-66. I-66 inbound was the normal parking lot with all five lanes solid and crawling. He tapped his Metro card on the turnstile and took the escalator down to the tracks. Being the last stop on the Orange Line, a train was waiting to go into the city. He walked on and grabbed an open seat.

The ride in was uneventful, and because he was going to the Capitol South Metro station, he just stayed on the Orange line. Riding the escalator up, he came out on First Street. He walked up the hill on First and crossed Independence, putting him in front of the Library of Congress. The day was already hot and sticky, but being in such great shape, he hardly drew a sweat.

He took a moment to admire the Neptune Fountain with its three massive bronze sculptures. A huge muscular Neptune in the center and two sea nymphs on either side. He loved the sound of the water splashing about the pool. Going up the stairs, he passed through security and then entered the Italian Renaissance building's Great Hall. The mosaic floor of marble was stunning, but nothing compared to the grand arches which supported the ceiling soaring 75 feet overhead. The ceiling was adorned with stained glass and aluminum relief decoration; it took your breath away. As he walked through the commemorative arch, he took note of an original Gutenberg Bible on display. A new technology, movable type, created about 1450, changed bookmaking forever.

Sandy entered the Main Reading Room and just paused to take it all in. He had come to the library many times in the past but was always stunned by this room. The massive domed ceiling rose 165 feet above the floor. Eight giant pillars stood tall, taking the weight of the eight arches which supported the dome. The dome was capped by a stained-glass oculus. Sandy reverently walked slowly to the circular desk in the center of the reading room. He took note of the librarian's name tag and said, "Good morning, Carol, I would like to request a book."

"Of course, sir, do you have a Reader Identification Card?"

"I do," and he retrieved the card from his wallet.

"If you've got the author and title, please go over to one of those computer terminals and get the call number for the book. Fill out a request card, and someone will retrieve it for you."

Sandy went to the computer and entered 'Water Gas' as the title and 'Richard Beckwith' as the author. The computer came back with the call number HD2763 .T67

19579. He filled out a card and returned it to the desk. "Found it, Carol, and here is the card. That was so easy."

"We will have someone retrieve it, and I would suggest taking a seat and stopping back here in an hour. Sometimes it takes longer, but it's quiet today with Congress in recess."

Sandy took a seat at one of the long tables that circled the central librarian's desk. Several chairs down was a very attractive young woman with a stack of books on the table, who appeared to be in her late twenties. Sandy retrieved a book from his backpack and began to read. The woman stood, which Sandy caught out of the corner of his eye, and he turned to look at her. She smiled and began to move in his direction. Sandy smiled back and said, "Wow that's quite a stack of books you're working on."

She continued to smile and said, "Yup, just another research project. Are you waiting for your books?"

"Yes, just one. It's kind of a mystery project for me."

"Can you watch my books. I'll be back in a few minutes."

About 5 minutes later the woman returned. She was athletic, tall, maybe five seven with beautiful strawberry blonde hair in big, long curls. Sandy stood and introduced himself. "Hi, I'm Sandy Powell."

She replied as she shook his hand with a huge smile, "Morgan Dutton, a pleasure to meet you, Sandy."

"Morgan, that's a beautiful name. Reminds me of my favorite breed of horse."

"Wow! We just met, and you call me a horse," she said with a grin and a chuckle.

"I did say beautiful."

"Yes, you did. So where did Sandy come from?"

"Well, actually it's short for Sandusky. My Dad spent part of his summers in college in Upper Sandusky, Ohio, and he had a special spot in his heart for those memories."

"Well, that's a great story. Mine is similar. My mother loved Morgan horses, so you hit it on the head. Well back to work. I hope your book turns up soon."

Sandy returned to the book he brought with him, but his thoughts weren't on his reading. He was thinking about Morgan. Her green eyes were captivating, and she also had a great figure, narrow hips, and an amazing smile that just radiated. Sandy also noted he didn't see a ring- possibilities.

****

Morgan likewise was thinking about Sandy. He was tall maybe six foot one and in really great shape – broad shoulders, narrow hips and a tight butt, close-cropped light brown hair, huge smile, and the most amazing blue eyes. They really sparkled like dark blue sapphires. She too noticed no ring or even a tan line if he had removed it for the day.

After about twenty minutes, Sandy approached the librarian, and his book had just arrived. She said, "It's part of the permanent collection so please return it here if you step away or need it back tomorrow."

"Thank you so much! I will do just that."

When he returned to his seat, he looked over at

Morgan, and she smiled back, saying, "Well it looks like your mystery is about to begin."

****

Sandy smiled back and said, "It started a few days ago and this seems to be the next chapter."

"Good luck, Sandy"

Sandy sat and looked at the book. A piece of kitchen string was around the book like a ribbon around a Christmas present, tied in a simple bow like on a shoe, at the front center. Sandy gently pulled the two ends of the string, releasing the bow. There sat the book, neatly handwritten.

The Water Gas
By
Richard Beckwith

Sandy reflected for a moment that his grandfather had many years ago tied that bow. Then, he opened the book and could see how the cover had been wrapped around an existing book. Turning to the cover page, he saw the book was *Autobiography of Benjamin Franklin*.

Sandy thought, ok, I didn't see that one coming.

On the cover page was the number 12. Sandy turned to page 12 and there was nothing there. He started to flip through the pages and saw words or letters underlined, and on those pages, there was a number on the top of the page. He flipped back to page 12, thinking he had missed something, but there was nothing there.

Sandy leaned back in his chair and gazed at the magnificent arch on the opposite wall and ceiling and tried to think. Morgan, quietly, in her best library voice whispered, "You look perplexed. Can I help?"

Sandy smiled and said, "Perhaps, but it's a long story." And then, in a moment of inspiration, he added, "Would you like to have lunch?"

She smiled back. Then nodding, she answered, still in her library voice, "I like the plan. I enjoy a good mystery."

"Are you up for a walk? The place I'm thinking about is about six blocks away."

"Sure," she said with a big smile, "Nothing like a nice long walk in August in DC. Well, that is if you're a horse."

"Do you like French food?"

To which she replied in perfect French, "Oui, mais bien sûr."

Sandy had this massive smile. "Ok, we're off."

Sandy and Morgan dropped their books off at the desk and walked out onto First Street. They headed east to Pennsylvania Avenue in no particular hurry. Morgan started, "So Sandusky, tell me your history."

"Well, I was born and spent my youth near Manchester, Vermont, near my great-grandfather's farm. When I was about six, we moved to St. Louis, where my father worked for what would become Boeing. He passed away several years ago, and my mom still lives there. No siblings. I went to Virginia Military Institute, and majored in biology. After VMI I was in the Navy, got married, became a SEAL, and did several tours in the Middle East. While I was deployed, we got divorced, with no kids. After ten years in the Navy, I received a medical discharge and became a schoolteacher in Fairfax last year."

"Wow, Navy SEAL, I can see that. Did you see any action?"

"Way too much, it never really leaves you. So, what about you?"

"Well, I grew up outside Ithaca in the Finger Lakes region of New York. My dad was a vet, mostly large animals, and now he teaches at Cornell. I went to Syracuse University and majored in Political Science and then went to Cornell for law school. I took a year off in between and lived with a friend in France. I took a job with a big firm here in DC doing intellectual property law and struck out on my own two years ago."

Sandy shook his head, smiling broadly, and replied, "So bottom-line you're brilliant as well as pretty."

"Awwww shucks," in a mock southern drawl, "You just know how to say all the right things to a belle."

They walked on, commenting on each other's lives, and soon arrived at Montmartre, a French Bistro on Pennsylvania Avenue in the Eastern Market neighborhood. The airy, light-filled space was known for its scrumptious lunch and dinner menu. Stepping inside the air conditioning was refreshing coming from the humid tropical steam bath outside.

They chose a table near the expansive window, and Sandy ordered a bottle of Perrier and Brie de Meaux with a baguette to begin. Morgan started, "So tell me about your mystery."

"Well, about a month ago my aunt passed away."

"Oh, I'm so sorry. Were you close?"

"Yes, she lived in Great Falls, and I saw her often. My grandfather, her dad, died many years ago in a hit-and-run accident. I never knew him. We all believed it was an accident. She left a letter for me which I received last week at the reading of the will. My aunt learned from my grandmother, just before she passed, that my grandfather's accident was really murder. Further in the letter, I learned there were secrets left by my grandfather before his murder. Based on her letter, I uncovered a note that he left which led me to a book at the Library of Congress and pleasantly to you."

"So, do you know why he was killed?"

Sandy stared into her bright green, emerald eyes. "Not yet, but hopefully, I will discover it. Perhaps it's in the book."

Morgan ordered a bistro salad and seared octopus, while Sandy chose the French onion soup and two dozen Mussels marinières and frites. They shared the mussels. The conversation drifted back and forth on their lives and related stories. Time slipped away, and at last, somewhat reluctantly, they headed back to the library.

After retrieving their books, they returned to their table. This time Morgan sat next to Sandy. Morgan remarked, "So you looked perplexed before we left for lunch; can I help?"

Sandy retrieved from his bag the deciphered note and shared it with Morgan.

As she looked down at it, she frowned slightly and asked, "So what does the 'Add 20' mean?"

Sandy replied, "That one has got me, plus it was separated a bit from the rest."

Morgan opened the book again to the cover page and said, "What if you add 20 to the 12 and turn to page 32?"

Together they turned to page 32 and the word 'Go' was underlined. At the top of the page was 17. They then turned to page 37, and the word 'to' was underlined. They turned and, looked at each other and in harmony, said, "WOW," and chuckled.

Several people shushed them for being so loud. They just beamed at each other.

Sandy began the tedious work of flipping through the pages and writing down each word or, in some cases, a single letter. The last number sent him to page 131, where he found a folded slip of paper inserted in the book with the blank side facing out. Sandy gently removed the paper and read it.

Hello, the fact that you are reading this letter means I must have been killed.

If you were not intended to receive this letter, I strongly advise you to stop reading now and simply return the book as it will place you in grave danger.

To the future person who is reading this now, the fact that you were chosen means that you are trusted. Please know if you continue on this quest, you may place yourself in harm's way.

With best wishes, God's grace, be safe,

Richard Powell

Sandy looked at Morgan, "Well another clue."

Morgan read the sentences he had written and then the note, "Wow, looks like an adventure. Want some help?"

Sandy looked thoughtful and slowly said, "Morgan, the note says grave danger. I don't want you to get hurt."

"I've got my knight in shining armor plus you're a SEAL; what can possibly go wrong?"

"Well," Sandy grinned, "In that case, would you grace me with dinner tonight, fair princess?"

"Ahhh," Morgan smiled, "A very gracious offer, but sorry, I've got plans. You see, I spent so much time today with this captivating knight that now I'm behind on my work for my client, and I will be up half the night catching up."

"Oh, I'm sorry to have kept you from your duty, milady."

Morgan beamed. "It was worth every moment. How about tomorrow night?"

"Perfect, can I pick you up at about six? What ethnicity would you prefer?"

"Well, like YOU, how about hot and spicy," she said in a sultry tone. "Let's do Indian."

It was Sandy's turn to beam. "I know the place - you'll love it."

They exchanged phone numbers and addresses, and Sandy was on his way to the metro while Morgan plunged back into her pile of books.

Chapter 15 Fairfax, VA

Sandy woke up a bit later than normal, knowing it might be a late night. Copper was ready to go, and they were off on his perfunctory five-mile run. Light rain made it cooler but just as humid, and they were both soaking wet when they returned.

He was busy all morning around the house, and by midafternoon he dressed in grey slacks, a white shirt, and navy sport coat, no tie. Knowing that traffic was horrendous on a Friday night, he left at 3:30 for the 20-mile drive to downtown. I-66 was not yet a parking lot, so he made it with plenty of time to spare. Shortly before six, he parked on Olive Street in Georgetown and found Morgan's home - a recently built Federal-style brownstone townhouse. The architecture was classic, and she had a middle unit. He rang the bell next to the bright red front door.

In less than a minute, she opened the door. She simply glowed, wearing a soft blue dress with a slight plunge at the neckline with a matching pleated skirt that stopped just above the knee. Her white open-toed shoes accented her beautiful legs.

Sandy caught his breath and took her hand as she stepped down from the threshold. "Wow, you look stunning."

"Well, my knight, you dress up pretty good too." She

tucked her arm in his as they walked together to his car. It felt natural. He opened the door, and she slipped comfortably into the Mazda. After he slid into the driver's seat, she said, "This is pure sport. I've never seen one like this. Sweeeeet!"

"One of a kind, it's a prototype. I had it shipped over from Japan in pieces. A friend is an executive at Mazda. I built it last winter."

They drove across downtown and parked in a garage across the street from the Bombay restaurant. After starters, Morgan had the shrimp moilee, and Sandy had the Adraki lamb chops. Dinner was amazing, and they enjoyed the small talk and getting to know each other. After dessert Sandy with a totally serious face said, "If you're free tomorrow, I was hoping you could join us at the farm for the next clue."

Morgan looked shocked. "Us!"

"Oh yeah, I always have my companion with me when I go to the farm."

"Your companion? I thought you were single."

"Oh, I am, it's my golden retriever, Copper."

Morgan punched him hard in the shoulder. "You've got a warped sense of humor."

"Ahhhh, just having a bit of fun," Sandy said with a big grin. "You should have seen your face."

"Love to join you and Copper. He is probably better mannered than you are."

Then she added, with a smile, "Ok, we're not done yet. Let's go to a club I know. It's not far, so we can walk."

"Sounds great - the night is young."

****

Ten minutes later, after walking north on Connecticut Avenue, they arrived at the Eighteenth Street Lounge. The place was full of people, and they got drinks and found a comfortable place to enjoy the music and chat. Morgan texted her best friend Vicky, and soon they had a whole group of people. Vicky and Morgan headed off to the ladies' room, and once inside Vicky said, "Oh my God, he is amazing! Not only is he a dish to look at but smart, witty, and fun to be with. He's a catch, and don't let him get away."

"I know! We only met yesterday, but already feel like I've known him forever. Plus, he's so nice and treats me like a lady. He makes me feel special

"Well, hang on tight! He's such a catch."

From time to time, Sandy and Morgan would get up and dance, and the next thing they knew, it was nearly midnight and time to call it a night. When they walked out, Sandy said, "Better hurry before the garage closes."

"No worries, we will grab an Uber and go to the garage first. That will get you there faster." And she laughed, seeing the concerned look on Sandy's face, "Ahh, my knight, never fear. I'll be fine. I've done this Uber routine once or twice before going home if you haven't noticed Georgetown isn't exactly on the metro line."

Sandy nodded. "Ok. But be ready for Copper and me to pick you up first thing in the morning."

"I can't wait"

****

Saturday morning, Sandy awoke early with Copper crossways on the bed. He groaned as he stroked the dog, rubbing Copper's ears.

"What's wrong with the dog bed?" he sighed. "You're too used to it being just the two of us, huh? BUT..." he said dreamily, thinking of Morgan, "With a little luck, we might have someone else, and you will have to sleep on your dog bed, buddy."

Then he jumped up quickly, startling Copper. "No run this morning, buddy." And Copper cocked his head, his ears pulled out inquiringly.

"We're sure to get plenty of exercise at Aunt Beth's farm." And with that, Sandy started for the shower to get moving on the day ahead.

Sandy and Copper made good time, and they enjoyed a traffic-less weekend morning drive on 66 from Fairfax to Georgetown. They surprisingly found a parking space on the street close to Morgan's house, walked up, and rang the bell.

Morgan came to the door, smiling widely. She wore skinny jeans and a teal polo shirt with light hiking shoes. "Come in," and looking down at Copper, she added, "Both of you. I hope you're hungry. I've got breakfast in the oven, almost ready to come out."

Copper greeted Morgan, wagging his whole body as happy as could be, and Morgan, smiling, leaned over to stroke his back.

Walking into her house, Sandy was blown away. It was like it was out of Architectural Digest. A brick wall ran from front to back, hardwood floors in the open-concept layout, and it was enhanced with tastefully arranged stainless and glass furnishings. They walked to the back, where the kitchen had a wall of cabinets, marble countertops, and a large marble island.

As they entered the kitchen, Morgan pulled something from the wall oven. She said questioningly, "I hope you like quiche?" She set it down on two potholders strategically set out on the counter.

"It smells amazing!" Sandy exclaimed as he ambled over and pulled her in tight. Giving her a generous kiss, he murmured in her ear, "You smell amazing too."

She laughed lightly, then pulled away and gestured to the island in the center of the kitchen. "Why don't you pour the coffee while I cut the quiche," she told Sandy. "And" with a grin at Copper, she said, "There might be a breakfast style treat of some ham for you too...that is," she raised her eyebrows and looked at Sandy, "If your dad says it's, ok?"

Sandy laughed. "You had him at 'treat' and 'ham'. He knows those words – now you've got to deliver."

Copper gave a guttural 'woof' in agreement, and Morgan laughed.

"No problem...let's eat."

They ate slowly, enjoying the sumptuous quiche Lorraine along with a delicious espresso blend of coffee and fresh orange juice while sitting at the breakfast bar on the large center island. Copper sat at their feet, enjoying the scraps of ham that Morgan had saved for him. When they finished, they made quick work picking up the kitchen and went out into the already warm and humid summer day to Sandy's car to make the journey out to Great Falls.

Chapter 16   Great Falls, VA

Sandy, Morgan, and Copper pulled up to Aunt Beth's house. As soon as they got out of the car, Copper was off running around the barn and the outbuildings. Sandy unlocked the door and turned off the alarm.

"Well, what do you think of my new spread?"

Morgan looked about. "A few updates and this could be a sweet home."

Sandy beamed. "This plus 60 acres in Great Falls, it could be whatever we want. Let's go see where the next clue leads us."

Morgan's heart skipped a beat, and she smiled from the inside out. She'd heard the 'we' and liked how it felt. They were going at warp speed in the relationship, but she'd never felt safer or more comfortable with anyone. It felt great. "Lead on Sherlock."

The clue they deciphered yesterday read:

"Go to the NE corner of the barn. Tilt up the middle shelf in the cupboard and pull the right side of the cupboard out."

Sandy unlocked the hasp and opened both big sliding doors. Inside was a collection of machinery and, on the right, stalls for horses or cows. They walked to the far end of the barn and in the corner stood a roughly eight-foot-high, four-foot-wide cabinet. Sandy cleared off the items on the middle shelf and put them on a nearby table. He then lifted the shelf and could hear a click. He pulled on the right side, and the cabinet rotated out, revealing stairs going down.

Sandy looked at Morgan. "Ok, I never imagined this was here. I'm going to go get a flashlight or two out of the car. Copper you stay with Morgan."

****

Copper sat and was happy to be with Morgan. When Sandy returned, he put a paint can in front of the cabinet to make sure it didn't close behind them. Then he entered the space and flicked a light switch on. Light shined down the stairs and below.

"Looks good so far. Morgan, you and Copper stay here while I check it out." Sandy carefully went down the wooden stairs and couldn't believe what he saw. It was a full laboratory. He looked around and could see no snakes or mice, and the place looked safe. He yelled up, "You gotta to come down and see this."

Morgan felt a rush of adrenaline and took a deep breath. "OK, a real mystery and what a Holmes to my Watson." She grinned, and she and Copper descended into the basement lab.

Down the center between the posts that supported the ceiling were black stone-topped tables covered with flasks, beakers, and assorted chemistry equipment. One wall had shelves with cardboard boxes and jars full of various chemicals. An antique desk and more workbenches lined the opposing wall. An exhaust fan was mounted on one wall, and Sandy guessed its exhaust came out in the stone well twenty feet from the barn. Sandy said, "Time for the next clue."

"SE corner, middle shelf, in the bottom of a box of papers are the details."

Sandy and Morgan walked to the far corner and pulled a box out and placed it on a black stone table noticing that there was surprisingly little dust anywhere. Slowly removing the papers in the box, they came to an upside-down laboratory notebook. They took it and all the papers below and set it aside. Together they opened and began to read Sandy's grandfather's lab notebook.

Sandy said, "This is it - why he was murdered. Let's take it to the house where it'll be easier to read."

The threesome went back up the stairs, turned off the lights, closed the cupboard, and put a few things back on the middle shelf. A few minutes later, they were in the house, sitting at the kitchen table.

"Sandy, the Navy must have built that for him. Remember, it was the height of the Cold War, and he was doing top-secret work for the Navy. Do you think the Russians had him killed?"

"It's certainly possible, but I would think the Navy would have removed everything from the lab."

She thought. "Good point, but it's a possibility."

"Let's look through his notes and try to figure out what his discovery was, and that may give us a clue to who wanted it."

After an hour, Sandy said he was hungry. They put

the notes and lab book in a kitchen drawer and locked up the house. Sandy told Copper to stay in the kitchen, and he and Morgan drove to Great Falls for lunch. The Old Brogue Irish Pub in the heart of Great Falls looked like a great spot. They ordered the Warm Crab & Avocado Crostini to start – a treat they both loved and remarked how the avocado was a great twist to the blue crab. For the main part of their meal, Sandy had an Angus burger and Morgan a grilled Reuben. Both were amazing. To accompany the feast, they each enjoyed a draft of Smithwick's Ale.

Sitting in a back-corner booth, they quietly compared notes on what they'd learned so far. Sandy remarked, "It looks like he discovered a way to produce hydrogen gas using a solution and electroplating."

Morgan replied, "Yes, and even more interesting he'd written a patent on it, so we can see if that patent was filed. That's pretty easy to do."

Sandy thought for a moment. "You know, I'm supposed to start teaching in about ten days. But now I think I'll take a sabbatical for the fall semester."

"Ok, why take a sabbatical?"

"This is going to take a bunch of research, and we also need to test to see if it even works. I don't need the money. I just inherited a small pile, and I may just sell the house in Fairfax and move out to the farm. What do you think?"

****

Morgan thought a moment. Her heartstrings pulled

again, thinking he had used "we" and valued her opinion about his life moving forward. "It's an interesting idea but pretty major. I'd sleep on that one for a couple of days. There's nothing you can do till Monday anyway."

"Great point."

"I've got an idea. Let's go back to the farm, gather up all the papers, then go back downtown. You can read through the pile, and I can get some work done, and we could order in some Chinese or something. We can pick up something for Copper."

"I love the idea, but are you sure about bringing Copper?"

"Sure, I've got a feeling he's going to be spending a lot of time at my place. We might as well get him adjusted."

Sandy turned on his million-dollar smile. "Well, I'm not worried about Copper adjusting. I'm worried about you seeing all the clumps of dog hair, and you throwing us both out."

"You don't have to worry about that; remember, I'm the daughter of a vet. I love dogs."

"Well then, it's a deal. But don't worry about Copper. Aunt Beth has dog supplies from when we visited. We'll pack up some from here."

And they walked out, two people falling in love on a beautiful Saturday afternoon.

Chapter 17   Georgetown, DC

They arrived late afternoon back at her house in Georgetown. Morgan directed Sandy to a parking area behind her house, and they entered through her small, fenced yard leading to the back door.

"This is convenient," Sandy remarked about the parking. Copper was on his leash, looking all around as Sandy carried in a small gym bag with dog food and bowls for Copper that they snagged from Aunt Beth's house.

The backyard was compact but lovely. Flowers and a small hedge were against the fence. A bluestone walkway gently curved from the gate to the rear door and patio. Comfortable furniture and a grill completed the area. In the far corner, a small pool provided a babbling sound of water running down over a pile of round rocks. Sandy, taking it all in, said, "This is like an oasis in the city, absolutely beautiful."

Morgan smiled, "I'm really lucky! A friend of mine from Syracuse is a landscape architect, and she designed it. And I've got a great gardener who keeps it so lovely. Let's go in first. We can come back out once we're settled."

Morgan entered the key code and the door unlocked. They entered the mudroom off the kitchen. A washer and dryer also occupied the space, as well as a coat closet.

Copper was sniffing everything as they entered. Sandy unhooked the leash and said, "You behave." Copper was off exploring the downstairs smelling everything, and then returned to the kitchen. Sandy set the bag in a corner and pulled out a water bowl for him.

"How about some cheese and crackers on the patio? The heat seems to have broken, and there's a light breeze. Would you like wine, beer, or something else?"

Sandy smiled, "White wine sounds great. Can I help?"

Morgan directed him to the wine glasses and the wine fridge under the counter while she got plates, cheese, and crackers. Sandy chose a New Zealand Oyster Bay Chardonnay, which he loved for being both vibrant and creamy.

As he watched, Morgan made quick work pulling out a creamy blue cheese, smoked gouda, and a sharp Vermont cheddar along with water crackers and some baguette slices. She arranged it all on a tray, and they were off to the patio. Copper was right on their heels and rushed out the door to explore the yard.

After a bit, Morgan said, "I really have to get some work done."

They returned inside, and she said, "I will be upstairs in my office; please make yourself at home."

"I will. I already feel at home," Sandy grinned, "I'm going to dive into the papers my grandfather left. Take your time."

Sandy sat at the dining room table and began to read from his grandfather's notes and papers. Morgan headed upstairs with Copper following closely behind. Several hours later, Morgan came downstairs, and Sandy smiled at her return. Copper was in tow and was the happiest dog on the planet.

He looked at her, "I think Copper has fallen for you. Looks like I'll have some big competition on that front."

Morgan felt her muscles deep down in that special place clench. "Oh, I think you're safe, mister. Any interesting discoveries?"

"Actually, yes. His notes and papers go into extensive detail, so we should be able to recreate his setup. There are a lot of details on the transformer he used that was acting differently. He was actually in the process of replacing it. And then there's this piece," he looked up at her. "You may find this interesting; I found a receipt from the Patent Office saying he filed it."

"Wow, that's helpful. I'll check Monday to see if it was issued, or what the status is for the patent. Would you like Chinese or something else?"

"Chinese sounds great. We can munch, relax, watch a bit of TV before Copper and I take our leave."

Morgan laughed. "Well, I certainly can't resist those puppy dog eyes... yours or Copper's. I'll get the menu and maybe some kind of a doggie treat." She winked as she left the room.

They relaxed, enjoyed their Chinese food feast, and watched a bit of a pre-season football game. Then the three of them walked slowly to Morgan's back door, where she and Sandy enjoyed a very amorous good night kiss.

Sandy sighed as they broke apart. "Until tomorrow then..."

"Mmm," Morgan murmured. "Plan on breakfast again."

"You got it," Sandy said as he and Copper disappeared into the gently lit backyard and slipped out the back gate to the car.

Sunday dawned bright and early. "First things first," Sandy said to Copper, and they went for a five-mile run; the refreshing day made it a pleasure.

After giving Copper his favorite Blue Buffalo breakfast and taking a quick shower, the two were ready for the drive to Morgan's for breakfast. Over delicious scones and croissants, they discussed the plan for the day. Morgan decided she really needed to get more work done.

Sandy nodded and said, "I think I'm going to sell the Fairfax house and take that sabbatical. So, I might as well start moving into the farm. What do you think?"

Morgan nodded thoughtfully, "I think it makes a lot of sense. You don't need two places to live, and I think it will take a lot of time to research and see about your grandfather's discovery."

Sandy grinned at that thought. "My house in the suburbs and my country home it does sound like a bit much, doesn't it?"

Morgan laughed. "And," she smiled wickedly at Sandy. "If you play your cards right, you could be looking at a great little place in Georgetown too..."

Sandy's eyebrows shot up. "Really?" he said as a grin spread across his face. "Well, by all means, let's explore this issue later. Would you be up to driving to the farm after you finish working? I'll go home and get some things packed so Copper and I can stay up there. I'll fix dinner – sunset on the farm?"

"Sounds romantic..." Morgan teased. "And, what a catch! Not only a SEAL but also a chef. I love the plan. I should be up there between 5 and 6."

Soon after, Sandy and Copper were on their way, driving over the Key Bridge and out the GW Parkway to 495, jumping off in Tysons, and taking 123 through Vienna to Fairfax. The day was a pleasant 70 and sunny with a breeze out of the north - a nice change from the heat and humidity of the last week.

****

Bob and Sally Lancaster had planned a weekend get away from the US Embassy in Abuja, Nigeria, to celebrate 20 wonderful years together. It would also give them time to catch up with friends at the Consulate in Lagos. While Bob's State Department salary was modest, the cost of living in Lagos was also cheap. The Oceanview Restaurant on Victoria Island had a reputation as the classiest and best seafood restaurant in town, so it was well worth it. They were seated off to the side of the restaurant in a quiet corner.

After they were seated, Bob glanced around and then whispered to Sally, "I can't believe who's seated next to us. Don't stare, but those are three of the richest people on the planet."

At the table right next to them were Harold Watson, Bryce Carrington, and Reginald Clark. They were the respective CEOs of Texas Oil, American Petroleum, and Sunco, the three largest oil and gas companies in the world. With the US antitrust laws, Bob was thinking these guys shouldn't be in the same city, let alone having dinner together. Bob focused on Sally but was also listening to their conversation, beyond curious.

****

HW began, "We should have reserved a private dining room. I hope we aren't recognized."

Bryce replied, "Nobody in this corner of the world knows who we are. I'm sure we're safe. We need to talk about what we should do with Ali Mohammed. We've paid him nearly half a million, BUT he's demanding more."

Reggie piped in, "I don't mind paying the money, but he isn't delivering. Actually, it's his vice minister who's aligned with our thinking about control of the various oil fields and tariffs. I think we've got to take Ali out."

HW was very uncomfortable with the direction this conversation was going. As the newest member of the Pinnacle Club, he was surprised at how matter-of-factly they discussed killing someone.

"Gentlemen, I'm not sure I can go along with this solution. Perhaps there's a better way to turn him in our direction."

Chapter 18   Fairfax, VA

Sandy called Jackson and gave him a full update on Morgan, plans to sell the house, and his grandfather's discovery.

Jackson said, "Well mate, it looks like you're over the moon in love and clearly off the eligible bachelors' list."

"Well, I think you just might be right, old friend. I don't think I've ever been so happy. I will keep you updated."

Sandy could hear Jackson's smile. "You'd better, mate!" And the two signed off, promising to stay in touch.

"Ok," Sandy thought to himself. "Let's get organized and work the plan."

He made a to-do list:

- Contact School about a sabbatical
- Find a real estate agent
- Line up movers
- Pack essentials for the week
- Move critical stuff to the farm
- Get cash from the attorney

Going down his list, Sandy first called Lezlie

Anderson, his high school principal, and told her about his plan to take a sabbatical for the fall semester. She totally understood and instructed him on what he needed to write. He should send it to her and the administrator for the county school system immediately. He got off the phone and wrote the letter while it was fresh in his mind.

I'll be able to mail it tomorrow, he thought.

Next, he called three well-known real estate agents and made appointments, also for tomorrow, to have them look at the house.

He then packed two suitcases of clothes to bring to the farm. He pulled out his footlocker and carried it out to the car. Next, he removed the false panel in the back of his closet, and extracted his small arsenal of guns: pistols, shotguns, and several rifles, and put them in cases. He packed a bag with shells and spare clips. All of this went out to the car as well.

Finally, he put in a call to his attorney, Gary Sutter, and updated him on his plan and discovery. He instructed him to transfer twenty thousand into his account at a local bank. Then he and Copper headed over to the farm to unload the car. He didn't trust leaving the weapons in the house, so he decided to hide the weapons in the lab. He knew he would need to get a heated gun safe soon if he kept them in the lab.

"We're on our way to our new home, boy," Sandy said to Copper. "I think you'll be very happy there!"

Copper gave his series of "Woofs," which meant he liked what he heard...or at least that's what Sandy took it as.

On their way out, Sandy stopped at a great butcher

shop in Reston and picked out two huge dry-aged tomahawk ribeye steaks. He went to another shop and got a bottle of cabernet sauvignon, several russet potatoes, asparagus, and a peach pie. Back in the car, he took Fairfax County Parkway north toward Great Falls.

Arriving about 5:30, Sandy had just finished unloading his car, when Morgan pulled in. After a warm and affectionate greeting, they sipped some wine while Sandy prepared the luscious steak dinner – happy that Aunt Beth still had a full tank of propane for her grill.

After dinner, Morgan brought in a bag and cleared space in the guest bedroom closet and dresser for some of her clothes. "You don't mind..." she asked Sandy shyly.

"Not at all," he beamed. "It's a bit of a drive...and there's plenty of room."

And the two sat snuggled on the back deck, watching as the stars came out, content to sit in each other's arms and talk.

****

Over dinner in Nigeria, Reggie looked disgusted, "You know HW, this is a tough business, and we've grown our companies to what they are by working together and secretly controlling the world's energy supplies. Sometimes, we're forced to make hard decisions to maintain our control. This isn't the first time, and I'm sure this won't be the last where the best solution is permanent."

Bryce looked HW in the eyes. "You'll see in good time that Reggie is right. It's never easy, but it must be done. With Ali out of the picture, Arsalan Aziz will be in power, and we'll have our oil at our price. Further, I believe we'll find new oil fields and will be pumping here for decades."

Reggie asked, "Everyone in favor of putting Arsalan in power."

All three nodded their heads, but HW remained uncomfortable with the development.

"I will reach out to Paragon and have them fix things," Reggie said.

Bryce looked around the table. "With that problem solved, we need to talk about the situation in Saudi and Indonesia while we're together. Aren't these prawns amazing?"

Bob was shocked at what he had overheard. It was unbelievable. He excused himself from Sally and went to the men's room. On the way back to the table, he secretly took a picture with his phone of the three men together.

The following day, Bob went to the airport, and with his diplomatic credentials, was able to drive around the private jets. He took pictures of all the jets' tail numbers. That afternoon he spoke with his boss and got the go-ahead to reach out to a former college roommate who worked at the Justice Department to share what he had overheard and securely emailed him the pictures of the men and the jets.

Bryan Park thought he'd heard everything until the call from Bob Lancaster. Bryan had been at the Justice Department for over 15 years, and while he was a prosecutor, he did have friends throughout the department. He reached out to Mark Taylor, a good friend who was in the antitrust division at Justice, and they agreed to meet in Mark's office the next day.

In Mark's office, Bryan shared what he learned from his former roommate about the meeting between Harold Watson, Bryce Carrington, and Reginald Clark. He shared a thumb drive with the pictures Bob had sent over.

Mark shook his head in disbelief. "If this is true," he began slowly, "And I've got absolutely no reason to believe it isn't true; this has massive implications. I'll talk to my boss, Melissa Pearson, and see if we can get a go-ahead to start an investigation. We'll take it from here. I really appreciate you and Bob putting this together. I'll reach out to Bob and remind him to keep this classified."

Shortly after the meeting, Mark called Bob Lancaster at the US Embassy in Nigeria. "Bob, thank you for informing us of what you saw and heard. I want to emphasize that the matter is highly classified. Please take some time to memorialize everything you saw and heard with as much detail as possible. I will be sending a DOJ agent down to interview you shortly."

A week later, Bob reached out to both Bryan and Mark to let them know that Ali Mohammed, the Nigerian Minister for Oil and Gas had died of apparent food poisoning.

Mark called Sarah Hughes, the US Ambassador to Nigeria. "Please have someone discreetly contact the person performing the autopsy on Ali and request they wait until someone from the US could attend the autopsy. Just tell the coroner that the US had seen recent attacks by Al Qaeda against leaders in other countries, and we'd like to confirm it was food poisoning."

"Will do."

Still moving quickly, Mark then reached out to a colleague at the FBI and requested a forensic pathologist be sent immediately to Lagos. He shared the developments with his associate.

****

Dr. Matthew French was unaware of the details but knew it was important when an FBI jet was standing by at Joint Base Andrews to fly him directly to Lagos. Normally, the dead can wait for his arrival. His instructions were to assist in the autopsy, collect specimens, and confirm the food poisoning assumption even if it was not.

After the 12-hour flight with a brief refueling stop in Puerto Rico, Matt was ready to go, and arrangements were made to meet with the coroner, Dr. Habib, at 3 p.m.

"Dr. Habib a pleasure to meet you. Could I have a few moments to review your notes before we start the autopsy?"

"Of course, Doctor."

He reviewed Habib's notes and saw that Ali had died approximately 12 hours after eating at a local restaurant. Ali had told his wife he was suffering from a headache, severe abdominal pain, and nausea. He died in bed. Within a few hours, he was transported to the coroner's morgue, and fluid samples were collected, and the body was placed in cold storage.

Ali's body was moved from the cooler drawer and placed on the examination table. Habib and Matt did a routine examination of the body, and there was no indication of any external trauma, as expected.

Habib suggested, "Let's prop the head and neck up and expose the brain, and we can take several samples."

After getting their samples, Matt remarked, "Nothing unusual here."

"Ok, I will do the classic 'Y' incision." Habib cut across near the shoulders and then cut down from the top to the groin. The Striker saw was used to cut through the ribs. Pulling the skin and ribs back, all the major organs were revealed.

"As I'm sure you'll agree, there's pulmonary edema of both lungs and congestion of the liver," Matt said.

"I concur, and this is common in food poisoning. Let's open the stomach to see if any food was still present and take several samples." They also opened portions of the small and large intestines.

Matt said, "Looks like you called it right, Habib. It certainly looks like acute food poisoning. I'll take my samples back to our lab and let you know our results in a week or so."

"Thank you so much, and it's good to know that it was not a result of terrorism. I hope you have a safe trip home."

"Very happy to help. Would you like me to assist in closing up the body?"

Habib replied, "No, I will have one of my staff close and prepare the body for the family. Again, have a safe trip home, and thanks for your assistance."

After Matt boarded the plane, he used a secure phone to reach his boss at the FBI. "It certainly appears to be arsenic poisoning, but we will have to run some tests when I get back to confirm. I left the coroner with the impression it was my opinion that it was food poisoning, and he concurred."

Chapter 19 Georgetown, DC

It had been a busy week for both Sandy and Morgan. Sandy was able to select an agent who recommended a few changes and suggested what should be moved out and what should stay for staging the house. Sandy lined up movers, and in two days, they packed and moved things the fifteen miles to the farm in Great Falls. Some of his things went into the barn or one of the sheds since he didn't need them right away, the rest were in the living room for now. By Friday, Sandy's house was ready for the staging company to come in and get it ready for the market. The photographer came in the afternoon, and by that night, the house was on the market with an open house on Saturday and Sunday.

Morgan had been equally busy supporting several clients' patent applications and revisions to get their product through the tangled web of USPTO. She also had several clients that were foreign companies supporting their efforts for US patent protection. Particularly challenging was taking the translated patents and converting them to acceptable English for the application.

They decided to go out for Italian at a nearby restaurant on M street, a short walk from Morgan's home. Over dinner, Sandy said, "I've got an idea, not sure if we can pull it off, but what if we went out to the Eastern Shore tomorrow morning. I know a place near St. Michaels right on the bay. We can rent a sailboat and go sailing tomorrow."

"Sandy," Morgan smiled, "Have I told you how much I love you? That sounds amazing. We both could use a break and it would be nice to get out of town."

Sandy smiled, feeling very good inside. "Consider it done!"

Sandy made a few calls from the restaurant, and soon they were all set for a weekend of sailing on the Eastern Shore. Both were up early, and two hours later they were in St. Michaels picking up the boat. Sandy walked up to a neat shack in front of the boatyard, carrying their bags, and poked his head in the open door. "Master Chief, how are you, sir?"

"Commander Powell, you're looking great, and who's this beautiful woman?"

"Chief meet Morgan Dutton. She's the answer to many prayers."

"I can believe that, and you were in luck when you called. I had a cancellation and was able to get you a Catalina 30 that will give you a great weekend. I don't need it back till midweek so enjoy. It's fully equipped with charts, fishing poles, and all the gear you need."

"Thanks so much, Master Chief, we plan to be back Sunday night or early Monday morning."

While Sandy got the boat ready, Morgan bought some food to eat onboard, and by ten in the morning, they were underway. Copper enjoyed the boat but mostly stayed in the cabin and slept.

They motored out of the harbor and were under full

sail after 15 minutes. With a gentle breeze out of the south, Sandy had to tack back and forth so they could sail south on the Chesapeake Bay. After a few hours, they found a quiet cove where they dropped anchor, ate some lunch, and took a dip in the warm water of the bay. Sandy and Copper swam a hundred yards to shore and ran around a bit, and Copper relieved himself.

They had a quiet afternoon sailing about the bay and then across to the western shore, where they docked at Chesapeake Beach. There they had a wonderful meal in a local crab house restaurant. The next day they sailed south past Tangier Island almost to the ocean before turning about and heading north to St. Michaels. It was very late by the time they returned to the dock, so they crashed on the boat that night, and after turning in the boat, left early Monday morning when the traffic was still light over the Bay Bridge. They arrived back at Morgan's house in great time.

As they unloaded their gear, Sandy watched Morgan with Copper following closely behind her into the house. He sighed contentedly.

Sandy thought, "We are definitely an item, it gave him a warm feeling inside. One of these days we should discuss the next steps..."

Monday evening, while they ate a quiet dinner, the real estate agent called to say she'd received three offers all above asking. Sandy chose one, and they celebrated.

Sandy's exploration into hydrogen gas was only just beginning. While there had been a lot unearthed since his grandfather's discovery, on first reading, it didn't appear that any method produced the volume of gas with so little energy input. The puzzle intrigued him, and he pushed hard all week at the Library of Congress learning, more and more about hydrogen and its production.

Brooke Tate was working at her station when an alert came through. Paragon, with nearly limitless resources, was like a mini version of the NSA. They'd installed backdoors in major systems around the world and were constantly monitoring traffic for keywords to determine if competitors to the Pinnacle Club had emerged.

Brooke's alert was that someone at the Library of Congress was doing a deep dive into hydrogen. The system was smart enough not to send up a flag if someone pinged one of the keywords once or twice, but only when it was more constant.

Brooke started her analysis. Pretty quickly, she was able to determine that the person had pulled up over 40 papers and articles on hydrogen gas and its production over the past three days. She had the IP address as the Library of Congress wireless network. She installed a tiny virus that would signal them whenever the device connected to the internet. So far, she'd been unable to break through the firewall on the device to pull down data off its hard drive. Brooke sent an alert to her boss, Lynn Nash, with the information she had.

Ten minutes later Lynn, sat down at Brooke's station and looked on with her at the three monitors with data on the suspect. Lynn asked, "Do you have any new information or made any progress breaking in?"

Brooke said, "I'm still trying to break through the firewall, but it seems pretty strong. I should be able to get through in the next thirty minutes."

Lynn looked at the clock on one of the displays and realized at most they had an hour before it was 5 p.m. eastern time. Lynn said, "I'm going to have Van come over and work with you. He's a black hat extraordinaire; if anyone can break it, he can. Heck, he probably designed the firewall."

"Thanks so much."

Van arrived shortly and slid in beside Brooke. Van was a pure techie, overweight, zooming on the caffeine from his nonstop energy drinks, and clearly needed a trip to the corporate shower. He quickly assessed the data on the three screens and then asked, "Can I take over for a few minutes?"

"Of course." Brooke rolled back from her station.

Van rapidly typed some commands and sent them through the ether to the device they were tracking. Before long, he cracked the firewall and slipped a different virus into the device. Through the crack, he also harvested some key data, including the device's digital fingerprint.

Van said to Brooke, "I'm going to leave the hole open so you can capture some files, but don't copy too much, or they may notice. I will be back in five minutes to close it, so move quickly."

"Thanks." Brooke quickly scanned through the directories, found some key files, and grabbed them.

She activated the camera and took a picture of the guy using it and thought he was kind of cute.

A few minutes later, Van returned and closed their opening. Brooke began her more in-depth analysis. An hour later, she had a pretty extensive background on the person using the device. She created her report and let Lynn know she was ready to review it.

Lynn sat with Brooke as she reviewed the report. "The user appeared to be Sandy Powell. He lives in Fairfax, Virginia, and has several bank accounts. He was researching hydrogen gas production for the past week. The intent was unknown."

Lynn looked at all they had and said, "Ok, let's keep track of him 24/7 for a week and see if this leads to something or if it's just another flash in the pan."

Brooke agreed with the assessment and began tracking. Unless something big happened, this was often the end of an assignment.

Chapter 21 Washington, DC

At the Robert F. Kennedy Department of Justice Building, things were spinning up fast. With the confirmation that Ali Mohammed had been murdered, this case became very real. Add to this the apparent involvement of three of the global leaders in the oil and gas business, and this situation became much more than an ordinary antitrust matter.

Attorney General Charles Caserta called Stuart Ervin, Director of the CIA, on a secure line. "Stuart, how are things at Langley?"

"Good, we're beginning to get clean intel on the terrorists around the world. Feels like the good guys are finally winning."

"Great, happy to hear that. I've got a situation that I need your assistance with. We just confirmed that the Nigerian Minister for Oil and Gas was murdered. We've got solid information from a State Department employee that leaders of the three largest oil companies sanctioned this action."

"Wow, that's news. How can I help, and what's in it for our little department?"

"Stuart, you know I'm always happy to share the stage for mutual accolades. I need your station in Nigeria to find out who murdered him and get the chain of command back to the oil companies."

"Ok, I will set the wheels in motion and keep you updated. Looking forward to being on stage with you if we put this all together."

****

Melissa Pearson entered the office of the Attorney General. It looked very much like a judge's chambers, dark wood paneling, a simple marble fireplace, a large desk covered with papers, and a whole bunch of photos and curios on the mantel and scattered about the room. A United States flag stood in a corner by a glass-paneled curio closet. The room felt very personal. Charles Caserta rose to greet her. He was five-eight with black hair, a rich smile, and his Italian heritage self-evident.

"Welcome to my office. I appreciate you jumping over the chain of command and sending this matter to me directly. I will personally smooth any feathers that may have been ruffled. The potential political nature of this means we need to keep it very tight. I've invited Assistant Deputy AG Rod Holloway to join us, and he should be here momentarily. Have a seat."

Just then, there was a light knock on the door, and Rod stepped into the room. Charlie continued, "Rod, thanks for joining us. As I mentioned to Melissa, I want to keep the circle on this tight. Rod, I want you to personally take the point on this investigation. Based on the sworn statements from Bob and Sally Lancaster I believe we've got probable cause. We can skip doing an assessment and begin a preliminary investigation.

Due to the nature of this investigation, I can imagine we could have several other agencies involved, including the CIA, State, and NSA. I would like you to request warrants from a magistrate judge to get the phone and other records for these three individuals and their companies. We should probably go back five years and see if we can find any correlation in their records. Additionally, I want a team assembled at the FBI to do a deep dive into the financial records to see if there's anything there."

At this point, Charlie paused, and with a grim smile on his face, turned to his Assistant Deputy AG and asked, "Rod, your thoughts?"

Rod was a former Air Force prosecuting attorney, his hair high, and tight, and the gray was beginning to show. "As I see it, there are two additional points that require immediate investigation. One is to determine, if possible, who poisoned Ali. Second, in Bob Lancaster's notes, he mentioned Paragon. So, I want a group at the FBI to try to determine who that is. I will coordinate with Lester Hodges at the FBI to get it started on their end."

"Excellent. I've got a meeting with the Director tomorrow, and I'll update him. Obviously, loop me in if we reach out to other agencies. I'm going to call Director Ervin at the CIA and brief him in right after this meeting. Melissa, I want you to report directly to Rod on this, and Rod, I want you to talk to her supervisor to smooth over the chain of command issue." Charlie stood, and it was clear the meeting was over.

****

After exiting the AG's office Rod said to Melissa, "Walk with me; we'll discuss the next steps in my office." They walked down the long corridor, turned the corner, and entered Rod's suite. Walking past his admin, he called out, "Hold my calls, please, Doris. Melissa, do you want anything to drink?"

"Yes, thank you, black coffee would be great."

They entered his office and sat at a table adjacent to his desk. A moment later, Doris entered with a large mug of steaming coffee. "Anything else Mr. Holloway?"

"No, I'm good. Thanks, Doris." Turning to Melissa, "I know your background is in antitrust, so I would like you to chase that rabbit. Let's start with the following assumption. First, let's assume they're working together. Next, make a list of the evidence we need to convict them on antitrust violations, say under the Sherman Act or similar. Next figure out who in the department, the FBI, or other agencies could collect that evidence and get back to me. I will help you assemble that team, and then we can collect the information."

"Excellent, I'll start on it straight away. And Rod," she said sincerely, "Thank you for your support in this investigation."

He nodded and smiled at Melissa as she stood and headed out of the office. "Let's hope we get to the bottom of this...quickly," he said.

And with the door still open, he called out, "Doris, do you have a second?" Doris stepped into Rod's office. "Can you ask Lester Hodges to meet with me at his earliest opportunity? Thanks."

"Absolutely. Is there anything else?"

"No, I'm good. I need about 30 minutes uninterrupted to pull some thoughts together. Thank you." Doris stepped out and closed his door.

★★★★

Over breakfast, Morgan said, "I'm happy with our life now that we're sleeping together. You know you're a quiet sleeper."

"Really good to know I don't snore or toss and turn."

"Well, there's the part where you've got your arm wrapped around me, and I try to move or go to the bathroom, and you just pull me tighter. I really like staying downtown during the week and escaping to our country home for the weekend. Yup, we're a bit spoiled. I like going for the morning run. I can eat anything and don't put on a pound," Morgan said.

"We're lucky that Glover Archbold Park is nearby, and if we go all the way and back, it's a nice six-mile run."

"How's Jackson doing?"

"He's great. He does keep complaining about how dry it is this year."

"I always thought that Australia was supposed to be dry."

"I guess not so much where he is in the Hunter Valley. Is Vicky coming for dinner? Anything, in particular, you'd like me to fix?"

"How about some kind of seafood."

Sandy grinned, "Your wish is my command."

"How's research going?"

"Industrial production is mainly from steam reforming natural gas. What they do at a chemical plant is combine methane with steam, aka water, at high temperatures with a catalyst creating carbon monoxide and hydrogen. The problem is it's very inefficient, so the resulting hydrogen is expensive, plus you get carbon monoxide."

"Wow, you're really getting into this aren't you? I thought you were a biologist," she said with a smile.

"Oh, but you know there's a lot of chemistry that goes along with a biology degree. I had to take organic chem in college. The cool thing is if my grandfather's process really works as efficiently as I hope it does, it changes the whole economic picture."

"So, do they create hydrogen using electrolysis?"

"Oh, yeah. But that's even less efficient than steam reforming."

Morgan looked a little perplexed. "So what would they use the hydrogen for?"

"They use hydrogen today to split long-chain petrochemicals into more usable products. They also use a lot of it to produce fertilizer. If we had a cheap source of hydrogen, we could switch from gasoline and diesel engines to hydrogen fuel cells to power cars, trucks, and lots of things. Even to produce electricity with the only output being water. No pollution."

Morgan quickly realized, "Hydrogen could totally change the way we work and create energy on a global scale."

Sandy sighed, shaking his head slightly, "That's probably why my grandfather was killed. Someone found out about what he was doing."

"But-" Morgan started to say, frowning...

Sandy cut in abruptly as if to cut off her questions. "So, how is your work going?"

Morgan smiled slightly and said, "I see what you're doing, and I'll let it go for now...but remember, we're a team, you know."

She held up her hand, as Sandy was starting to protest, and quickly said, "My work is great. I'm actually a bit ahead, so I thought I would take some time this week to begin researching your grandfather's patent."

"What do you mean... research? We've got his patent; can't we just file it?"

"Well, over the years, others may have invented something similar, so I will look at existing patents and literature to see what's out there. Then I need to craft the claims to weave through the existing information, so they're unique. It's more or less what I do every day."

"You know, sweetheart, you're pretty amazing. I'm truly a lucky guy."

"Yes, you are, and it seems to me you've been getting lucky a lot lately."

Sandy said in a husky voice, "For sure and no complaints from me."

Rod went to his desk, pulled out a yellow legal pad, and started making some notes.

What do we know? There was a meeting between the CEOs of the three largest oil companies in the world in Nigeria. They're all US companies. They discussed joint problems with Ali Mohammed, the Minister for Oil and Gas. They also discussed paying him, but he wanted more. They talked about problems in Saudi and Indonesia. A week later, Ali was murdered. They mentioned Paragon would fix things.

What are our next steps? Rod started a list.

- Who is Paragon – FBI to investigate
- Who killed Ali – FBI, State, CIA, and Nigerian government. Can we trust the Nigerian government at this point? No, we have no idea how high the infiltration goes, so we need to do this without their help at this point. Nigeria doesn't know that Ali was murdered. He crossed them out. Have to use the CIA to investigate – follow the money.
- Need in-depth profiles on Harold Watson, Bryce Carrington, and Reginald Clark – three separate FBI analysts, so the investigators don't

see the correlation. - FBI

- Need briefing on their companies and subsidiaries. – FBI
- Need warrants - Dean Mclaughlin to draw up a request
- Need five years of telephone records to see if there are matches – NSA & FBI
- Follow the money – can we backtrack from Nigeria to find out where the money tree came from – FBI analyst
- How did Watson, Carrington, and Clark arrange their travel and where did they stay, who coordinated the meeting. Clearly not the first meeting. Can we see if travel plans align on other dates – FBI and FAA
- Political implications – make sure that's included in the profiles

That afternoon Rod met with Lester Hodges, Deputy Director of the FBI in his office. "Lester, how are you?"

"Good, what's up that you need to meet rather urgently?"

Rod said, "We've got an interesting investigation, and I'm going to need a bunch of your resources. My gut feel is this could be huge, and it could have some serious political implications."

Rod spent the next thirty minutes reviewing his notes and requests for the Bureau to investigate. They discussed the involvement of other agencies and agreed they needed a bit more evidence, even if it was circumstantial, before getting this too far out of their control.

Lester agreed to get a small team and multiple independent analysts working on various aspects. They both agreed, at this point, they didn't want too much coordination so that people couldn't see where it was leading. The more people in the dark at this point, the better.

****

At breakfast on Friday, Sandy said, "When we go out to the farm tomorrow, I think I feel comfortable testing Grandpa's invention. You know, see if it works."

Morgan smiled. "Sounds good. Plus, we've got the swatches and samples to look at for our remodel."

Saturday morning, they were off, and Copper loved riding along with the top down. The farm looked great, but, as usual, the lawn grew exponentially. Something about the Northern Virginia weather, and he made a mental note that he needed to mow the yard this afternoon.

He and Morgan left Copper on the porch and went to the barn, opened the cupboard, and descended into the basement. Sandy turned on the fan, and cool air was replaced with fresh air from outside.

From Grandpa's notes, Sandy knew to look on the shelves under the staircase to find the box with the ingredients to build the electrolysis setup. "This is pretty cool to think this sat here for about forty years hidden away."

"Even if it doesn't work, it's incredible."

Sandy and Morgan carried the boxes over to the table in the middle of the room. They took notes Sandy had written from his grandfather's directions and began to assemble the electrolysis tank. Pretty soon, they had it assembled, water and chemicals in the tank, and the transformer hooked up. "Why don't we just turn it on for a minute and see if anything happens?"

"Ok, sounds good to me, but remember your grandfather mentioned getting blown across the room when he put a match near it, so just keep it quick. Then we can set up the cover and put the hose into the pail of water."

"Great idea." Sandy turned on the transformer, and immediately bubbles were created near the plates in the tank. He quickly turned off the transformer. He and Morgan did a high five.

"All right, time to get the lid on the tank and set up the hose and try that."

After making sure the lid was on tight and the hose secured, Sandy turned on the transformer, and it began bubbling away. Sandy held a lighter near the end of the hose, and they had a powerful flame shooting out from the hose.

"We did it. We're making hydrogen; this is too cool."

"Very cool! Ok, I'll turn off the transformer. I remember from his notes that he couldn't get it to work with another transformer, and he felt that was part of the equation. Let's see if we can find the other transformer."

After fifteen minutes of searching, they found another transformer that looked like the first one. According to the plate on the bottom, it was the same model number, so this had to be it. They hooked it up, turned it on, and they only saw a few bubbles.

Morgan said, "Let's check to see that it's working."

They found a meter and hooked it to the transformer wires, and sure enough, it was working. Then they hooked the first transformer up, and it had the same reading on the meter.

"This is strange. It must be something we aren't seeing," Morgan said, shaking her head and frowning.

Sandy sighed. "Well, you're right. I'm going to have to do some digging into this situation. How about we close this up and go back to the house." He smiled, "I feel a nice evening of barbequed ribs, roasted potatoes, and a wedge salad coming on."

Morgan pecked his cheek. "Any moonlight and stargazing with that meal?"

"I'm counting on that."

Sandy and Morgan cleaned up a little bit, turned off the fan, and headed upstairs. They carefully closed the cupboard.

Sandy thought for a moment. "I want to see if I close the cupboard behind me if I can reopen it. Just wait here in case I can't get out."

****

Danjuma and Ismail were police detectives in Lagos, but they were also undercover CIA agents. They enjoyed double-dipping, and their day jobs gave them both cover and a great deal of latitude to gather information. Their CIA station chief had advised them that he had it on good authority that Ali Mohammed,

Nigerian Minister for Oil and Gas, had been murdered by poisoning. They needed to find out who at the restaurant the evening before his death had delivered the poison, and more importantly who paid to have it done.

After a few days of observation, it became obvious that Faruq Eze had been paid off. While he still worked at the restaurant, he'd just purchased a new TV and furniture. He was also seen haggling over the price of a car. Danjuma and Ismail entered Faruq's shack on Odunnukan Street at three a.m. The shack had two rooms, one for sleeping the other for cooking and relaxing. Faruq's wife shrieked when the two men entered their bedroom. Danjuma told her to be quiet while Ismail pulled a sleepy Faruq from his bed. Together they cuffed and dragged him out of the house and pushed him into the back of their unmarked police car.

They took him five kilometers away to a deserted dark road bordering the Lagos Lagoon. Dragging Faruq from the car, Ismail punched him as hard as he could in the stomach doubling him over, and he fell to the ground. They stood him up against the car. "We know you poisoned Ali Mohammed and got paid for it. Who paid you to do it?" Ismail asked.

Faruq gasped for breath, "I don't know." Ismail hit him again and they stood him back up against the car.

"We need to know who paid you, or this doesn't end well for you."

"He was English. He comes to the restaurant from time to time. He was about 1.7 meters tall, slight build, strong English accent, brown hair, and eyes."

"Where did he meet you, and what did he tell you to do?" Danjuma asked.

"He met me behind the restaurant in the afternoon and gave me a large sugar packet and told me to put it on his food and make certain he got that plate. Then he handed me a thick bundle of One Thousand Naira notes. About three and half million Naira. He said if I didn't put the powder on his food, my family would die a terrible death. Then he walked away. That's all I know."

"If you see this man again, call me, immediately." Danjuma handed him his police card. They removed the cuffs and put him back in the back seat of the car. They drove him back and dropped him off a block from his home. "Don't speak to anyone, even your wife, about tonight. Ever."

Sandy stepped back into the space behind the cupboard and pulled it closed. He heard the click and noticed a small latch on the back of the cupboard. When he turned the latch, he heard the click and was able to open it again.

"Ok, now I want you to lower the shelf and see if it still works."

Again, he pulled the closet closed. "Ok, please lower the shelf." He heard Morgan lower the shelf and noticed there was a mechanism that moved when she lowered it. He turned the latch again - click. The door was unlocked.

Stepping out he said, "This is good to know that we won't get locked in the basement." He showed her how the latch worked on the backside of the cupboard.

They walked over to the house, and Copper was wagging his whole body, so happy to see them back. They went into the house and got some more water for Copper. As always, he was glued to Morgan.

As they walked through the house, Morgan said, "Beyond a few minor things, this is a great house. Your aunt had great taste with the kitchen remodel, so it's really up to date, and with the layout and four bedrooms and two baths upstairs, it really is lovely. I think some bathroom updates," she pointed to the box with paint and flooring samples on the kitchen island, "is all it really needs."

"I agree. So, we just have to figure out what to do down the road," he said. "You know, it's kind of remote. I'm going to find out if we can improve the internet and also have the security system upgraded next week to add some cameras so we can keep a better eye on things when we're downtown."

"I think that's a really good idea, especially with what we know is in the basement of the barn!"

Sandy thought for a moment. "I need to mow the yard. It shouldn't take me more than an hour. Are you ok just hanging around?"

"Of course. Copper and I'll check to see if there are any rabbits and may do a little gardening in the flower beds. You take your time, and we'll see you soon."

Sandy headed off to the barn to get the John Deere tractor out, and Morgan and Copper went around to the front of the house. An hour or so later, they all met up on the front porch. Somehow it was already five o'clock.

"Well," Sandy looked down at his watch. "I'm afraid it's too late for our delicious barbeque – we won't be eating for hours!"

"We can have it tomorrow," Morgan said. "Go out tonight?"

A knowing look came over Sandy's face. "Yesss," he said slowly. "And, if you'll excuse me for a minute, I'll make a quick call for a reservation."

"Sounds fancy." Morgan raised her eyebrows. "I'll just go upstairs to freshen up a bit."

Sandy nodded and walked out onto the deck while Morgan went upstairs to the master bath.

After Sandy cleaned up, he and Morgan settled Copper in until they returned. A few miles away, tucked off a local road, they pulled into the gravel parking lot of L'Auberge Chez François. Sandy parked and put the roof up on the car, and they walked in.

Sandy remarked, "You won't believe this, but this is a very coveted restaurant and consistently ranked in the top 100 in the DC metro and even top 100 in America."

"Wow, out here off the beaten trail!"

"Yup, fortunately, I know the owner and was able to get us a table on short notice." Just then, the hostess returned to her stand.

With a very French accent, she said "Sandy!!! How are you and who is this lovely woman?"

"Marie, allow me to introduce you to the love of my life, Morgan Dutton. I'm surprised to see you, seating guests."

"A pleasure to meet you. You're a very lucky mademoiselle to capture this guy. Our wonderful hostess became ill today, so I'm stepping in."

Morgan replied with a grin, "Le plaisir est pour moi et oui j'ai beaucoup de chance. Je ne vais pas le laisser partir." *(The pleasure is for me and yes, I'm very lucky. I won't let him go.)*

Marie smiled. "Bien pour vous. C'est un hic." *("Good*

for you. He's a catch.")

"Ok, you two enough talking behind my back."

Marie led them back to a quiet table on the side of the restaurant.

"I will let Jacques know you're here with your love."

"So now I'm the love of your life. That's a huge upgrade."

Sandy glowed, and he grinned from ear to ear. "Well, you are, and I'm very lucky."

After dinner but before dessert, Jacques and Marie came to the table. Greetings were shared and hugs around. Jacques expressed his sadness for the loss of Sandy's aunt, and he insisted that they come back again soon on a Monday for lunch when the restaurant was closed so they could relax and catch up. Sandy and Morgan happily agreed.

A week later, Danjuma's cell phone rang. It was Faruq. "The man is in the restaurant eating lunch."

"Don't do anything. Don't even look at him. We will be there in a few minutes."

Danjuma and Ismail pulled up to the restaurant and parked in front. They walked in and up to the obviously English man.

Ismail said, "Please stand up. You're under arrest."

The man stood and started to speak when Ismail shook his head and said, "Not here, not now."

They walked him out of the restaurant with his hands handcuffed behind his back and placed him in the back of their car. They drove across town to Tin Can Island, pulled into a sea of shipping containers, and parked.

It was a sunny 90-degree day when they got out of the car. Danjuma opened the door to a 20-foot shipping container. The heat rolled out the open door. Danjuma and Ismail yanked the Englishman from the back seat and walked him to the container. They pulled out his wallet and a roll of bills from his front pocket. The man yelled, "What're you doing? What're you doing?"

Neither one said anything. They pushed him into the container, closed, and locked the door. Returning to their car they drove off. The man in the container heard the lock being put on the door and heard the car drive off. He sat up in the darkness, slid his butt across the floor and leaned against the container wall. It was getting really hot, and he thought, this is a shitty way to die.

About midnight, the agents returned to the container. Leaving the car running and the lights on, they unlocked the container and opened both doors. "Oh my God, it really stinks in here," Ismail said.

The Englishman was on the floor in a fetal position. They both walked back to the car and got three folding chairs from the trunk. They set up the chairs inside the container. One chair facing the car and the other two facing the single chair far enough apart that they wouldn't block the glare from the headlights.

Together they pulled the man erect and led him to the chair facing the car. As they walked over to their chairs, Ismail pulled a roll of bills from his front pocket, and peeled off the top one, and handed it to Danjuma. "You were right, he soiled himself." They both chuckled.

Danjuma said, "Ok, what's your name, and who do you work for?"

"Who are you? Why am I here?"

Ismail said, "I told you he wasn't going to cooperate."

He walked over and pulled the chair out from under the Englishman, who collapsed to the floor. Danjuma stood, folded up the other chairs, and they started to leave the container.

"Wait, wait, I'll tell you everything you want to know."

Ismail looked at Danjuma. "I don't think he has had enough time to think about this. I think he'll be more trustworthy tomorrow night. Let's just go."

The man was curled up on the floor and sobbing. "Please, I will tell you all you want to know."

They calmly walked back and set up the chairs again. They lifted him off the floor and put him back in his chair.

Danjuma started again, "What's your name, and who do you work for?"

"My name is Harry Atkinson, and I work for Global Research here in Lagos."

Ismail was writing notes, and Danjuma asked, "Where's your office located?"

"39 Obafemi Awolowo Way, Agidingbi."

"What does your company do?"

"We do background research on mostly the oil and gas industry."

Ismail stood up. "See, I told you he would just feed us a line of bullshit. Let's go."

Danjuma said, "Let's see if he gets a bit smarter and if not, I'm with you, and we can come back tomorrow night. So, Harry, this is your chance to be brilliant or not. Totally up to you."

"That is what we do and then other projects."

Danjuma continued, "So, why did you have the Minister for Oil and Gas murdered?"

"Murdered?"

"I told you, he is having that credibility problem. Let's go."

"Ok, it was a project ordered by headquarters. I don't know why."

Taking a different tack, Danjuma said, "So how many people work in your office on Awolowo Way, and what are their names."

"Five including myself," and he told them their names.

"Do you have any other offices in Nigeria?"

"Not that I know of."

"Are you the boss of this office?"

"No, Bob Jones heads the office."

"Where's headquarters?"

"I don't know. I just work there, and my only contact is with my coworkers."

"Ok, Harry, this is all good. We're going to take you downtown, so we can talk further, then we'll book you for murder."

"Wait, you can't charge me with murder. I didn't kill him."

"Right Harry, that's like the guy with the smoking gun saying, I didn't kill him, the gun did."

Danjuma and Ismail dragged him out to the car and put him in the back seat, then pulled a black hood over his head. They went back, got the folding chairs, and drove not to police headquarters but rather to a CIA safe house. Another CIA operative dressed as a local cop began questioning Harry.

The next day about 10 a.m., a CIA team went to the office dressed as Lagos police. They entered the office and arrested four people, including Bob Jones. They were led out of the building in handcuffs and placed in separate cars. As soon as they left the office, another team of three entered the office and removed all the file cabinets, computers, and any loose papers. It was like the office had been vacuum cleaned. All the material was transported to the CIA office at the embassy.

Bob Jones and his three staffers were all placed in separate rooms at the safe house, and one by one, they were questioned.

Danjuma and Ismail started the interrogation of Bob Jones, who was handcuffed to the desk, by informing him he was being charged with conspiracy to commit murder, and they already had a confession from Harry Atkinson.

Ismail turned his laptop so Bob could see it and hit play. The screen showed a man with a noose around his neck drop from a platform and struggle for five minutes while he was slowly and clearly painfully asphyxiated.

Bob was visibly shaking from what he watched.

"See, here in Nigeria, we hang people for murder. We've got compassionate hangings that are swift, or we've got less compassionate hangings. Kind of depends on how helpful you are. It's even possible if you're really helpful that we could get your charges reduced. So, we'd like to know, who you report to at headquarters?"

"I don't know his name or where headquarters is even located."

"Bob, see, you're not being helpful, and that doesn't have a good ending for you."

Danjuma, now playing bad cop, said, "Let's just send him to the general population and let them soften him up for a few days. He can be a bitch to a whole bunch of those thugs and see if his memory comes back."

"Works for me," Ismail said. They stood and headed for the door.

****

Rod Holloway had Dean McLaughlin prepare the applications and affidavits and received warrants against Watson, Carrington, and Clark and their companies and affiliates. Since the individuals and companies were located in different states, the warrants were obtained in different District Courts. All the warrants were sealed due to the nature of the alleged crimes. Rod passed this information over to Lester Hodges at the FBI.

****

Melissa Pearson summarized the elements to build an antitrust case in a brief memo to Rod Holloway.

From: Melissa Pearson

DREW THORN

To: Rod Holloway

RE: Antitrust Approach

Core to any antitrust action are three laws; The Sherman Act (1890), Federal Trade Commission Act (1914), and the Clayton Act (1914). There have been minor revisions, but these are the basis for antitrust action. Separately and together, they prohibit:

Price fixing, i.e. predatory and discriminatory pricing

Conspiracy to monopolize

Restraint of trade

Anti-competitive mergers

Limitation of competition

Should the department prove that the companies' leadership endeavored to work together to achieve one or more of the above acts, we would have a strong case to bring against these companies. Settlements in a case like this could be substantial, as shown by the recent class action settlement against Enron of over $7 billion.

I believe one avenue to pursue would be to determine the price-fixing of finished products such as gasoline, jet fuel, and diesel fuel. This would include coordinated price reduction allowing one or more of these companies to acquire competitors.

Another avenue would be to demonstrate their conspiracy to monopolize the industry. It would require the DOJ to find documents or testimony clearly showing their joint efforts to control the industry.

Should you need further information or clarification, please contact me. Melissa.

B ob Jones shouted, "Wait, I can tell you some things."

"Ok, tell us about headquarters," Ismail said.

"I don't know much. We're pretty isolated. My boss's name is Todd, and he has an American accent."

"Ok, how do you contact him?"

"It's all through encrypted email. I never call him, and he rarely calls me."

Ismail asked, "How do you get funds?"

"We've got a numbered account; I don't know where, and we transfer funds to a local Nigerian bank which we use for payroll, expenses, and other things."

"Do you bribe officials with those funds?"

"Sometimes, it depends on the person. For example, we paid Ali Mohammed nearly half a million US over the past two years. We also paid Arsalan Aziz, the Vice Minister, about $250,000 US and others."

"We'll need a list. So, if you were paying Ali, why have him murdered?" Ismail asked.

"He was not doing what we told him to do."

"And what did you want him to do?"

"We wanted certain companies to win the leasing rights in various oil fields, but he was awarding contracts to other companies."

"Bob, here is where we are. I appreciate you're beginning to cooperate. I'm going to get a pad of paper and pen, and I want you to write down everything from when you first met these guys through today. Every single detail, account numbers, passwords, names, everything you can think of. We will arrange for you to have a comfortable, safe cell, and we will come back tomorrow and review your notes."

****

Dylan Harrison got the call early on a Wednesday afternoon from Lester Hodges' office to come to his office at 4 p.m. for a short meeting. Hodges was Deputy Director of the FBI, and Harrison was multiple levels below. Dylan had no idea what was going on but was understandably nervous. Arriving ten minutes early, he waited in the reception area.

Precisely at 4 p.m., Lester walked into the office area and greeted Harrison. "Dylan, come to my office."

"Yes, sir."

"Have a seat. I've got a small project I want three of your analysts to work on. I've secured access to the FAA plane registration records and the flight log database. While much is public information with this access, you may get more and certainly easier analysis. The usernames and passwords are on this sheet of paper, as well as specific instructions for what we're seeking. It's critical that the three people assigned to this project not know what the other person is working on. This is a highly classified project. The people you select must have a TS-SCI clearance."

"Ok."

"Dylan, I want five years of flight records of dates, times, and airports for all planes owned or used by American Petroleum, Sunco Power, and TXO anywhere on the planet. Each analyst will work up the data for one company independent of the other two. When the data is assembled, I want you to take that information and determine where there's overlap for two or all three companies. You'll report directly to me. If you've got any issues, come directly to me. Are we clear?"

"Crystal, Sir."

"This project is your only priority. I want a comprehensive job, but time is of the essence. I've already spoken to Jodie Harper, and she knows you're working on a classified project for me directly. Good luck." Lester stood, shook hands with Dylan, and sat back down.

Meeting over, Dylan turned and left the office.

Thank God I wasn't called on the carpet for something, he thought. And, I'm sure glad he cleared it with Jodie, so she isn't looking over my shoulder on this.

Back at his cubicle, Dylan thought of who'd do the best job and keep it quiet. He picked Leo Gibson, Hannah Cox, and Erin Palmer. He sent out individual emails for meetings tomorrow morning and afternoon.

****

Lester Hodges asked Amber Dean to meet him in his office at 9 a.m. tomorrow. Amber was a 35-year-old senior agent, a Caribbean black mother of two middle-school kids who enjoyed binge-watching boxed sets and yoga. She was known in her department for delivering on challenging cases.

"Amber, thanks for coming up. We've got reason to believe that Harold Watson, Bryce Carrington, and Reginald Clark are conspiring together. Their names may not ring a bell, but they're the CEOs of the three largest oil and gas companies in the world. You don't need to know the details, but here is what I need your analysts to do. I want you to drill into their phone records: office and cell and see if you can find them talking to each other over the past five years. These guys travel internationally, and we know of one international meeting recently, so if you need assistance from NSA, just let me know. This is a highly classified project, so make sure the people you assign are cleared and understand this isn't to be discussed. While we don't need them, we do have a search warrant for each of the individuals and their companies. Contact Dean Mclaughlin at DOJ if you've got any questions on the warrants."

"Sounds like fun, love a challenge like this."

****

Lester also had teams assembling a brief on the individuals and the companies, as well as looking at their financial records.

Morgan asked, "Would you like some coffee?" as she, Sandy, and Copper walked into the kitchen from the backyard in Georgetown.

"That would be awesome, thanks!" Sandy smiled and looked up as he was taking off Copper's halter and leash. "We had a great run this morning. How do you feel?"

"Really good. You're getting me in great shape. Now I can eat anything I want, and I don't have to worry about putting on a single pound. Oh," Morgan looked over from the sink where she was filling the drip coffee pot with water. "I forgot to tell you I finished the research on your grandfather's patent, and I'm ready to file it."

"Awesome, do we file it in his name?"

"Nope, it has to be in your name since your grandfather passed away many years ago, and if we used him, it would be invalid due to the elapsed time. But we'll always know it was his invention. Have you had any luck with the transformer issue?"

Sandy nodded, "I think so. I contacted a friend of mine, and he recommended a guy who's a genius at electronics. I set up a meeting for tomorrow. I'm going to bring both transformers and see if we can figure out the difference and if we can buy or build a transformer like the one that's producing the hydrogen. So, I'm going to run out to the farm today and pick them up. Would you like to ride along?"

"Sorry. Wish I could. I've got a couple of things I must do at the patent office, and I'll drop off your patent today. If the electronics guy discovers something novel, we can amend the patent after it's filed but still maintain the filing date." Then, with a huge grin, she added, "So, you're going to get help? I thought you'd be an electronics wizard as well as a hydrogen expert."

Sandy just smiled and didn't bite. The coffee was ready, and they relaxed at the kitchen table and watched the morning local news. Being DC, the bulk of the news was on the political diatribe that DC thrived on.

Morgan reflected, "This drives me nuts how they can all carry on about things and act like they're actually doing something."

"It's politics, if they weren't politicians, they'd be actors, which is really what most of them are. Overpaid actors."

After that, they both headed off in different directions.

Copper, as always, loved riding up front in the car with Sandy, and soon the twosome was at the farm.

"A bit like old times," Sandy said as he rubbed Copper's ears. Copper looked up into Sandy's face, gave his happy "Woof," and Sandy laughed. "Ok," he said to Copper as they disembarked from the car. I'll take off your leash and let you run around but don't go too far. We're not here for an overnighter this time!"

Copper gave several excited barks and started running around, sniffing out whatever small game had been nearby.

Sandy shook his head and smiled. Then went to work. "Start with the basement in the barn." And he headed over to the barn and went down into the basement, happy he had checked the locking system. Not that I plan on getting locked in down there, he mused, but it's a lonely place to get stuck if something did happen that way.

Once down in the barn basement, he labeled and collected both of the transformers his grandfather had been working with. It didn't take long and before he knew it, he was walking back to the house where he noted that the new internet line was installed on the side.

I've got to thank Ben. Another thing off the list. He went inside to check out the connection.

Ben Schmidt was the son of Kurt Schmidt, Aunt Beth's closest neighbor. The two had grown up together – their families very close. The Schmidt family stepping up to help the Powell family after the death of Dick. Sandy enlisted Ben's help to look after the place when he was in DC. That included being at the house during the install of the new internet system.

As Sandy went inside, he thought about all the happy memories in this house that had been in his family for generations.

He smiled. I wonder if Morgan and I will make some new memories – new Powell generations in this house. He certainly hoped so.

He went into Aunt Beth's office and read Ben's notes about the system – the password was Copper13 – too easy. He would have to change that no matter how much he liked it.

Well, he thought positively, it will be easier for Morgan and me to come out here and work, even this far out, now that we've got high-speed internet. Next, he continued ticking off the list in his mind. I need to schedule the new security system installation for next week. Maybe I'll come and take Ben and Kathy out to lunch to thank them. Kathy was Ben's wife of 40 years and a wonderful, down-to-earth woman. A good friend to Aunt Beth. He went out to the car through the back door off the kitchen and was happy to see Copper just standing by the front door, waiting to go in.

"Copper!" The dog raced toward him and, with perfect timing, jumped into the front passenger seat.

"You're too used to this," Sandy said to his canine companion. "You know now it's reserved for Morgan."

Copper just ignored him and settled comfortably into the seat.

They got back from the farm around three just before rush hour, when traffic went crazy.

A moment later, Morgan walked in the door and, upon seeing him, a mysterious smile came over her face. "I've got an idea for dinner. I want to celebrate."

"Ok, I'm game. In fact, I'm always game."

"I want to take you out tonight. Let's say six."

"I'm all yours," and he remembered his daydreaming at the farm earlier and thought, "you've got no idea how much I'm yours."

****

Later at the Bombay restaurant, Morgan said, "Do you know what tonight is?"

"I'm guessing, another wonderful dinner with the most beautiful woman on the planet."

With that wicked grin of hers, Morgan said, "Yes, well, there's that. Silly, tonight is our anniversary. It has been three of the most wonderful months of my life. Thank you, Sandy, for making my life so amazing."

"Well, dittos to that, but it's you that completes me. I love you, Morgan."

Her heart raced, and she felt warm. "I love you too."

****

The next morning, Sandy drove out 66 and took the cut-off to the Dulles Toll Road. Exiting at Reston, he quickly found the convenient parking garage at Fountain and Freedom and walked the short distance past the fountain to the building. Riding the elevator to the fourth floor he knocked on the unlabeled door to 4138. A moment later the door opened.

"Hi, you must be Sandy," Jake Nichols said.

Nichols was built. He looked like he lifted daily. High and tight brown hair accented his chiseled face. "You got me, a pleasure to meet you. You come well-regarded."

"Come on in. Hope I can help."

"Thanks. Were you in the service?" Sandy asked.

"Oh, yea. Rangers 75th and you?"

"SEALs."

"You guys get all the press. We just get the fun," Jake said with a cheeky grin.

After a quick coffee, they went to the back. Jake had an insane lab with instruments, devices, and all sorts of things in the large room.

"Wow, this is quite the setup."

"This is my toy land. I'm really lucky. I don't go to work. I just have fun every day. Companies pay a ton of money to figure out how to reduce the amount of current drawn by their device. Battery life is everything."

Sandy began, "Too cool. My challenge is a bit unusual... I need to understand why these transformers are different."

"No problem. I'm happy to help, plus Rich told me you were a friend, and that means a lot."

After an hour with incredibly complex oscilloscopes hooked side by side to each transformer, Jake said, "The difference is this transformer has an underlying, call it a buzz, on the line. This means when you look at the signal on the scope, this one," he pointed to one of the transformers, "Has one clean line while the other has a fuzzy line. When we zoom into the fuzz, you can see the harmonics on the line. This is caused by one of the components going bad."

"If I got a brand-new transformer, could you make it create that 'buzz' consistently?"

Jake replied, pointing inside the transformer, "Yes I need to modify this Zener diode, see, the barrel-shaped piece. And this other barrel-shaped element."

"Ok, what's a Zener diode, and what's the other barrel-shaped piece?"

"Simply the other barrel-shaped piece is a rectifier diode which only allows current to pass in one direction. It essentially converts AC to DC. The Zener diode allows the current to flow in the opposite direction at a specific threshold. Do you want me to go into detail?"

Looking a bit lost, Sandy said sheepishly, "Oh no, you lost me at the diode."

"Bottom line, this old transformer has kind of failed. That said, I can build one for you that will deliver the same 'buzz' as the old one."

Sandy was ecstatic. "Ok, order whatever you need and build me three of them that perform like the old one."

"No problem, give me two weeks, and I'll have them ready for you."

Sandy beamed. "Just let me know how much and I will send over the funds for the parts and, of course your time as well."

"Will do, it won't be much - parts for these things are pretty inexpensive these days. I'll give you a call when they're ready. Can you leave the transformers so I can test against them?"

"Absolutely, see you in a few weeks." Sandy headed

to the door and looked back, a thought just occurring to him. "Jake," he said, "Let's keep this on the q.t. I don't want anyone else finding out what we're doing."

"My lips are sealed since you're a SEAL." Jake gave him a grin while Sandy groaned.

"Yeah, well, hey, thanks, so much – see you in a couple of weeks."

Paragon's tracking of Powell's laptop led them to realize he operated in five different locations: three in DC and two in Virginia. Lynn authorized an in-depth digital research project on Powell and assigned another person to work with Brooke. They knew his locations, where he grew up, that he was an only child, that he recently sold a house in Fairfax and had inherited his aunt's farm in Great Falls, that he was a former Navy SEAL, that he taught biology in the Fairfax County school system and most importantly, that he was continuing his research at the Library of Congress and online.

Brooke Tate got another alert. She picked up the phone and called her boss Lynn Nash. "Lynn, do you remember the guy we've been tracking on the hydrogen?"

"Sure, the guy in Virginia?"

"Yes, that's him. Well, he just filed for a patent on hydrogen gas production."

Lynn thought a moment. "Well, that changes things. Clearly, he isn't working on a thesis. Ok, send me the link to his file, and I will take a fresh look at it. Great work."

Lynn sent a secure email to headquarters with her

assessment of the situation. Todd Peterson read through the profile on Powell and the current status. He sent an email to Harriet Campos in the Washington office.

Harriet, please begin a 24/7 agent coverage of Sandy Powell, details attached, and give me a brief in a week. Todd

Harriet assigned three of her agents to discreetly follow and collect on-the-ground info on Powell.

****

Leon Davies, former DC Police detective, began his surveillance of Powell. He had a pretty complete dossier on him supplied by the research team in California. Using freeware and knowing Powell's cell phone number, he quickly got the GPS location of his phone. Driving around the neighborhood, he finally spotted Powell's car in the back alley behind Morgan's townhouse. Sitting a discreet distance away, he watched the car through his shift and saw him, a woman, and a dog leave through the back gate at seven in the morning. They were headed west through Georgetown towards the river. Leon got out of the car and did his best to keep a hundred yards behind as they began their run. Middle-aged and seriously out of shape, Leon very soon tired of trying to keep up. He decided to return to the car and watch for their return.

About half an hour later, he watched them return from the run, enter the backyard, and he assumed entered the back of the townhouse. He couldn't see for certain because of the high fence surrounding the backyard. An hour later, Karen Young called Leon to confirm his location and to relieve him from the watch. She arrived within 15 minutes, and Leon drove off.

****

She sat all morning and saw nothing. As a former CIA operative, she was used to sitting and watching for hours. Generally, the most boring part of this job, still it was a good-paying job.

Karen called Harriet about noontime and gave her an update, "I haven't seen anything all morning. I wonder if they went out the front of the townhouse?"

Harriet agreed with Karen's assessment and said, "You're probably right. I'm going to assign another person to watch the front during the morning and afternoon. You might as well take a short break, come back, and watch the back for the afternoon just in case they're inside and decide to leave in a car."

Karen walked a couple of blocks to M Street in Georgetown and caught lunch at a Vietnamese restaurant. One of the great things about this job was no one cared about expenses, unlike her former government job, where everything had to be documented and within guidelines. She loved the job. It paid well, had a company car, and she was almost always home for her kids. She handed off the watch to Verna Elliott about 6 p.m. Fortunately, this assignment was close to her home in Falls Church, Virginia.

Verna had an uneventful evening watching the rear of the house. She did see lights going on and off upstairs, nothing unusual. The next morning while Leon watched the rear, Ivan Hammond watched the front. About the same time as the previous day, Leon watched Sandy, the woman, and the dog go for their morning run.

****

Sandy noticed the shiny black Escalade parked down the street, and it seemed out of place. Cars rarely parked in the alley because they all had spots off the alley. Also odd was someone sitting in it. Maybe it was his sixth sense, polished in Afghanistan, kicking in. When they returned the car, and driver were in the same spot.

Leon updated Ivan that they'd returned. About an hour later, Ivan watched as they left out the front door and advised Leon. Knowing the specific address in Georgetown, Paragon had begun assembling information on Morgan, and they now knew with certainty which cars on the alley belonged to Sandy and Morgan.

****

Harriet Campos was surprised when she saw Morgan Dutton's name associated with Sandy Powell. She knew Dutton and had met her once. On occasion, they'd use Dutton's firm to discredit a patent filing. Small world.

****

The next day Leon and Ivan switched places, so Leon was watching the front. Despite being a cold, blustery November day, the three went for their run at the normal time. Sandy took note of the blue Chevy truck sitting almost in the same spot as the Escalade yesterday. On the run, Sandy said to Morgan, "Someone on the street is being watched."

****

Rod Holloway had scheduled a meeting of the various people working on the oil executives' case. He had named the investigation 'Operation Valdez' after the huge oil spill that occurred years earlier in Prince William Sound, Alaska. The team assembled in an executive conference room.

Rod kicked off the meeting by thanking everyone for attending, reminded them of the secret classification, and then asked Lester Hodges, Deputy Director at the FBI, to have his person provide a brief on the three CEOs and their companies. Lester looked at Tiffany Flores and nodded. Tiffany walked to the front of the room and delivered a PowerPoint briefing on the men, Harold Watson, Bryce Carrington, and Reginald Clark. Then she went through the highlights on the companies; TXO, American Petroleum, and Sunco, noting that the three companies emerged about 1915 from the breakup of Standard Oil due to antitrust legislation.

Rod then asked Diana Scott from the CIA to provide an update on the situation in Nigeria. Diana now moved to the front of the room and opened her PowerPoint presentation with a summary of the sworn statement from Bob Lancaster and his wife. She then reviewed Matthew French's autopsy results which clearly showed that Ali Mohammed had been poisoned by a massive amount of arsenic. She then put up a photo of Faruq Eze. She told them that Faruq had been paid to poison Ali's food, subsequently. He had been interviewed and arrested.

Diana then briefed the room on what they learned from Harry Atkinson, the man who paid Faruq and gave him the arsenic. The interview of Atkinson led them to his office in Lagos and the interviews of four other people who worked with Atkinson. The CIA was able to access the staff computers and email. Jones so far hadn't given them his password. Beyond the name, Todd, they'd been unable to determine who the parent company was. They did know that funding for the office came from a numbered bank account in the Cayman Islands. She closed by saying the five people from the company were being held at the CIA safe house and thought they were being held by the Nigerian police.

Rod remarked to Diana, "Please reach out to your counterpart at Treasury who's active with the Financial Action Task Force. FATF monitors progress to stop money laundering, and the UK is also a member. Leverage that to get the detailed ownership and transaction records for that numbered account in the Caymans."

"Yes, sir, will do."

"If you've got a problem, call me directly."

Morgan was surprised. "Really, how do you know that someone is being watched?"

"I noticed an SUV with a guy sitting just down the street yesterday, and today there's another truck sitting in almost the same spot with a guy just sitting in it."

Morgan said, "I guess it could be anybody on our block. Do you think it's a security detail for someone? We do have some wealthy, important people in the neighborhood."

"I don't think so. They didn't look like security detail-type vehicles. My guess, some private eye is watching somebody." When they arrived back at the house, the truck was in the same spot with some guy sitting and watching. After freshening up and having a light breakfast, they headed off in opposite directions. Morgan had meetings downtown and went out the front as it was easier to catch a bus than drive and park. Sandy went out the back to his car.

Leon saw Morgan leave the house out the front door. She was walking east and turned right, heading down the hill to M Street. Leon pulled out of the parking spot, drove slowly down to the corner, watched her cross M street, and wait at the bus stop. He pulled down the street and was able to stop in front of someone's garage entrance. Not a legal parking spot, but he would only be there for a few minutes. Leon saw her get on a city bus and head for downtown. He followed the bus, which was a bit tricky with all the morning traffic. He was able to see her get off the bus and enter an office building on K street. There was no way he could stay parked in downtown DC and wait for her return. He updated the team and went home to rest before his next shift.

Meanwhile, as Sandy backed out of his parking spot, he noticed the truck start up, and as he headed west down the alley, he took note that the truck pulled out and began to follow at a distance. When Sandy got to 33rd, he turned right, not the way he needed to go, and sped quickly north up the street. He was almost two blocks away when he saw the truck turn to follow in his rearview mirror. He sped up the next two blocks and turned left, continuing north on Wisconsin Ave. Several blocks up, Sandy pulled into a small parking lot and backed into an open spot with a car blocking him from the view on Wisconsin. As he suspected, the truck drove by him a few minutes later. Sandy waited a minute, pulled out of the parking lot, and headed south on Wisconsin back in the direction he needed to go.

Ivan updated Leon and Karen that Powell had given him the slip for the moment. It was time for Karen to take over the watch. So, she used the cell phone GPS locator software to discover that Powell was now headed west on the GW Parkway.

****

Next, Rod asked Amber Dean to review what they'd found in the analysis of the phone records. Amber had lived for decades in the US, but her colorful Caribbean accent was a delightful undertone to her presentation.

"We gathered the past five years' cell phone records for the men and looked for numbers they'd dialed in common as well as noting if they'd called each other," Amber explained. "Over the past five years, we found only a few numbers in common, and the majority of those were other wealthy people or politicians that they appeared to know independently. We're still investigating the other phones. The overlaps occurred with Bryce Carrington and Reginald Clark. There was only one overlap with Harold Watson, and that happened about a month ago. That call was a three-way conference call."

Rod thought a moment. "Wait a minute, Tiffany, when did Watson become CEO of TXO?"

"Sir, he was elected by the Board of Directors to become CEO in June of this year."

"Who was the CEO prior to Watson?"

"That was Jacob Holden, great-grandson of Malcolm Holden, the founder of Texas Oil and Gas."

Rod announced, "I'll get a warrant for Jacob Holden's information with regards to this conspiracy later today. Each of you'll do a deep dive into Holden for your respective areas. Lester," he turned toward his colleague. "Can we now cover the information on the executives' flights?"

"Absolutely, Dylan, would you be so kind as to brief us on what your team discovered?"

Dylan Harrison stood and moved to the laptop at the front of the room and opened his PowerPoint. "We were quite lucky in that all three companies primarily use the jets they own and on a limited basis use rentals. Each CEO has a preferred jet which made it easier. We looked at five years of data on these jets and were able to find common airports. Since corporate jets can often land in smaller fields, we used a 50-mile radius to account for the jets landing at different but adjacent airports. For example, one might land at National while another landed at the airport in Manassas."

He continued, "Over the past five years, we saw nearly 30 occasions where two or all three jets landed and took off within 48 hours of each other at the same or adjacent airports. On average, they were together about once per quarter. Some of these coincidences coincided with Congressional testimony or meetings with senior government officials."

Dylan continued, "We then had local FBI agents pose as IRS agents to go to the Fixed Base Operator to get the manifest of the people on the flights, and we were able to confirm Bryce Carrington and Reginald Clark were on those flights and in one case Watson. We will go back and look for information on Holden, sir. Some of the flights were international, so we went to Customs and Border Protection at DHS and were able to review the entry and exit of the individuals and confirm the use of the specific jets."

Lester said, "Excellent job Dylan, we look forward to your update concerning Holden. Nina, can you give us an update on the financial information on the case?"

Nina Craig stood but didn't move to the front of the room, "Sir, we're dealing with three multi-billion-dollar international public companies. Each of these companies has tens of subsidiaries and thousands of subcontractors many of which are located offshore. We haven't seen any irregularities, but that doesn't mean they're not there. All their financials are audited, but again that doesn't mean a great deal. With companies this big, there are a million places to hide slush funds. With regard to the three executives, we reviewed their tax returns, and they're all independently wealthy, but their returns appear to be in order, and all were prepared by respected firms."

"Thanks, Nina. Good job. Jordan, can you brief us on the price-fixing analysis?"

Jordan moved to the front and put up her PowerPoint. Jordan Vasquez was a late-twenties woman with a huge smile and almost waist-length reddish-blonde hair. "We looked at the pricing of several common products of the three companies. This included gasoline, diesel, natural gas, jet fuel, and heating oil. Since these companies are international, we looked at historic prices in multiple markets, the United States, Canada, Japan, and the European Union. We also looked upstream to see if the acquisition of mineral rights or leases changed.

Rod interrupted, "Excuse me, what do you mean by upstream?"

"Excellent question, sir. The oil and gas business are generally thought of in three broad sectors: upstream, midstream, and downstream. Upstream consists of exploration, drilling, and pumping from established wells. Midstream is the transportation from the well to the refinery and includes trucks, pipelines, rail, and ships. Finally, downstream is the processing of crude oil and gas into finished products. This sector also includes the commercial distribution of finished products."

Jordan moved to the next slide in her deck. "As we can see here gasoline prices tend to be adjusted seasonally for two factors. We see peak prices from the refineries when they switch from primarily gasoline production to heating oil, and we also see price changes in anticipation of higher demand due to holiday travel not only in the US but overseas as well." She went on to the next slide, which drilled into a day-level pricing chart. "When we look at the price adjustments by the three companies and their competitors, in nearly every instance globally, the three companies adjusted their prices within hours of each other while competitors took three to five days to adjust their prices in response to the move."

Rod asked, "Does this demonstrate anti-competitive price-fixing?"

"I don't believe this information alone could prove that, but it's much more than circumstantial evidence."

Jordan continued, "When we look at leases and acquisition of mineral rights, we can see a pattern in various fields where prices were pushed lower, and one of the three companies made an acquisition. We're going to have local agents make some inquiries into specific acquisitions to see if there was an influence to push the price lower."

Rod then asked, "Melissa, from an antitrust perspective do we have a case?"

Melissa replied, "Sir, we're building one, but I don't believe we've got enough evidence at this time to go to a Grand Jury, to get an indictment. We need a smoking gun."

Rod stood and moved to the front of the room. "Everyone, your teams have all done an excellent job with this investigation. I believe we're beginning to uncover a conspiracy to control the oil and gas business both here and internationally. As I mentioned before, I want you to add Jacob Holden to the investigation, and we will secure the required warrants later today. Lester, do you need anything to get wiretaps on the cell and office phones for the execs?"

"I think I've got all that I need, I'll call you later today to confirm."

"All right, everyone, keep up the good work, and expect to meet again in a week to give us an update." Rod left the room with Lester right behind.

Lester said, "I think you're right, and this could be huge. I'll keep you updated." As they approached the elevator bank, Lester's security detail appeared.

"Thanks, and again your team is doing a great job. I'll brief Charlie, and I assume you'll update the director."

"Of course." Lester entered the elevator with his detail. Downstairs they headed back for the short walk to the FBI building. Before crossing Pennsylvania Avenue, Lester turned around and looked at the inscription above the door, 'The Place of Justice is a Hallowed Place,' and he thought it appropriate for this investigation. The quote attributed to Francis Bacon about 1600 spoke to justice interpreting the law and not writing the law. They were implementing the law. Then he thought, if this plays out, there's going to be a shit storm of politics because these guys were in everyone's pocket.

Bob McCall knocked on Todd Peterson's office door and entered. As CFO at Paragon, it was McCall's job to keep the finances of their global operation running smoothly. This meant managing funds for each office in separate numbered accounts based in the Caymans. The offices would draw funds for operations and payroll, and if extraordinary funds were needed for an operation or a bribe then a secure email requesting the amount and use of the funds was sent to headquarters.

Todd looked up from a pile of papers and said, "What's up, Bob?"

"Our Lagos, Nigeria office didn't pull their normal weekly funds from the account for the past two days. Have you had any communications with them?"

Todd thought for a moment. "No, not since we had them run the op on the minister, and they confirmed it went as planned."

"Well, something isn't right. Suggest you look into it."

"Good point, Bob. I will check it out. Thanks for the update."

Todd thought about the procedure they'd put in place when an office went offline. It had only happened once, years in the past. Todd decided not to send anyone from headquarters because they'd stand out like a fly on a wedding cake. The best solution was to send Nick Keller.

Todd trusted Nick. He was an Arab, so moderately dark skin but spent most of his years in London, so he spoke 'proper' English, which would fit in well in Nigeria, a former English colony. Keller was now based in their Abu Dhabi office in the United Arab Emirates.

Nick received the secure email from Todd with instructions to fly ASAP to their office in Lagos and investigate. Details, including staff photos and bios, were in the attachments. One of the many things Nick liked about the job was the unlimited budget. He booked a first-class ticket from Abu Dhabi to Lagos. The best way to get there was to fly Etihad direct about an eight-hour flight. He arrived at about 8 p.m. and went to the InterContinental Hotel. He planned to check out the office the next morning.

After a light breakfast, he grabbed a taxi and went to the office about 30 minutes away. The street was full of ramshackle buildings, many of which looked like a strong wind would blow them over. Hundreds of people were walking on the street since the sidewalk was blocked by parked cars, and there was a constant throng of taxis and a few cars narrowly missing the people. The office was on the fourth floor of a better-than-average but still rundown building. He found an open-air coffee shop across the street where he could watch to see if anyone entered the building that looked like the photos he had memorized.

After an hour of not seeing anyone, he crossed the busy street and entered the building. He was surprised to find the lift working and took it to the fourth floor. The office door was locked, so Nick took his lock-pick from his rear pocket and thirty seconds later was in the office. The office was empty except for the furniture. He looked around, but there was nothing.

The CIA office received an alert that someone had tripped the motion detector and entered Global Research's office. They had a high-def video of the person entering and looking about the office. The second hidden camera recorded him leaving the office space 15 minutes later.

Nick sent a secure email to Todd advising that the office was empty with no sign of anyone. Todd replied with his thanks and said to return to the UAE.

****

Most patent applications are not published for 18 months following their filing and therefore are unavailable for the public to review. Paragon had inserted a virus in the system at USPTO so it could receive notification of a patent as soon as it was filed and entered into the system. Paragon no longer had to pay a patent examiner to watch for patents. Technology certainly had its benefits.

Todd Peterson was reading the analysis of the Powell patent filing and realized he had an actionable event. He called Harriet Campos in Washington to get an update on Sandy Powell.

"Hi Todd, how are things in The Big Apple?"

"Good, I was looking to get an update on Sandy

Powell. It appears his patent has some merit."

Harriet said, "Well, no real events to report. We've been watching him 24/7 as well as his girlfriend Morgan Dutton, whom by chance I've met, and we've used her as a patent attorney in the past. Powell seems to be living with her. We've been tracking their cell phones' locations. For the most part, they stay in downtown DC. With a few trips to Reston and a rural property in Great Falls. From what we can see, he is continuing his academic research on hydrogen gas production. Is there anything you want us to do with him?"

Todd reflected, "No, we're good. Continue the surveillance, and I will reach out if there's a change."

Todd sent a secure email to Watson, Carrington, and Clark briefing them on the Powell case and patent and requested their recommendation on the next steps. The next day he received Carrington's recommendation that they acquire the rights to the patent for $250,000 and assign the rights to one of their offshore shell companies. Watson and Clark concurred with the approach.

Todd emailed Harriet and asked her to have one of her agents make an offer.

****

The CIA had DHS review the Lagos customs tapes to find this new person's entry into the country on the premise that he was a potential terrorist. Now that he was flagged, it was easy to tag Nick Keller leaving the country on a flight to Abu Dhabi. The Lagos CIA office advised their office in the UAE, and they were there when his flight landed. They didn't pick him up but watched to find out where his office was.

Sandy had prepared an incredible filet of salmon with a mayonnaise and Old Bay dressing. He also had sides of asparagus with hollandaise sauce and new potatoes for Morgan and Vicky. They were all enjoying the get-together over several bottles of the buttery Cakebread Chardonnay.

Sandy excused himself to go to the bathroom and went upstairs. Vicky immediately asked Morgan, "So, how's it going?"

"I've never been so happy." Morgan beamed. "It just feels so right and comfortable. He's definitely the one..." she trailed off, a dreamy look on her face.

"You're so lucky. I'd die for that. So, what's next?"

"We're just enjoying being together and trying to figure it out as we go. Sandy is continuing his research on his grandfather's discovery. He has the farm in Great Falls, and we've got my place. I think he'll go back to teaching next semester, but we've got to see where things are at. He doesn't need the money at this point."

Sandy was returning from upstairs, "So, have you girls got it all figured out?"

Morgan tossed her curly hair and smiled. "Sure do. We're doing the dishes since you were the awesome chef you always are."

"Great! I've got an idea; if you can knock off early on Friday, let's fly out to St. Louis and see my mother. I'm long overdue, and she's dying to meet you. There's a direct flight out of National at 2:40 on Friday, and we can be back on Sunday afternoon."

"Great idea. I would love to meet her and learn more about your secret past."

Vicky chimed in, "Well, off to meet the mother, do you think she'll pass muster?"

"Are you kidding? My mother will love her more than Copper does."

"That isn't possible. That dog absolutely adores her," Vicky said.

"Oh, I know. He hardly pays any attention to me anymore. Well, unless I'm going for a drive. Then he loves me."

Morgan had a perplexed look. "So, what're we going to do with Copper while we're gone?"

"No worries, one of my former students loves to watch him when I travel. I'll drop him off Friday morning, and we can collect him when we get back, or I'll get him on Monday morning."

Friday noontime, they grabbed a cab and were soon checking their bags, off to catch their flight. About three hours later, they picked up a rental car and were off to Sandy's Mom's house about 20 minutes from Lambert Field. They pulled up to a beautiful old brick Tudor with a huge oak tree in front. Sandy said, "This is the Kirkwood neighborhood, and the house backs up to the Greenbriar Country Club."

"What a beautiful house and a nice established neighborhood."

Sandy and Morgan grabbed their bags as Sandy's mom Barbara, opened the front door. They approached the house on the brick walkway. Barbara was about 5'6" with blue eyes like Sandy, a big perfect smile, and short brown hair with gray highlights. "Sandy, Morgan, I'm so happy you came for a visit!"

"Hi, Mom, let me introduce you to Morgan Dutton, my better half."

"Morgan, so wonderful to finally meet you. Sandy has told me a little, and you're even more beautiful than he described. Please come in and make yourselves at home. I was just going to get some crackers and cheese, and Sandy can fix some drinks. We have some unusually warm weather, so we can sit out on the deck."

Sandy and Morgan dropped their bags in the entryway, and Barbara took their coats to the hall closet. The front hallway led straight back to the kitchen. The rear of the house had been remodeled recently to one large open space with a family room and fireplace on the left and a large kitchen with white and black veined marble countertops to the right.

As Sandy headed into the family room, he asked, "Morgan, Mom, what would you girls like to drink?"

I will have a scotch on the rocks if that's what you're having," Morgan said.

His mom replied, "I'll have a glass of Woodford Bourbon on the rocks, if you please."

Morgan stood at the kitchen island while Barbara prepared a decorative platter with crackers and various cheeses. Sandy returned with a tray that held the drinks along with the bottles of scotch and bourbon. He set it down on the island and handed Morgan her glass of scotch and the glass of bourbon to his mother. He grinned at them as he saw the look on their faces and a mutual glance at each other.

"What?" he said trying to sound innocent. "I'm preparing for refills – makes it easier."

Then he grabbed the platter of cheeses and cocked his head toward the backyard.

His mother shook her head and laughed, and they followed her out the French doors to the deck.

The lawn sloped down towards the golf course, providing a beautiful view of the fairway and part of the lake. Morgan remarked as they sat down, "What a beautiful view of the course."

Barbara was just beaming, "Oh yes, except we had to replace the glass with impact-resistant windows several years ago. It didn't used to be a problem but with the new clubs, more than a few players overdrive the dogleg, and our house gets hit nearly every day. So, tell me about yourself and how you two met and, well, just everything."

After about an hour Barbara said, "Sandy, I've got some steaks in the fridge. Would you be so kind as to fire up the grill while Morgan and I pull together the sides?"

"Happy to Mom." Sandy picked up the cheese platter and headed into the kitchen, followed by the women. The conversation was light and delightful as they prepared the meal, and since the weather was still cooperating, they decided to eat outside. After dessert, they retired to the family room for sambuca with roasted coffee beans and quiet jazz in the background.

On Saturday, Sandy toured Morgan around the area where he grew up and went to high school. Saturday evening, they went to "The Hill," the famous Italian neighborhood in St. Louis. Charlie Gitto's Restaurant presented a two-story building in a semi-residential neighborhood, very different from the hustle and bustle of Georgetown. The dining was elegant, and the food, they all agreed, was stunning.

Sunday morning, Sandy and Morgan made a bacon and asparagus quiche combined with Jarlsberg cheese which added a light nutty flavor to the dish. Adding toasted Italian bread that they bought last night on "The Hill" completed the brunch. Still surprisingly warm they enjoyed breakfast on the deck. While Sandy was inside attending to a "Honey-do" project for his mom. Morgan and Barbara chatted.

"Sandy makes me so happy. I always feel safe and protected with him. He completes me."

Barbara just grinned. "I can't ever remember him this happy. When he was married before, it never felt like a fit. He is over the top in love with you, and I'd love to have you as a part of the family when you're ready."

"Oh, I'm already there. I'm just enjoying each moment, and when he's ready, I will be there for him. Thank you so much for making me feel so welcome."

"I think it's you that completes him. You're a perfect

match, and I know because I was so lucky to have mine. If you ever have a doubt, call me immediately. I'm there for both of you."

The trip to the airport and back to DC was quiet. A bit tired and looked forward to enjoying some one-on-one time with Morgan, so he decided to pick up Copper Monday morning.

By Monday evening, based on the thoroughly enjoyable trip to St. Louis, they agreed they should go to Ithaca for Thanksgiving so that Sandy could meet Morgan's family.

Chapter 31 Washington, DC

Harriet Campos at the Paragon Washington office got the update Friday afternoon that Powell had flown to St. Louis. Karen had followed Sandy and Morgan's cab to National. Several hours later, they'd located his cell phone in St. Louis. The assumption was they were going to see his mother, and there was no need to fly a team to St. Louis to watch him.

Harriet sent a text to Jason Roberts to stop by her office first thing Monday morning. Jason knocked on her door at 8 a.m. "Jason, good to see you. How have you been?"

"Great, keeping busy with the assignment on the guy at the Department of Energy. How can I help?"

"We've got an inventor we've been watching, and the decision has been made to make him an offer of $250,000 for the rights to the patent he just filed. I sent you his background through secure email, and I'd suggest you set up a meeting for tomorrow morning at a coffee shop he frequents in Georgetown. You're our best sales guy, so convince him it's a great offer, and he should accept it. We aren't in a rush, but you know how we like to deliver for our clients."

"No problem, I'll make him an offer he can't refuse," Jason said in his best Godfather imitation.

****

Sandy was cleaning up the breakfast dishes when his cell phone pinged that he had a text. He snatched it off the island, expecting it to be from Morgan, but it was an unknown DC number.

Meet me for coffee on Grace Street at 10 something to discuss – Jason

Sandy had already planned to go to Grace Street for their incredible roasted coffee and continue reading on hydrogen gas production. He was more than curious who this Jason was but felt comfortable since they were meeting in the very public coffee shop. Subliminally he knew if there was a threat, he was trained to handle it. He sent a quick text to Morgan.

Meeting an unknown Jason for coffee on Grace Street – film at 11 LY SP

Ok – let me know – Love YOU Too MD

Sandy went out the front door of the townhouse with Copper and glanced at the black Escalade parked about a block away to the west. They turned east and then headed down to M street. Then they crossed M and continued south on Wisconsin Avenue crossing the bridge over the Chesapeake and Ohio Canal, then down half a block and turned right onto Grace Street. Grace Street was a combination of new and old brick brownstones turned into high-end office space, restaurants, and some condo lofts. Since it also was the alley behind the shops on M Street, there were multiple overhead doors to docks for those buildings.

Sandy and Copper headed up the stairs and entered the coffee shop. The fragrance of the freshly roasted beans and the pulled espresso almost assaulted him as they walked back to the espresso bar. "Good morning, Chip," Sandy said to the barista.

"Sandy... my man. You and Copper are looking great. The usual?"

"Yes, please, and I'll get a roll to share with Copper."

Several minutes later, his triple shot latte and sweet roll were ready, and they headed to a quiet corner in the back. Many days they'd sit in the small courtyard behind the coffee shop, but it was a bit chilly today. He sat against the wall facing out towards the pastries. They were intentionally early. So, he quietly sipped his latte and wondered who this Jason guy was and what he wanted.

About five minutes to ten, Jason walked over to the table where Sandy was seated. "Hi Sandy, I'm Jason. Very nice to meet you." Jason was slender, clearly not an athlete.

Sandy stood and gave him a full-on man handshake and noticed the slight wince when he squeezed a bit more than necessary. "Nice to meet you. Have a seat. You don't look familiar. Do I know you?"

"No, thanks for taking the time to meet me. I will cut to the chase. I represent a client that would like to purchase the exclusive rights to your recent patent."

"Ok, that's interesting. Especially since it hasn't even been issued yet."

"They believe it has real merit, and we're prepared to offer you $250,000 for you assigning all rights to their company."

"What if the patent doesn't get issued because of prior art or if the invention doesn't work?"

Looking Sandy straight in the eye, "No problem, you get to keep the money, and they'll assume all cost and liability to perfect the patent and the technology."

Sandy thought a moment. "Who's the company?"

"I can't say at this time, but obviously that would all be shared when the contract is executed."

"Ok, well, this is interesting. I'll have to think about this and get back to you. Can I reach you at the number you sent the text from?"

Jason smiled and looked at Copper who'd moved so he was between Sandy and Jason. "Yes, that's my cell. Beautiful dog."

"Thanks. Yes, he is and very protective. I will get back to you next week. It's an intriguing offer."

Jason and Sandy stood up, and Jason almost reluctantly reached out his hand. They shook and Sandy didn't put the full squeeze on since he had already established who was on top. "I look forward to your call. Have a great day."

Sandy and Copper walked back to the townhouse where Sandy texted Morgan.

Jason has a client that wants to acquire the patent for $250K

Headed to Reston and the farm C U tonight LY S

Morgan texted back.

Say what!!! Drive safe look forward to discussing tonight LY M

Sandy drove out 66 and took the connector to the Dulles Toll Road. Several minutes later, he pulled into one of the many parking garages surrounding the Town Center. He left Copper in the car and went to Jake Nichols's office on the fourth floor. After catching up with Jake, he took a box with the original transformers and the three new modified ones and went back to the car.

Twenty minutes later, they were at the farm. Sandy went into the house and got food and water for Copper and then went to the barn with his box of transformers. Opening the cabinet, he went down to the basement and set everything up on the worktable. As always, he started with the old transformer. He ran it for a minute, and it was producing copious amounts of gas. Then he tried each of the new transformers, and they also produced huge amounts of gas. The answer was clear. The combination of chemicals plus the harmonics of the transformer power split the water molecule into oxygen and hydrogen.

Back at Morgan's townhouse, Sandy prepared sautéed chicken thighs, which he sliced into strips and presented over a simple romaine Caesar salad. "I tried out the new transformers that Jake had modified, and they worked perfectly. We've got a new way to produce hydrogen very cheaply."

Morgan was so happy. "Sandy, this is amazing! You solved it. So, you're the resident expert on hydrogen gas production. What does this mean?"

"Well, first, I didn't exactly solve it! It was a combination of my grandfather's investigation and notes, along with Jake's modification of the transformers. But, as to your question, it will change everything within ten years."

Morgan nodded, and Sandy continued.

"Imagine we no longer use fossil fuels to power everything from cars and trucks to generating electricity across the world. Assuming we can create small hydrogen plants everywhere, you don't haul fuel to a gas stations you make it right on site. Same for a power plant. You'd produce it where you need it. The conversion of hydrogen gas into electricity produces water. So, at an electric utility, you'd capture most of the water, recycle it, and produce more electricity. Even in a desert, you wouldn't need a lot of water. Vastly less carbon in the atmosphere, the whole global warming thing is no longer an issue."

Morgan shook her head, clearly impressed by what she was hearing.

Sandy laughed and kept going. "One gallon of water would produce 1,200 gallons of hydrogen gas. In the past, it's taken more energy to produce hydrogen than the energy created by burning the gas. But my calculations show that this production method is insanely efficient. Because of the harmonics, it results in a lot of energy for very little input. This will change the world."

"Wow, you're a genius, one of the many things I love about you. Tell me about your meeting this morning."

"Well, it was kind of strange. First, I get this text out of the blue from this Jason guy suggesting a meeting at the coffee shop on Grace Street. How did he know I get coffee on Grace Street? Then we meet. Basically, he says he has a client that would offer me $250,000 for the rights to the patent regardless of if it's issued or if the technology works."

Morgan thought for a moment. "How did he know about the patent?"

"I didn't ask, and he didn't say. I guess his client saw it on the web or the USPTO website."

Morgan said, "Well, patent applications aren't generally public for 18 months after they're filed. There are lots of exceptions, and the rules are complex, but on average, patents aren't published for at least a year. The 18-month rule applies where the priority date is the same as the filing date. Bottom line, there's no way they should know about your patent unless you shared it with someone, and they shared it with this company."

Sandy frowned. "I haven't shared anything about the patent with anyone, not even Jackson. So, it had to come from some other source. Any chance someone got it from you or your office?"

"No, I'm very careful with all my work to keep it very confidential, and the files are secure. They had to have gotten it from the USPTO."

Sandy pondered. "I didn't feel like the guy was trustworthy, and Copper was great. He sat there between us, and he was not his usual jovial self, so I guess he had the same impression."

Hearing his name, Copper looked up expectantly, his tail brushing the floor rapidly.

Morgan laughed. "I think he feels deserving of a treat since he was so great." She reached into the dog biscuit canister on the counter and tossed Copper a treat. Copper caught it and snarfed it down.

Sandy grinned, then quickly looked serious again. "So, what do we do with the offer, however they discovered the patent?"

"Well, what do you think the discovery is worth, say in ten years?"

"Billions or more. As I said, it changes the world."

Morgan looked him straight in the eye, smiled, and said, "Well, we don't need the money; my thought is we simply say no. Not for a million dollars."

"I totally agree. I'll let him know next week."

Sandy didn't mention that he thought they were being watched, not wanting to alarm Morgan, but it did weigh heavily on his mind.

Chapter 32   Washington, DC

Diana Scott reached out to Rod Holloway and Lester Hodges to provide them with a brief update on the Valdez case. They met in Rod's office at the Department of Justice.

"Obviously," Diana began, "What I'm sharing is very sensitive, so I didn't want to just put it in an email. We're still working on the people from the Lagos office. We know that Bob Jones heads the office. We haven't turned them over to the Lagos police, but they believe they're already under arrest. Jones has yet to provide us with his password. We're still trying to break him."

Rod and Lester nodded as Diana continued, "As you know, we captured all the documents and computers in their office. We sent the computers to Ft. Meade. We also set up cameras and motion sensors. Last week we caught Nick Keller breaking into the office. We were able to find him entering the country the day before on the customs tapes at the airport. And the day after the break-in, we were able to watch him get on a flight to Abu Dhabi in the United Arab Emirates. We put a team on him and have located his home and office. He works for a company called UAE Research Limited, and we suspect that it's linked to the Nigerian company through a parent company which Jones told us Todd operates."

"Excellent work," Rod said. "What're the next steps?"

"Well, since we're in the UAE, we've got to be a bit more careful than in Nigeria. I've asked the NSA to try to get anything we can on both Keller and the company. I had one of our technicians attach monitors on the office phone and internet lines, so we're starting to assemble data. But it appears the important stuff is all encrypted. This creates a challenge for NSA, but they're working on it. I hope we've got more information next week."

Diana thought for a moment, then added, "Oh, and I did reach out to Treasury, and they're working the terrorist angle to get transaction data on the numbered account in the Caymans. Nothing yet, but I haven't heard we hit a roadblock, so hopefully, more next week."

Lester suggested, "Is there anything you need us to help with at this point?"

"No, I think we're doing all we can. Thanks. Have a great Thanksgiving, and hopefully, the whole team will have more after the holiday."

Chapter 33   Georgetown, DC

Sandy, Morgan, and Copper all loaded up in Sandy's car and were off before noon Wednesday for their trip to Ithaca. Morgan was really looking forward to introducing her folks to Sandy as well as seeing them herself since it had been almost a year since she took a trip up north.

They headed out of town, with a million other people.

As they were passing the Gettysburg exits, Morgan asked Sandy, "Have you ever been?" pointing at the signs.

Sandy recalled. "Yes. A very moving experience with my parents. You?" he asked Morgan.

She smiled. "Yes – the same type of experience with my parents. It's interesting though," she continued, "Many people fail to realize that Gettysburg is as far north of Washington, DC as it is."

"And" Sandy continued, "That more men died in the three days of the battle of Gettysburg than in the entire Vietnam War. In many ways, the Battle of Gettysburg was the turning point in the Civil War where General George Meade's army defeated General Robert E. Lee's Confederate troops."

"Well, far or not, we're really lucky to be living in a

place that's so full of history – even if it's a bit of a drive," Morgan said.

Sandy agreed and they resolved to take advantage of the historical treasures of the area when they got back.

"Maybe a once-a-month outing to a historical venue or museum..." And they both fell into a contented silence.

The divided four-lane highway was relatively quiet despite being a long holiday weekend, and they rolled north now, listening to tunes and just relaxing. Sandy noticed a white Lexus sedan following about half a mile back. He pulled off in Dillsburg at the Wendy's to grab a quick bite for everyone, including Copper. He noticed that the white Lexus had also taken the left-hand turn and was parked at the adjacent gas station.

When they pulled out of Wendy's parking lot and turned left on 15, the Lexus followed a short way back. They took Google maps suggestion and took Hwy 581 east through Harrisburg, crossing over the wide Susquehanna river and then turning north on Interstate 83 to connect with Interstate 81. The Lexus remained a reasonable distance back. Just after the split where 83 continued east to Allentown and they headed north on 81, Sandy turned off at the Love's Truckstop and pulled up to a gas pump.

Morgan looked surprised. "We've got plenty of gas. Why did you stop?"

"I think we've got someone following us, so I wanted to see what they do. Don't look around, but there's a white Lexus parked over on the side of the gas station. I'll bet my pension; it'll stay there until we leave. Do you need a pit stop?"

"Good idea. And I'll take Copper for one when I get back. Why do you think they're following us?"

"My guess it has something to do with the strange offer on Tuesday."

Sandy topped off the gas, and when Morgan returned, she took Copper on a leash to do his business. Shortly after leaving the gas station, the Lexus resumed following them.

Sandy asked Morgan to look up Rudy Zimmerman's number on his cell phone and call his mobile. Morgan hit dial and put the phone on speakerphone.

Rudy answered the call. "Sandy, you old washed-up SEAL, what're you up to these days?"

"Hey Rudy, just the happiest guy on the planet."

Rudy shouted back, "Well, that must mean you've finally met a gal that'll put up with your crazy stunts!"

"Yup, that's right. You nailed, it and she's sitting right here next to me. Need a huge favor."

Zimmer replied, "What? Do you need me to walk you down the aisle, mate?"

"Not yet." Sandy grinned. "But I can picture you in pink and carrying flowers."

Zimmer laughed. "So, what's it that gives me the pleasure of this call?"

Sandy's smile turned into a slight frown. "Well, I'll make a long story short. I'm on 81 just north of Harrisburg, and I've got a car following me. I wonder if you could have someone pull them over. So I know who they are and slow them down to get a bit of distance."

"No problem, always happy to help." Then Zimmer said, "Do you owe a loan shark some money or something?"

"Nothing like that. I think they're trying to pressure me on an invention I just came up with."

"Cool, I can see you as a creator. Give me about 10 minutes to find out who's in that sector, and I'll ask them to call you on your cell directly. Then you can give them the details."

"Thanks, Rudy. I owe you one!"

"No problem, man! Can't wait to see you at the team get-together in April. Keep the wheels down and call if you need anything else."

Sandy said, "See you in April, and again thanks so much." Then the call disconnected.

Morgan asked, "So who's Rudy?"

"Rudy was part of my SEAL team. We saved each other's lives multiple times, and now he's a Pennsylvania State Trooper."

"Good friend to have. Your team is really tight."

"After what we went through together, we'd literally lay down our lives for each other. It's a special bond."

About five minutes later, the phone rang. "Hi, this is Sandy Powell."

"Officer Francis here," a pleasant female voice came from the speaker. "I just got a call from Zimmer, and he said you could use my help. I guess you two go back a ways."

"We sure do, and I appreciate your help. I've got a white Lexus that's been following us since Washington.

We're just passing exit 100 on 81 north, and the car is about half a mile behind us."

"Ok, it will take me about 15 minutes to catch up to you. I'll give you a call when I get close."

"Thanks so much. Talk to you soon."

About fifteen minutes later, Sandy's phone rang again. "Hi, this is Sandy."

"Hi, Officer Francis again. I'm about a mile back. Could you speed up to about 80, and we'll see if the Lexus picks up the pace? Then I have a good reason to pull them over."

"No problem, almost at 80 now."

"Great, did they speed up?"

"Yes, just like you suggested."

"Ok, I'll pull them over, get a picture of the driver, registration, and the license and send them to you as a text. I imagine after I get all done with them, they should be tied up for at least 30 minutes. Of course, if they have wants or warrants, it could be days," she said with a chuckle.

A few minutes later, they received a text from Francis saying she had her.

Sandy reduced his speed back to a comfortable 65, and they continued north to New York. There was a good deal of traffic, but it was not bad considering the holiday weekend. And, while cloudy, the roads were dry, and thankfully no snow or slush. They received a text from Officer Francis. The text included a picture of Karen Young's driver's license, registration, license plate, and a photo of her behind the wheel. Francis had included there were no wants or warrants, and she hoped the information was helpful. Morgan texted back a thank you.

Sandy said, "We'll have to try to check her out when we get home."

"For sure, you really think she was following us?"

"I'm pretty sure, but it could have been a coincidence," he said to reassure Morgan while thinking to himself, I'm sure.

At Whitney Point, they finally left I-81 and took Route 79 west for 30 miles to Ithaca. Morgan took over navigation from Google maps and directed them across town on Stewart Ave below the Cornell Campus to Cayuga Heights and her parents' home.

The house was a Frank Lloyd Wright Usonian style of architecture. Single story with long thin lines, the roof was only gently sloped, forming a low peak. It was built from long thin concrete blocks that were staggered in and out between courses creating long parallel lines. The windows on the side facing the street were only 18 inches high and just under the eaves. Every ten feet along the wall were pencil-thin pairs of windows from the ground to the eaves encased with stained mahogany trim. A short wall in front of the house created an enclosed patio, and they used the same style of block to blend with the house. Everything worked together to accentuate the feeling of length, thinness, and lightness. The house was stunning. In keeping with this architectural style, the front door was off to the right of the house under a flat porch roof. Morgan led the way with Sandy and Copper right behind. She pressed the doorbell next to the dark red front door, and a moment later, her mom, Betty, opened the door with her dad, Clint, close behind.

Morgan gave her parents hugs then said, "Folks, I want you to meet Sandy and Copper."

Sandy moved to shake Betty's hand, but she said, "Oh no, Mister, I want a serious hug," with an ear-to-ear smile. Like Morgan, Betty was tall and thin, with significantly more red hair in a short cut, and bright green eyes.

Clint rescued Sandy from the lingering hug and shook hands.

"So glad you both could join us for Thanksgiving. It's nice for the family to get together for the holiday. Please come in."

The front entry was a simple wall opposite the door that was open on the left, with a closet to the right. Walking around the wall, Sandy was stunned by a wall of glass facing the back lawn.

His jaw dropped. "Wow! That's an amazing view, and you even see some of Cayuga Lake from this vantage point. Did you have this house built?"

"Yes, many years ago, one of my clients was a professor in the Architecture School, and he wanted to build a house inspired in part by the Frank Lloyd Wright modernist approach. We had this property, and it all just kind of worked out. We love it."

Sandy nodded appreciatively as Clint continued, "We've added a large garage off to the right but basically changed very few things about the house."

It felt like touring a museum; every detail was stunning. A transom above the windows was fashioned in stained glass that played with the light from the backyard. The floor-to-ceiling windows had a latticework of tall, thin, and square frames of black steel holding both clear and opaque pieces of glass. Everything was framed in rich mahogany.

"I'm going to let Copper out if you think he'll stay in the yard?" Morgan asked.

"He'll be fine. I'm sure he'll sniff everything, but a good run around will do him good after the long ride. He'll come back as soon as we call him."

Morgan opened the door to the deck overlooking the backyard, and Copper was off and down the stairs like an arrow from a bow.

Betty suggested, "Let's relax for a minute and catch up. Would anyone like a drink?"

"Well, it's after five o'clock, so I'll have a scotch on the rocks, thanks," Clint replied.

"Sounds great, me too," Sandy said, feeling himself relax in this new but important environment.

Betty and Morgan headed off to the kitchen while Sandy and Clint got acquainted and discussed recent events. The women returned shortly with drinks and a plate of veggies. The sunset was amazing and Copper, as always, settled at Morgan's feet. Sandy felt very much at home, and Morgan's parents made him feel welcome.

The next morning after enjoying Betty's cinnamon monkey bread, Sandy and Morgan drove over to the Cornell Campus for a nice long run. Everything was quiet with all the students at home for Thanksgiving break. Sandy marveled at the 'Old Stone Row,' the original campus buildings built in the 1860s. The buildings were a French Second Empire design with arched windows of limestone and colored slate Mansard roofs. At the northwest end of the arts quad sat the modern and amazing Johnson Art Museum designed by I.M. Pei, best known for his glass pyramid entrance to the Louvre in Paris.

When they got back to the house, everyone fluttered around the kitchen, preparing for Thanksgiving dinner. Betty had picked up all the fixin's from Wegmans. A brined turkey was the centerpiece with roasted parsnips, pan-fried Brussels sprouts with honey and balsamic vinegar, mashed potatoes with turkey gravy, and, of course, sausage stuffing. The day before, Morgan had quietly suggested to her mom to let Sandy do the cooking.

Clint remarked how nice it was not being an active veterinarian since invariably some cow would have a difficult delivery halfway through Thanksgiving dinner, or some other emergency would arise requiring his service.

On Friday, Morgan gave Sandy a tour of the area. Driving up the west side of Cayuga Lake, she took him to the overlook for Taughannock Falls, the highest waterfalls east of the Rockies. She showed him the 215-foot falls cascading from a deep gorge into a massive amphitheater surrounded by soaring cliffs of sedimentary rock. She also took him to Buttermilk Falls, where the creek gently flowed over ageless layers of sandstone and shale. Since the day was unusually warm and sunny for November, Sandy suggested, if her parents liked steak, they could pick up some nice thick ones, and they'd fix dinner for her folks. She loved the idea.

Friday night, Sandy and Morgan hummed around the kitchen, pulling together a wonderful dinner. Sandy bustled back and forth to the grill while Clint and Betty sat at the island, watched, and chatted.

By Saturday midmorning, the two said goodbye to Morgan's parents. Sandy thanked them profusely for the lovely time.

"Not at all, dear." Betty smiled and gave him another big hug. "It was our pleasure."

Once again, Clint reached out with his hand, saying with a sincere smile, "And don't be a stranger. We'd love to have you come back." And he gave his daughter a knowing look and a wink.

Morgan grinned and gave her dad a slight nod as if to say "You get it..."

Then, she took Copper's leash and headed to the car. The trip back was uneventful without a lot of traffic since it was only Saturday.

"I wish we could have stayed another full day," Sandy said to Morgan as they were driving along 81. "But the traffic tomorrow will be horrendous."

Morgan nodded in agreement. "We've got a full week coming up - including your new task of checking out Karen Young."

After days of interrogating the people from the Global Research office, the CIA team had little more than when they started. It was clear that Bob Jones was the only person who'd contact up the chain of command, and yet he seemed to know only the mysterious 'Todd' and insisted he had never met the man or knew where he was based. Funds flowed through the numbered account. While the staff had shared their passwords, there was no useful data on those machines. All they had were research notes on various oil companies.

They did have Harry Atkinson's confession to pay and supply the arsenic to Faruq Eze. He'd quickly thrown Jones under the bus saying that Jones had directed him to make the arrangement. So, they could put them both into the Lagos legal system. The challenge was they didn't want anyone to know they had them, so Atkinson was kept at the safe house until they were ready.

Bob Jones, the leader of the office, was the key. He was the only one getting the critical information and emails. Danjuma and Ismail had tried to break him for days, and it was not working. They decided to use the container again. In their experience, 99% of the time, one day was all it took. The next morning, they handcuffed him behind his back, put on a blindfold, and put him in the back of a windowless van. As far as Jones knew, they were Lagos police.

They drove him over to the Tin Can Island and put him in the same container used on Atkinson. Ismail said to Danjuma as they were dragging Jones into the container, "You know this thing is really starting to stink in here from the dead bodies. We need to air it out."

"Yeah, you're probably right, but Jones here won't care when it's all over." They removed the blindfold so Jones could see for a few minutes where he was but left the handcuffs on.

Jones started to scream, "You can't leave me here to die! You just can't!"

Ismail replied, "We can, and we will. Goodbye, Mr. Jones." They slammed the door closed and padlocked the container. They could hear Jones sobbing inside. They drove back to the safe house.

As before, they returned in the evening with the folding chairs and sat Bob Jones in a chair facing the headlights. He began talking very rapidly.

Danjuma said, "Slow down, Mr. Jones. We're going to take you back to the police station and get all your information. If there are any gaps or unanswered questions, we'll just bring you back here for a longer stay. Are we clear, Mr. Jones?" Danjuma asked.

Jones nodded, whimpering.

Ismail remarked as they dragged him from the container, "He soiled himself. God, he really stinks. We better hose him down when we get back before we start to question him."

"Yeah, you're right. He reeks." They pushed him into the back of the van and put on the blindfold. They hosed him down in the garage and dragged him into an interview room in his wet clothes. They sat him in a metal chair and handcuffed him to a desk.

Ismail started the interview. "Let me be perfectly clear. We don't care about you. If you give us the wrong answers, you're going back for an even longer visit at our version of Club Med. Who do you report to?"

"I told you before; his name is Todd, and I think he's in New York, based on his accent. Can I have some water, please?"

Danjuma replied, "We'll get to the water in a while. So, you've talked to Todd. What's his phone number?"

"As I told you, I don't know. I never call him. If I need to talk, I send a secure message, and he calls me back."

Ismail continued the interrogation. "Which gets us to the next question, what's the password for your computer and the secure email and any other passwords we may need."

Bob Jones thought for a moment. "I have a non-disclosure agreement. I don't believe I can share that information with you."

Danjuma looked at him and smiled. "Did you hear that, Ismail? He has a non-disclosure agreement. Well, that changes everything. Clearly, the company will be upset if he tells us."

He started to yell at Jones, "Do you think the

company will care when they find your dead body at Club Med!"

Both stood up and started to unshackle Jones.

"What're you doing?" Jones asked.

"We're taking you back to Club Med, you idiot. Clearly, we wouldn't want you to violate your non-disclosure agreement. Stand up."

****

Back home on Saturday night, Sandy and Morgan relaxed and watched a movie. Sunday morning, they slept in. Since it was a cold and sleety day, they relaxed and watched football enjoying traditional football game snacks of pizza and wings.

Monday morning, Sandy sent a text to Jason.

Let's meet on Grace Street at 10 just let me know what day works for you

A few minutes later he got a reply.

Tomorrow is good, see you then Jason

He spent the rest of the day finding out what he could about Karen Young. He knew from her driver's license that she was 5'5," had brown hair, brown eyes, and weighed 135. In her driver's license photo, she had short brown hair, but that was three years ago. From the photo taken by Officer Francis, he knew she'd kept the cut but added blonde highlights. She lived in Falls Church, Virginia, in the Pimmit Hills area. Sandy knew the area because a few of his former students lived there.

After paying for a record search, Sandy learned that Young had worked for the CIA but now worked for OI

Research. This aligned with the car's registration which was owned by OI. The only thing he could discover about OI was that it had an 'A+' rating from the Better Business Bureau, and they were in Tysons Corner. He had their address on the registration. OI had no customer reviews, no apparent website, a dead end. All in all, nothing exceptional except she was following him.

Jones now truly feared for his life. "No, wait, I'll give you the passwords."

Ismail slid a pad of paper and a pen in front of Jones. "Start writing and make sure you get them right. Any screw-ups and we will give you pain like you can't even imagine and then take you to the container."

"I'll get them right. Can I have some water, please?"

Danjuma left the room and returned with a bottle of water. He set it on the table but didn't give it to Jones. "When you finish, you can have the water. Make sure you write carefully."

As soon as they had the list of usernames and passwords, Danjuma left the room. The computers had been flown over to Joint Base Andrews and been driven the 30 odd miles to NSA at Fort Meade, Maryland. The staff computers had been unlocked, and all the data was copied off to other drives. There was nothing but research notes.

As soon as the technicians at NSA had the passwords, they unlocked the Self-Encrypting drive and copied all the data to several spare drives that they controlled. Then they began unlocking the encrypted emails, and there was a treasure trove of data. They sent word to Lagos that they were into the computers and the passwords were correct.

Now they needed the last bit of crucial information. Danjuma held the bottle of water. It was clear that Jones was dehydrated. He had dry skin, was breathing rapidly, and his eyes were sunken. "We need one more thing, Mr. Jones." Danjuma said Jones' name with a mocking tone. "We need the details and passwords for the bank accounts. Write them down, now."

Jones just stared at the bottle of water. He took up the pen and wrote down the information on the numbered bank accounts in the Caymans. Danjuma sent a secure email to Diana Scott at CIA headquarters in Langley, Virginia. As soon as Diana had the passwords and other details, she began diving into the bank accounts to see the transaction details.

For now, they were done with Jones. They gave him the water, took him out of the interrogation room, and handed him over to a guard so he could shower and change into fresh prison garb. All in all, a good day for the good guys.

****

Tuesday morning, Sandy and Copper returned to Grace Street, and he was lucky to get the same table in the back. As expected, Jason arrived a few minutes early, they shook hands, and Jason sat across from Sandy.

"Thanks for coming, and I'm glad we can get this wrapped up. I thought about it and decided I'm not interested in selling the rights to my patent and invention.

Jason looked troubled. "I'm very sorry to hear that. My client doesn't accept no for an answer. Perhaps I can suggest he increase the offer."

Sandy looked him in the eye. "I wouldn't be interested at a million dollars or even ten million. You should understand that if this proves out, as I believe it will, it will revolutionize the whole world. I won't get into details, but bottom-line, I'm not going to sell."

"Ok but let me warn you this won't end well for you if you fail to sell."

Sandy got an even more stern look. "Is that a threat?"

"No, simply a promise." Jason stood, turned, and walked away.

****

Jason called Harriet and delivered the news. "He isn't interested in selling at any price."

"Ok, I'll pass the news up the line. Thanks, and I guess, for now, go back to your guy at the Energy Department. I'll let you know if we need anything further. Again thanks."

Harriet sent a secure email to Todd in New York that the answer was no.

****

In New York, Todd Peterson was thinking things weren't going well lately. First, the Lagos office looked like everyone just left. He had to send someone from NY to find a new office and hire new staff to keep things running down there. Then he got the news that

Powell said no to the offer of $250,000 to buy the rights. Now the most difficult thing he knew was coming. He needed to meet with the Pinnacle Club to update them on these events. With very few exceptions he never met with the CEOs, but this was one of those times. He put a call into Bryce Carrington's office requesting a callback.

Later that afternoon, his cell phone rang. "Hi, this is Todd Peterson."

"Todd, this is Bryce. What's up? It must be important for you to call."

"Thanks for calling back. We've got several developments that have just come up, and I think we need a face-to-face meeting of the club and myself."

"All right, but this doesn't sound good. I'll call the others and figure out a place and time where we all can meet and let you know. I assume your schedule is flexible to fit into our availability."

"Of course, sir. Just let me know where and when, and I'll be there."

Bryce called his admin into his office. "Cindy, I need to know my availability later this week when I can get away for the whole day. Look to see what can get moved around on my calendar."

Cindy returned a few minutes later. "Mr. Carrington, I can clear your calendar without too much trouble for Thursday, Friday, or Saturday."

Bryce used his cell phone to make a conference call to Reggie Clark and HW. "Gentlemen, sorry to interrupt your day, but Todd has asked that we meet with him, if possible, this week. Can you check your schedules and get back to me? I'm free Thursday, Friday, or Saturday." Both agreed to get back to him in fifteen minutes. They agreed on dinner in Miami on Friday night at Estiatorio Milos.

Bryce called Cindy. "Book the jet for Friday afternoon. Tell them we're going to Miami. I need to be downtown no later than 6 p.m. And make a reservation for a private dining room at Estiatorio Milos and obviously car service."

Rod Holloway held another briefing on Operation Valdez. He opened the meeting by saying, "I believe we've made substantial progress and I look forward to each of your updates. Lester, please let's begin."

They stayed in the same format as the previous briefing. Lester Hodges asked Tiffany Flores for an update. Tiffany presented a bio on Jacob Holden the previous CEO at TXO who became Chairman of Texas Oil and Gas in the spring.

Diana Scott from the CIA had a lot of new information. "First, we were able to break Bob Jones the leader of the Global Research office in Lagos. As a result, we got full access to his computer and secure emails. These files and emails clearly show a connection to a higher authority, a person named Todd. This correspondence covers the past five years and shows a clear pattern of working to either obstruct or influence the oil and gas industry in Nigeria. It names several oil and gas companies based in Nigeria that have either lost contracts or other companies that have gained contracts at what would appear to be very lucrative arrangements. Our CIA office in Nigeria is trying to dig deeper into the companies that have benefitted to determine if they're related to the three companies identified in the Valdez investigation."

She paused and looked at the attentive and serious faces of those in the room, then continued, "The people who worked for Global Research continue to be detained by our CIA office but believe they're being held by the Lagos police. We will have to transfer them soon to the police, but we don't want their whereabouts to be public at this time. It would appear the crimes have only been committed by Bob Jones and Harry Atkinson. The other staff members appear to only be researchers. In addition, we've also been able to clearly establish that Global Research was directly involved in bribes and murder of officials in the Nigerian government and this direction came from Todd. To date, none of the information goes as high as the President of Nigeria but certainly to some of his direct staff."

Rod Holloway raised his eyebrows and said, "Todd must be getting orders from somewhere..."

Diana continued, nodding at Rod, "Well, we were able to track Nick Keller from his break-in of the Lagos office to his office in Abu Dhabi which appears to be a related company in the middle east. We've got wiretaps installed on their phone and internet lines but all information that could expose the links has been encrypted and NSA is still working to break the codes. This office is significantly larger than the Lagos office and we estimate nearly twenty people work in this office. Since we lack evidence of a crime, we haven't been able to detain or suggest the arrest to the UAE government. We could grab Keller and see if we could get him to talk if you recommended that course of action."

"So," Rod said, "No evidence? No money transfers..."

Diana looked at him and said, "We also got access to the numbered account in the Caymans and can see the incoming and outgoing wire transfers. The outgoing transfers were all to Global Research's account in Nigeria. We've also collected the past five years' records from that account and are researching those transactions. Now that we know the numbered account that fed money into the Lagos/Cayman account we will attempt to get access to that account. So that's where we're at as of today. Any questions?"

"Excellent update and please pass along our thanks to your team. I would suggest picking up Keller and see what you can learn but of course, that should come from your Director and it's Stuart's call. Next up?"

Lester said, "Amber what have you learned?"

Amber took over at the front of the room, "When we included Jacob Holden in our analysis, we could see a pattern of calls about once per quarter between the three CEOs over the past five years."

Dylan Harrison was up next and like Amber when they added Holden to the flight information, they could see overlap at least quarterly. With the FBI interviews of the FBOs, they had the manifest for most of the flights showing the executives in close proximity to each other. They'd updated the international information from CBP which showed that international travel was aligned multiple times.

Nina Craig said there was no new information on the accounting review. Jordan Vasquez also had no new information.

Lester now introduced the newest member of the team. "I would like to introduce Patti Allen. She's managing the wiretaps on the executive phones. I think she's got some really great news."

"Hi everyone. We've been monitoring the executive phones and this morning had a breakthrough. This morning there was a call from Bryce Carrington's cell to a Todd Peterson. Peterson said they needed a face-to-face meeting of the club. Shortly after that call, Carrington called Watson and Clark saying they need to get together. Fifteen minutes later they agreed to meet on Friday evening in Miami. We picked up the call from Carrington's admin making arrangements for his jet and making dinner reservations at Estiatorio Milos in Miami for Friday evening at 6 p.m. in a private dining room."

Rod very uncharacteristically pounded his fist on the table and said, "Now we've got them! Lester, obviously you need to assemble a team for this. I want pictures of them getting off the planes, pictures entering the restaurant probably through a backdoor, video, and full audio of the meeting. Now that we know this mystery guy is Todd Peterson maybe we can figure out who he is."

"I totally agree. I will have the Miami office get on this within the hour and I will get someone working on Todd Peterson as well. Patti, did we get a phone number for Peterson?"

"No, caller id was blocked, and we didn't have time to triangulate the location."

Rod stood up, "Again everyone you're all doing

outstanding work, and let's stay on this. We're getting close."

Chapter 37   Houston, TX

B ryce Carrington stepped out of the open rear door of the Lincoln Town car at the FBO at Hobby Airport and walked a few feet to his Gulfstream G-650 ER. His flight attendant, Shirley, a stunning 32-year-old with long wavy brown hair and just enough makeup to turn any eye, was at the foot of the stairs.

"Good afternoon Mr. Carrington. We're ready to depart when you're ready. Will anyone else be joining us today?" She already knew the answer but wanted to make sure plans hadn't changed.

"Nope, just us. Thanks so much." He poked his head into the cockpit. "Ed, Carla, good to see you. I'm ready to go, thanks."

Ed, the captain, turned his head around. "Glad to have you aboard, sir. Should be smooth most of the way. We may get a few afternoon thunderstorms near Miami. We'll do our best to avoid them."

Bryce took his customary seat on the left of the plane, a large leather recliner. Shirley had closed the front door, and the twin engines were spooling up. A few minutes later, they were taxiing to the end of the runway and were off to Miami. With a top speed of nearly Mach one, they'd be on the ground in about an hour and a half.

As soon as they were airborne, Shirley came back. "Would you like anything, Mr. Carrington?"

"Thanks, Shirley. I'll have some Perrier with lime, and do we have any sushi today?"

"Yes, sir, I thought you might like some, so I just got some delivered fresh from Takumi. I will bring back an assortment for you.

Bryce opened his laptop and began reading a report from Vietnam on new discoveries in the Nam Con Son Basin located offshore in the south of the country. The reports were very positive, and he wanted to discuss progress with the others tonight. He thought for a moment about what was going on at Paragon that caused this urgent meeting. What seemed a short time later, they were on the final approach to Miami International.

Carrington's town car pulled up next to the jet, and he walked over and entered the open rear door. Thirty minutes later, due to heavy traffic, they drove over the Causeway to South Beach. The car pulled up to the back entrance of Estiatorio Milos. The one-story modern building faced 1st Street, but they used the alley behind to enter through the kitchen. The maître d' rushed into the kitchen and escorted Bryce to the private dining room. The room looked like a library, and two stewards stood patiently by the wall.

Todd Peterson and Reggie were already at the table, and they stood as Bryce entered. "Todd, Reggie, good to see you both. I hope your travel was uneventful."

Reggie grinned. "Always good to see you, Bryce, even if I've got to fly cross country or around the world to connect."

"Bryce, it's been a while, thank you for putting this meeting together on short notice." Todd shook hands with Bryce.

A moment later, HW entered the room, and everyone shared pleasantries. Drinks were ordered, and after a few minutes, Bryce took the lead. Bryce asked the stewards to leave the room and said that they'd call them when they were ready.

"So, Todd, what's so urgent and important that we need a face-to-face?" All the men focused on Todd.

"We've got a few developments, and with the...shall we say... sensitivity, I wanted to brief you in person. First, the inventor, Sandy Powell, who we discussed via email, has rejected our offer of $250,000 to acquire the rights to his patent and his invention. He told our agent he wouldn't even consider $10 million for the invention. He said it will, 'Change the World.' We had our resident scientist look at the patent again, and he believes Powell may be right. His invention could produce copious amounts of hydrogen gas at almost no cost."

Reggie's jaw dropped. "Shit, that could put us out of business. We all know that the only reason hydrogen hasn't displaced oil as an energy source is that the cost to produce it's so high. Yes, we produce a lot of hydrogen from natural gas, but the process and handling are expensive."

Bryce thought a moment. "Reggie is right. So, Todd, what're you recommending?"

"I think we need to eliminate this threat. We can delete the patent as if it was never entered into the

USPTO system. As near as we can determine, he hasn't shared the idea with anyone except his girlfriend who filed the patent."

HW looked shocked. "We can't just eliminate the guy and his girlfriend. It was bad enough in Nigeria where no one would know. These are Americans. We can't just knock them off."

Reggie replied, "HW... as I told you in Lagos, this is a tough business, and the reason we've been, and still are on top is that we make the tough decisions."

"Well, I for one vote NO to doing any harm to this guy. We need to get him to accept a reasonable offer."

Bryce looked at Todd. "For now, just put some pressure on Powell. We can up the offer to $5 million and see if that works. Keep us posted on the status. Anything else?"

"Yes, the office in Lagos is offline. We don't know what happened, but all our people in that office have disappeared without a trace. We're working to reopen the office with new staff, but it's strange; they're all gone."

"Do you mean like abducted by aliens gone or what?" HW asked.

"Kind of like that. We had perfectly executed the plan to eliminate Ali Mohammed, the Minister of Oil and Gas. The medical examiner said it was food poisoning, and a week later, our office is empty, and the people are totally missing."

"Do you think someone figured out the plan and grabbed your people?" HW asked.

"Reality is we don't know. I don't see how that could have happened, but at this point, we simply don't know."

"Any other problems, Todd?" Bryce asked.

"No, that's it. All of our other projects are running smoothly, and we will figure out this situation in Nigeria."

Reggie looked around and said to Todd, "I've got a great idea. I want you to get in the papers in the next few days. We need some professor to say that all these solar panels, because they're black, are going to contribute to global warming."

Bryce sat back and gave a hearty laugh. "That's the best one I've heard in a long time. It's perfect. Run with it."

HW looked kind of stunned. "Do you really think some professor will say that to a newspaper?"

"It's easy, you just wave some money under their nose. Those liberal professors are just like politicians; they'll do anything for research money," Todd said with a chuckle.

Bryce, HW, and Reggie all stood and thanked Todd for the update. He was dismissed and left the room.

After he left, Bryce suggested they order dinner and continue the conversation. The food at Estiatorio Milos was extraordinary and well worth the trip. The restaurant was world-famous for its Mediterranean seafood dishes.

Over dinner, Bryce brought up concerns about how Peterson seemed to be losing control of Paragon. Reggie pointed out several different projects that were running smoothly, and overall, they were a good investment. Bryce seemed unconvinced. HW stayed on the sidelines and continued to think about how extreme solutions seemed to be taken as a matter of course.

The conversation switched to mutual projects. Bryce started the conversation by discussing their joint development of several fields in Indonesia and Vietnam. He felt they were in good shape and would continue pumping in the proven fields, and exploration was ahead of schedule.

Reggie brought up developments in Kirkuk, Iraq, and how the Paragon paramilitary had repelled several potential attacks to disrupt the wells in that field.

HW asked about how the development in Iran was going and was the new company there able to work around the sanctions.

Bryce said it was going well, and the new company was structuring a deal to virtually move the oil through a Russian shell company.

Next, they turned to the timing of the spring price shift. Bryce said, "Listen, we've got the right guy in the White House and our usual support in Congress, and we're looking ahead to the next election this fall. I think we need to keep prices low and just do an 8 cent per gallon increase before Memorial Day. Memorial Day is the 31st this year, so let's roll up prices on the 20th, and we can roll them back 4 cents on July 10. Then a full 10 cents on September 10 through the midterm election. This will keep the economy in good shape and help the people we need to be elected. If we see things aren't going our way, we can adjust."

HW thought a moment. "I like the plan, and I can certainly live with those numbers." Reggie nodded his head in agreement

They all had baklava with strong Greek coffee followed by ouzo after the delightful meal. Reggie and HW left separately for the airport. Bryce was staying over at the Fairmont on the beach to see friends in the morning. He had reserved the Fairmont Suite, which was the size of a small house. He really enjoyed going out on the balcony and listening to the sound of the waves gently rolling in. Tonight, as he sat on the balcony, he could hear some of the Friday night sounds from South Beach and loved the smell of the salt air.

Chapter 38 Washington, DC

Lester and the team at the FBI were over the moon happy with all they'd collected. They had pictures of all the executives getting on their jets and off in Miami. All had landed at Miami International, making it even easier. They had photos of each of them, including Todd Peterson, entering the rear of the restaurant.

Before the meeting in Miami, the FBI had met with the IRS and knew the names of everyone who worked at the restaurant. They knew the maître d', Nick Praxis, was over $100,000 in debt to the IRS. It was rather simple for the FBI to approach him, suggest his IRS problem could go away, and get access to the private dining room. They installed four high-definition cameras and multiple microphones in the room. They also installed two cameras in the rear kitchen, so they got a video of the executives entering and leaving through the rear.

Lester called Rod on his cell phone and gave him the good news. They agreed to have a joint meeting with the Attorney General and the Director of the FBI, hopefully Monday, schedules permitting, to discuss the next steps.

Monday afternoon, after moving a few meetings around, the senior group assembled. Charles Caserta, the Attorney General, took the lead for the meeting. "I understand we've put together some solid evidence on these three oil executives. Rod, can you brief us?"

Rod shifted in his chair. "Actually, I would like Lester to bring us up to speed on the developments from Friday evening. He deserves most of the credit."

Lester began, "This really was a joint effort across several agencies that all came together to create a really strong case." He turned on the projector and showed a picture of all three executives. "Harold Watson, Bryce Carrington, and Reginald Clark have conspired to commit murder and have thwarted antitrust laws to work in collusion to create joint ventures and fix prices. We have pictures, audio, and video evidence." Lester flipped to the video with pieces of the conversation on Friday night that clearly demonstrated the damning evidence they'd collected.

Charlie was shocked. "Where did you get this? It's amazing!"

"We knew that they'd planned a joint dinner on Friday night in Miami. We convinced the maître d' to allow us to install covert cameras and audio equipment in the dining room. We also had agents at various airports photograph their departures and arrivals on Friday."

"Who's the fourth guy in the video?" Charlie asked.

"That's Todd Peterson. We're pulling together information on him and his company as we speak."

Meredith Drake, Director of the FBI, interjected, "We believe this is only the surface of this case, and it could go a lot further."

Charlie said, "Ok, what are the next steps?"

Rod suggested, "I think we need to keep digging. Clearly, we've got more than enough evidence to take this to a grand jury and get indictments, but I totally agree with Meredith and Lester that there's a bunch more we can get. Once we indict and arrest these three guys, the whole thing will go underground, and we'll have a hard time discovering more. I'd like to suggest we spend a few more weeks doing discovery."

"Ok, I agree. Dig deep, fast, and by the book. These guys will have the best legal talent in the country, so any loose thread, they'll unzip the pillowcase. Meredith, I think we need to brief the President so he can get in front of this."

"I would recommend we wait two weeks to see what else gets unearthed. We both know that 1600 is like a bucket full of holes. It will find a way out," Meredith said.

Charlie said, "You're right. Ok, let's plan to get together in two weeks and see if we've got more. Lester and Ron, please pass on a 'job well done' to the team. This is amazing."

Todd thought all weekend about the meeting. On one hand, he was pleased that he had shared the bad news with the execs. On the other hand, he was very concerned with HW's reluctance to take strong measures against Powell and that he had influenced Reggie and Bryce. He needed to solve the problem in Nigeria as soon as possible. So, he called two of his best people in New York and had them on a plane on Sunday afternoon.

First thing Monday morning, he called Campos in Washington and told her to have her agent meet with Powell and up the offer to $5 million. Harriet called Jason and gave him the updated information on the offer to Powell.

A client has a new offer can you meet tomorrow at 10 on Grace Street

Not really interested but yes will meet tomorrow

Sandy and Jason met as planned. "My client would like to revise his offer to $5 million for the rights to the patent and invention. Same terms as before. If it doesn't work, you get to keep the money."

"What about your threat?"

"I apologize. I was caught up in the moment and frustrated. My bad."

"Ok, I don't think it will change my mind, but I want to sleep on it and will text you tomorrow."

"I can't ask for more than that, thanks." Jason stood and left the coffee shop. He felt like it might happen, and he updated Harriet.

After Sandy got back to the townhouse, he texted Morgan.

They upped the offer to $5 million let's talk tonight L S

Ok have an awesome day LYM M

LYM????

Love YOU MORE silly

On Monday, Sandy had prepared a basic beef broth from scratch, using bones he picked up at the butcher. He roasted the bones and then cooked them down to make the broth, which he let simmer overnight. After getting back from Grace Street, he sautéed a pile of onions and combined the broth to make a French onion soup which simmered all afternoon. To this, he added a spinach salad with a zesty tomato and bacon dressing. A nice comfort food dinner on a chilly winter's night. They discussed the offer and agreed they didn't want to sell.

Sandy texted Jason.

Sorry not interested at any price, thank you for the generous offer

They will be unhappy to hear this proceed at your own peril

****

The news went up the chain of command, and Todd told Harriet to put the screws on Powell but not to kill him. Harriet contemplated this and decided that Leon would be the best one to crank things up on Powell. She thought it too bad that Dutton was involved in this situation; she seemed like a nice bright attorney.

The next morning as Sandy, Morgan, and Copper began their run. They turned into the alley and saw the black Escapade hit the gas. It was heading towards them at a high speed. Sandy pushed Morgan back towards the fence, Copper jumped after her.

The car screeched to a halt. The driver lowered the window. Wearing a black ski mask, only his steely eyes showed. He yelled, "You should've taken the offer! We show no mercy!" He took off, turning right at the end of the alley.

Sandy turned. "Are you ok?"

"Yes, I'm fine, just a little shaken, and Copper is ok too."

"Let's get in the house and come up with a plan."

"Ok, not sure what you mean about a plan."

Inside, sitting at the kitchen table, Sandy looked like a commander prepared for war. He was quiet and thoughtful. It was a side of Sandy that Morgan had never witnessed, and it both scared her and made her feel safer than ever.

"I've had a suspicion for the past month, since we filed the patent, that we were being watched and possibly being tracked. I saw the white Lexus twice in Ithaca but didn't want to alarm you. I've seen that black Escalade several times in the past month. They may have tracking devices in our cars. Today they're so small you'd never find them. They could also be tracking our phones and laptops. It's very easy to do. We've got to go to ground; while I figure this out."

"What do you mean, go to ground?"

"Disappear. We've got to disconnect from the web, and I need you to be out of sight for a little bit. My first priority is to keep you safe from harm."

"Sandy, I'll be ok. I'm a big girl."

"This could get ugly fast, and I want to know you're safe while I sort this out. Don't question me on this. I love you and will do whatever it takes to protect you."

"Ok and I love you for that. I always have since we first met. So, what's the plan, Captain?"

****

The FBI New York City Headquarters received orders from Lester Hodges to drill deep into Todd Peterson and his company without letting him know he was under investigation. They'd trailed Peterson after his return from Miami and knew where he lived; now they needed to find his office. Cliff Black had been assigned to run the team, and he gathered eight of his experienced agents for the task.

They were able to watch Peterson leave his apartment building on the Upper West Side of Manhattan and take a taxi to a low rise building a block east of Times Square on 46th Street. The agent riding shotgun jumped out of the car and followed Peterson into the building, joining him on the elevator. Peterson scanned his key card in the elevator and pressed 5. "Can I help you?" Peterson asked.

The agent looked perplexed. "Sorry, no, I'm going for a job interview. Is this 140?"

"No, this is 144."

"Ok thanks, walked in the wrong door, and I'm already late."

They got to the top floor. Peterson walked off the elevator, turned, and said, "Good luck."

The receptionist could be heard saying, "Good morning Mr. Peterson."

The agent took a mental picture of the space beyond the door. A typical office with a receptionist facing the elevator and a sign behind her reading 'Paragon Group.'

Sandy looked thoughtful. "The plan is first I need backup, so I'm going to get Jackson here as soon as possible. I trust him completely, and we can cover each other. I need you to call Vicky and see if you can stay there for a week or so. There's no way they know where she lives. I'll take Copper to Fairfax."

"No! Absolutely not. I want Copper with me! That's final Mr. Powell, and I know Vicky will be ok with it. Her cat will have to get used to sharing the space. Where are you going to go?"

"I guess tonight I'll stay with you and Vicky, and then we'll play it by ear. Why don't you give Vicky a quick call and see if she's ok with it and say that we'll be there about lunchtime? Then pack a bag for at least a week. I'm going to call Jackson."

Morgan would be lying to herself if she said she wasn't a bit scared. But she knew Sandy was capable and knew what to do. "Ok, will do." And she bounded upstairs to call Vicky and start packing.

Sandy dialed Jackson even though it was midnight in Australia. "Hey mate, sorry to wake you."

A bit groggy, Jackson replied, "No worries, what's up?"

"I got some bad shit going down here, and I need

your help."

A bit more awake now. "Say what, bad shit? You ok, mate?"

"Yeah, for the moment. I need you backing me up. Can you catch a flight tomorrow?"

"Sure."

"Book it, business class, all the way to DC, and I'll pay you for the ticket. I need you somewhat rested when you arrive. I'm getting a burner phone today. I'll text and email you my new number. Use that number to let me know when you'll land in DC. I'll meet you at the airport. Probably best to fly into Dulles."

"Slow down, mate. I'm just getting my pants on, and I need a pencil and paper. Give me a minute."

Sandy could hear him taking a leak and flushing the toilet. "No worries, buddy, standing by."

"Ok, I'm at the kitchen table. Go ahead."

Sandy repeated the information he'd given earlier and continued, "Pack for a few weeks and make your return ticket a few weeks out. We can always change it when we figure things out." Sandy thought for a moment. "You better bring your gear. This could get heavy, and as you know, better to be prepared when you walk into a shit storm."

"Ok, I can't pack any weapons. You know it's Australia, not the Wild West of America."

"No worries, I've got an arsenal. Got to run. See you in a day and a half."

"Cheers, mate, keep your head down."

****

Back downstairs and in the car, the agent who'd followed Peterson into the elevator called headquarters and reported the name and location of the company. This was a big break in the investigation. Now that they had the name and address, a whole group of people in New York and Washington set out on a mission of digital discovery.

Another lucky break occurred when they checked for Paragon job openings. Paragon was hiring for an experienced analyst and a field agent. Two FBI people applied online for jobs that morning. In addition, they called the number listed and asked if they could interview right away. The analyst was able to get an interview that afternoon and the field agent the following day. While everything was fake, their resumes were impeccable, and they both started on Wednesday morning.

Having two people inside was huge. Marsha Cohen was an attractive effervescent five-foot-two ball of energy that came through in the interview. Paragon hired her as a hacker but didn't realize she would be hacking Paragon, not other companies.

Billy Vaughn, at five-eleven, was slim but with a muscular build. Looking like he just walked out the gate at the Marine training facility on Parris Island, he even had a buzz cut. Vaughn was an experienced FBI field agent with an eidetic memory, like having a living video recorder.

****

Sandy went upstairs and joined Morgan in packing.

He was thinking through the next steps. When they got downstairs, he said, "We need to empty the fridge of anything that might go bad in case we're gone for a few weeks." They poured milk down the drain, put a few items in the freezer, and made up a bag of trash that Sandy took out to the bin. He put the bin on the street and took note of the white Lexus parked down the street. This would work well for his developing plan.

Back inside, he called for an Uber van. Five minutes later, they had one outside. They loaded bags, laptops, Copper, and his food and bowls. It took a couple of trips. Once in the van, they headed for National Airport. Sandy casually watched to see if they had a tail, and it looked like they did.

At the airport, they asked to be dropped off at the pickup side. There were always free airport luggage carts to grab, so they grabbed two and loaded everything onto them. Inside the airport, Sandy and Morgan turned off their cell phones. Sandy told Morgan the plan. "We're going to take the walkway over to the parking garage and get another Uber. We can take the Uber to the Walmart near Mt. Vernon and pick up some supplies, including two new cell phones."

★★★★

An hour and a half later, they were at Vicky's apartment in Alexandria, Virginia, about five blocks from the King Street Metro. Vicky helped them cart all the stuff into her roomy two-story two-bedroom apartment. Copper loved the golden-colored Persian cat whose fur almost matched his. Queen Latifah didn't share the affection and hissed a few times at Copper, who just laid on the floor and watched her longingly. Clearly, he hoped Latifah would come around and want to play. Morgan took him out through the backdoor so he could do his business.

Once everyone was settled in, Morgan and Sandy gave Vicky a brief update. Sandy sent Jackson a text with the new numbers. Sandy then said he had to travel out to the farm, would be back about dinner time, and not to worry.

Morgan thought that's easy for you to say, but put on a brave smile and said, "We'll be fine!"

Wednesday morning, together with one other guy in a Paragon conference room, they went through a mountain of HR stuff. Filling out forms, getting assigned corporate IDs, and all the usual stuff. The new hires met with their managers just before lunch and joined their teams for lunch on the company.

Marsha was assigned to gather information on new oil discoveries offshore in North Carolina. Specifically, to find companies with data on the fields, get into their systems by whatever means, extract it, and copy that information into the Paragon system. They gave her an Iraqi secure IP for the hacking and told her to make certain nothing could lead them back to Paragon.

Billy got assigned to a team watching a new UN diplomat from Saudi. Their mission was to find any dirt possible and document everything. Pictures or videos were the best. They were instructed to catch him at a strip club or drinking, so Paragon had leverage on him.

Lester worked with DOJ, and they were able to get the needed warrant for Todd Peterson and The Paragon Group. Even while that was happening, the

FBI offices in NY and Washington were building files on the company. Through the IRS payroll records, they had a list of every employee that worked for the company for the past ten years. They had details like Social Security numbers and were able to look up current addresses. In addition, they knew when they started and, more importantly, when they left the company. Another group of analysts was pouring through the Paragon tax filings, which told them the big picture of funds flowing in and out of the company. Revenue all appeared to be coming from several foreign companies. This was handed off to another team to dig into those foreign companies.

Marsha had been able to penetrate most of the systems and copy the data to an external drive. Todd's secure emails were copied as well. So far, NSA hadn't been able to break the code. Marsha was able to get the bank and account data for the three New York banks they were using.

Warrants in hand, the banks provided 10 years' worth of detailed transaction records on the accounts to the agents. The analysts now were able to identify the multiple numbered accounts in the Caymans where Paragon was wiring money.

Lester asked Charles Caserta to reach out to the Director-General of the UK's National Crime Agency to get access in the Caymans to the list of numbered accounts they now had information on. Fortunately, they were all at one bank. The case was building, and it was way bigger than they'd imagined.

Sandy walked from Vicky's apartment toward the King Street metro. A lot was going on, but he felt Morgan would be safe at the apartment. Just before the station, he ducked into the small Starbucks on the ground floor of the Hilton on King Street. First, he called Gary Sutter, his attorney; thankfully, he was in and available.

"Gary, Sandy Powell, I need a big favor."

"Sandy, good to hear from you. How are things working out?"

"Good. We filed the patent, and I'm still figuring out what to do with the farm. I've got a group that wants the invention, and they're starting to play very rough. I would like you to rent an SUV tomorrow morning and list me as a second driver. I'm concerned they may be watching my credit card transactions, and I need to move around without them following me."

"Okay, shouldn't you call the police?"

"I don't have enough to go to the police, and that would likely make things worse."

"Gotcha, no problem. I'll get one first thing in the morning, and you can pick it up at my office any time after nine."

"Thanks! That's great and make sure you get all the

insurance. See you tomorrow."

Sandy's next call was to his local bank in Fairfax. He had been doing business there for years, and they'd always been terrific. He asked for the branch manager.

"Hello, this is Anita Curtis. How can I help you?"

"Hi Anita, this is Sandy Powell. I've got several accounts with you. I'd like to withdraw $20,000 tomorrow morning in cash. I wanted to give you a call ahead so you could have it available."

"We can handle that, and I'm glad you called in advance since we'll have to order it delivered here."

"Yes, I totally understand. Would 10 a.m. give you enough time?"

"That'd be more than fine. I assume you want that in $100 bills."

"That's perfect. See you tomorrow, and thanks, Anita."

Sandy sipped his venti latte with an extra shot and thought about all that had transpired over the past few months, as well as the most recent developments.

He thought, what's the best next step? These guys weren't going to just go away, they'd never stop chasing him. By slipping away they were just postponing the inevitable.

****

Harriet Campos called her team together that had been covering Powell in their office in Tysons Corner. "So, what's the status?"

"I followed them to National with a pile of luggage," Karen replied.

Verna piped in, "From there, they've up and disappeared. We haven't seen their cell phones since they went to the airport. Maybe we scared them away."

"Leon, anything?"

"No, ma'am, I've been watching the townhouse. I installed a couple of cameras and motion detectors front and back. And nothing. My guess is they likely skipped town, and all we can do is wait till their cell phones come back on."

"All right, I'm going to have our group put them on a watch list. Even if we scared them away, they must be somewhere, and we need to find them. I want all of you to work out a plan to see if they go to any of the places we've known them to frequent, just in case they're still in town. Let's plan to get together here in three days at the same time as today and see if anything develops." Harriet then called Todd in New York and gave him an update. Todd told her he would have the tech group put them on a watch list.

★★★★

Sandy sat in the Starbucks thinking and sipping his coffee and put his military training to use. "We must go on the offensive and take it to them, not wait for their next response. Step one, find out what we can about the enemy."

There was no need to go to the farm today since he would be out in Fairfax tomorrow. He made a quick call to Morgan on the new phone, and she answered on the first ring. "Just wanted to let you know I'm on my way back to Vicky's apartment. Is there anything you need?"

Morgan could be heard asking Vicky if she needed anything. "Nope, we're good, see you soon."

When Sandy got back, he asked Vicky if he could order some stuff on her Amazon account because he didn't want to use his credit cards or Amazon account. Then he went online using Vicky's computer and ordered four GPS tracking devices. He told Vicky he would pay her tomorrow. They had a quiet evening and turned in early. Vicky would be back at work tomorrow, and Morgan would be housesitting with Copper.

About nine the next morning, Sandy gave Morgan a hug and a kiss goodbye and said he would be out for the day and be back late that night with Jackson. He told her she needed to stay out of sight, for now, use only her new phone and Vicky's computer. Sandy walked over to the King Street metro station and caught a Blue Line train to Rosslyn, where he switched and picked up the Orange Line to Vienna. He took the escalator up and walked across the bridge over 66 to the north. He hailed a cab and was on his way to Gary Sutter's office just north of Reston, about twenty minutes away.

At Gary's office, they exchanged pleasantries, and Gary reminded him if he needed anything to call him at any hour. He insisted that Sandy be careful and if it got ugly to call the police. Sandy thanked him, and with the keys, Sandy jumped in the Chevrolet Tahoe then headed south to his bank in Fairfax. At the bank,

Sandy picked up the $20,000 in cash. The two small bundles were less than a half-inch thick each. Back in the car, he peeled a thousand dollars from one of the bundles and put the cash in his front pants pocket. The balance of the bundle he put in the glove box and locked it. The other bundle went in the compartment between the seats. Not totally safe, but it was better than carrying it all on himself.

Sandy grabbed a bite to eat at his favorite restaurant in Fairfax, EastWind Vietnamese on Main Street. He had a spring roll and their awesome seafood pho, just enough to fill him for the afternoon. After lunch, he took the $10,000 bundle, went to Walmart and bought three prepaid MasterCard cards, loading two thousand on one and one thousand on the other two cards. He also bought a new laptop for Morgan. Next, he headed back north to the farm.

Before arriving at the farm, Sandy logged into his surveillance system to check the cameras and motion detectors he'd installed a month ago. Nothing looked amiss, and there had been no activity on the motion detectors. Just to be safe, he drove past the farm and about a mile down the road. There were no vehicles around. He turned around and drove back. Sandy parked a bit away from the barn because he planned to move some of the machinery out of the barn so he could park the Tahoe inside out of sight. After moving the tools and Ford 8N to an adjacent shed, he backed the Tahoe inside and closed the rolling doors. He walked over to the house and went inside to check that all was well. Nothing appeared to be disturbed, so he locked up and went back to the barn.

He entered the basement through the magic

cupboard. All was as he had left it. He grabbed his emergency bags and took them upstairs to the SUV. He went back down, gathered up his firearms, and loaded them into the Tahoe.

He rolled open the barn doors, drove the SUV out, and closed up. He headed to Herndon to grab a bite to eat while he waited for Jackson's flight to arrive from San Francisco in a few hours. Jimmy's Old Town Tavern in Herndon was perfect since it was a few minutes from Dulles. He ordered their amazing award-winning wings and the grilled salmon salad. Sandy checked in with Morgan and then relaxed and watched some pre-recorded football on the overhead TVs.

Just before 7 p.m., Jackson called and said he had just touched down. Sandy headed for Dulles Airport, a few minutes away, and parked in the cell phone lot.

The phone rang, "Bloody hell, mate, it's freezing cold out. I think I'll go home."

"I've got a gray Tahoe. What number door are you at, you wimp."

"Number Six, mate, and hurry up – Oh my God, how can you live here?"

Sandy pulled up to door six and jumped out in the mild 35-degree evening air. Jackson rushed over with his three bags as Sandy opened the tailgate. After a quick hug, they jumped in the SUV, and Sandy pulled away from the curb, headed for DC. He called Morgan to let her know they were on their way. Sandy brought Jackson up to speed on all that was going on as they drove down 66 and took Route 1 down past the Pentagon and National Airport to Alexandria.

Sandy parked in the lot near Vicky's condo, and they carried Jackson's bags in. "Hi gals, I would like you to meet my best friend, Jackson. Jackson, meet Morgan and Vicky."

Jackson, at five-ten with short brown hair and bright brown eyes was built like a soldier coming out of basic training. With his full-on strong Aussie accent, "Hi, so you're the one that captured his heart."

"Yup, that would be me. Of course, he actually started it all."

"And you must be the hostess with this great condo."

Vicky grinned and blushed like a high school teenager with a first crush. "You got me there. Please make yourself at home. What can I get you to eat and drink?"

"If you have it, I'd love scotch and just some biscuits and cheese. They had pretty good food in the front of the plane."

Copper had given Jackson the once over, was pleased with the new visitor, and settled as always at Morgan's feet. Vicky's Queen Latifah was nowhere to be seen and was still pouting at having this big furry dog inhabiting her house. In her own feline way, she was plotting a way to disgrace this creature.

"Biscuits?" Vicky said with a puzzled look.

Sandy translated, "Crackers here, biscuits Down Under. Next, we'll have to run out and get a jar of Vegemite for his breakfast toast."

Morgan piped in, "What's Vegemite?"

"Oh my, you haven't lived until you've had a

Vegemite to start your day. It's a thick dark brown spread made from leftover brewer's yeast with a few special ingredients you put on toast," Jackson said.

Sandy wrinkled his nose. "Takes a bit getting used to. We'll have to get a jar at Wegmans."

They sat around the family room and chatted into the night. Vicky finally stood and announced, "Sorry gang, I've got to turn in. I have to be at work in the morning." Then turning to Jackson, she added with a tired smile, "I'll get some blankets and towels for you. I wish I had another bed; you'll just have to pull out the bed from the couch."

Jackson smiled back. "No worries! Just appreciative of the place to crash."

Morgan yawned. "I should turn in as well." She and Vicky headed off upstairs to get stuff for Jackson.

Upstairs Vicky whispered, "Oh my God, he's a dream!"

"Oh yeah, talk about a catch. Maybe we each got one. Wouldn't that be cool?"

"Let's see how this goes. Australia is a long way away."

"True enough, but still worth checking out."

"I'm sure I'll be dreaming about him tonight."

Back downstairs, Sandy told Jackson the plan. "Tomorrow, we're going to get you rested up and maybe show you some of the sights. And then the next day, we'll take it to them. You know the drill; live the time zone you're in. So, try to get some sleep. And again, thanks for dropping everything and coming over."

"Of course, I came. What else would I do? I like the plan."

The FBI's New York office supporting the people in DC was building their case. With Marsha Cohen on the inside, they had a copy of virtually everything on the servers. The encrypted email files from Paragon still hadn't been cracked.

They knew the type of research being conducted focused on the oil and gas business or other energy-related fields. Information was amassed from around the globe. It was amazing how much had been gathered, and it went back years. They also had reports on hundreds of companies and individuals, which included photos that could be used as blackmail, especially of government officials both here in the US and others around the world.

Billy Vaughn was stunned by the bravado of the team watching the UN diplomat from Saudi. Within a few days, they had incredible photos of him, drinking at a topless bar and taking a hooker up to his apartment. They even had a video of him dancing nude about his apartment with the naked hooker. Once they had the goods on the guy, they approached him and pressed him into service to swing deals within Saudi that Paragon wanted. Clear-cut extortion.

****

Lester sent out an email calling the team in for a quick update. The next day at 11 a.m., they assembled in the executive briefing room at DOJ. Diana Scott from the CIA provided a brief on Nigeria. "No new developments in the Lagos office. All the individuals remain in custody at the CIA safe house and believe they're in jail. We haven't received any new information from them. We've had no luck using Treasury and FATF to get access to the Cayman bank accounts."

Amber Dean said there were no new phone calls between the CEOs and Peterson since the meeting in Miami. She also said they were now monitoring Jacob Holden, the former CEO and now Chairman of Texas Oil.

Cliff Black video conferenced into the meeting in DC. "We've been very lucky to have Marsha Cohen on the inside at Paragon," he reported. "We've been able to copy virtually their entire database, and it's like finding King Solomon's mine. Fortunately, the information is very well-organized. We could have a team of fifty work through the files for a year. What we do know is that they've dirt on lots of politicians and corporate executives around the world that could be used as leverage. They've done deep penetration into competitive companies also around the world. With the data we have, we know there are multiple numbered bank accounts in the Caymans. What we still lack is the transaction details within those accounts."

Lester thought for a moment. All eyes in the room were on him as he sat forward. "Cliff, who's leading the analysis of the data from New York?"

"Brenda Bates, sir."

"Thanks, I'll reach out to her directly. I want her to see if we can find the two ministers' names in Nigeria in the files, and there was another name mentioned in the conversation in Miami. What was his name?"

"Sandy Powell, sir," Amber said, recalling her review of the video and audio tapes from the Miami meeting.

"Right, thanks, Amber. Diana, can you email the information we have on the two oil ministers in Nigeria to Brenda. If you have trouble finding her in the system, call my admin, and she'll connect you."

Lester stood. "Ok, everyone, great job. It's clear we've got a lot and likely more than enough to make arrests and go to the grand jury for indictments. I'll put pressure to get the transaction details in those numbered accounts, which will tie all of this together. Thank you and keep on this."

Lester knew they were close, but they needed the information from the numbered accounts in the Caymans and the encrypted emails to have an open-and-shut case. They also needed to take this to POTUS. Lester sent a brief update to Rod, Charles Caserta, and Meredith Drake and emphasized the need to get access to the accounts.

Chapter 44   Alexandria, VA

The next morning, Morgan logged into the office system with the new laptop Sandy had picked up and was once again able to get some work done. Jackson, while tired, got up, and fortified with fresh coffee, did a casual tour of the DC sights with Sandy. Sandy's package arrived from Amazon, and they tested the GPS transponders and software on their phones. Sandy fixed a wonderful dinner, and Vicky did her best not to flirt with Jackson, although the chemistry was obvious. Everyone turned in early because Sandy had an early day planned for himself and Jackson.

Well before dawn, Sandy and Jackson drove off in the Tahoe for Falls Church. They had Karen Young's address from the photo of her driver's license and the license plate for her white Lexus. Driving through the quiet streets of Pimmit Hills, they quickly spotted her Lexus parked in the street. Sandy drove around the block and stopped well before her house. Jackson jumped out and casually walked up to the car. He crawled under it and attached the GPS tracking device with the waterproof magnetic case near the rear bumper.

Sandy and Jackson drove to the 24-hour Coffee Shop in Tysons and waited for the world to wake up. At about 7:30, they noticed her GPS started to move, and they watched as it was driven toward Tysons Corner. They leaped into the Tahoe and arrived just before she did at what Sandy suspected was her office, based on his research and the address on her car's registration. Jackson jumped out when she'd parked and walked over to the entrance to the office building arriving at the door just before her and opening the door for her. He followed her to the elevator and rode up, exiting with her on the fifth floor. He watched her enter an unmarked office and pushed the button to take the elevator back down.

In the parking lot, Jackson climbed back into the Tahoe and gave an update. Sandy said, "Let's sit and see if anyone else I think is part of the group shows up." About ten minutes later, they saw Jason Roberts exit his BMW and walk towards the building. "Bingo! Got another one. He's the guy that made me the offer. We need to tag his car. Why don't you follow him up and confirm it's the same office? We can tag the car later."

Another 15 minutes passed, and the black Escalade pulled into a parking spot. While not 100% certain, Sandy was pretty confident it was the same guy that threatened him a few days ago behind the townhouse. Again, Jackson followed him up the elevator and confirmed he went to the same office. Since they were in full view of the office building and it was broad daylight, Sandy drove around the parking lot and parked close to the back of each car so Jackson could slip out and attach the GPS to each car. Now came the waiting.

Sandy suggested, "Hey, let's go get some breakfast."

"Sounds great."

They drove over to a favorite, the Silver Diner near the mall in Tysons Corner. Over a delightful breakfast, they discussed the plan. Sandy asked, "Do you think we could mount a camera on a wall near the door to the office to record who comes and goes?"

"Possibly, but it would have to look like something that should be there. Anything but a camera."

"Good point. Let's see if we can find something that could work." Sandy began searching online for a solution. He found a hidden camera that looked like a smoke detector but actually was a hidden HD recorder. He showed it to Jackson. "What do you think?"

"I think that could work great."

While they were eating breakfast, they noticed that the cars were leaving all about the same time. "Must be the meeting is over. It should be interesting to see where they go. I'll order the camera for overnight delivery."

They relaxed, enjoyed a terrific breakfast of very fresh ingredients, and casually watched the cars head for downtown. Thirty minutes later, the cars had all come to rest. The black Escalade was parked behind Morgan's townhouse. Jason's BMW was near the Department of Energy. Karen Young's car entered a parking garage downtown, and they lost its signal.

"Well, it's no surprise that they continue to watch Morgan's townhouse. Clearly, they don't know where we are at this point. Do you think we should kick the hornet's nest?"

"My advice is let's wait till we get the camera up and

get more data on who else works there. Plus, we need a plan past kicking the bees. What do we do next besides getting stung?"

"Good point. Glad we've got the trackers. At least we know where they are and that they don't know where to look for us." Sandy smiled. "This is going to be fun."

****

The next day, they took the smoke detector camera and went back to the office. Jackson wore jeans, a work shirt, and a light jacket and looked like a maintenance guy. Carrying a ladder in from the parking lot, he went up the elevator and installed the smoke detector with a clear view of the office door. He was able to link it to an unprotected guest wireless point for one of the tenants in the building and 10 minutes later was loading the ladder into the back of the Tahoe. He climbed into the front seat. "Well, can you see the office door?"

"Perfect, and we can see what it captures today. Clearly, the best views are when they leave the office, and we can see their faces."

"Agreed, glad it's working. So, what do we use as leverage after we kick the proverbial beehive?"

"My only thought is to capture them on tape with a threat and go to the cops. I can't picture how we can threaten them with anything else. You got any ideas?"

"Well, mate, you're probably right. We could piss them off enough to shoot them, this being the Wild West here in the USA." Jackson's eyes twinkled at the thought.

They went back to Vicky's condo and watched the office door over the internet. They kept notes on the comings and goings from the office and now knew that about six people worked in the office. No names, but they'd recorded the faces. No one seemed to take notice of the smoke detector attached to the wall.

That evening, Sandy fixed a scrumptious chicken marsala over fresh fettuccine. Vicky remarked, "Morgan, you're so lucky to have a chef for a boyfriend. So, what about you Jackson, do you cook?"

With his curl-your-toes-deep Aussie accent, he responded, "Well Luv, I'm a fire bloke. I love to cook on the barbie. How about I do prawns on the barbie tomorrow night?"

Vicky glowed. "You're on. I can't wait."

Over dinner, they discussed the situation. Morgan summarized things. "First, this isn't a military operation. We have good reason to believe a company, or a very wealthy individual is behind it because of the offer that was made on behalf of a client. So, while this group in Tysons made the threats, they're simply middlemen to the client. I think you're on the right track. We need to get them to threaten you and record it. Then we can go to the police, and we'll have a case against them. If multiple people make the threat, then we can extend the case to the company, and perhaps, and this is a stretch, extended the case to the company paying the people in Tysons."

"I'm so happy you're an attorney." Sandy took another sip of the incredible Australian wine Jackson had picked out on their drive back. "I need to order a tiny camera microphone recorder so we can get these guys on tape. Jackson, let's see if we've got their home locations on the GPS. I've got an idea of how to approach this."

As Sandy went to the laptop to search Amazon, Vicky piped in, "Oh my goodness, you do love shopping on Amazon."

"Of course, they have everything, and it's here tomorrow or the next day."

"Ok, Jackson and I have an early start in the morning again, so we better wrap it up for tonight."

Jackson nodded in agreement. "But I'll help clean up a bit first."

Jackson joined Vicky in the kitchen, and the two were obviously enjoying each other's company as they cleared the dishes and put things away.

Early the next morning in the dark of predawn, Sandy and Jackson drove to the locations of the GPS trackers for Jason and his BMW. Jason was parked in a lot behind a group of townhouses in a trendy section of downtown Vienna, Virginia. It was impossible to tell which townhouse was Jason's. Next, they drove to West Falls Church, a few miles away. Following the GPS, they spotted the black Escalade parked in the driveway of a large house on Robinson Place. Jackson wrote down the house number, and they turned around and headed back to Vienna.

While Sandy waited in the SUV, Jackson went into Artisan Caffe and Roaster in Vienna and got two lattes and pastries to go. They drove back to the parking lot near Jason's car and waited, hoping to catch him emerge from his townhouse.

"My God, mate, this is the best coffee I've had since I got here. You need to mark them on your map as special!" Jackson exclaimed as he drank the rich, smooth drink.

"Yeah, you're right. An amazing cup of Joe. Do you know where the expression 'Cup of Joe' came from?"

"No, mate, but I'm certain you'll enlighten me." Jackson chuckled.

"Well, there are several theories. I prefer this one. Just before World War I, Secretary of the Navy Josephus Daniels, commonly known as Joe, banned all alcohol from all Navy ships. So, sailors called coffee a cup of Joe since it was the strongest thing they could get. It was also a subtle way to voice dissent to the policy."

"Good one. Had to know you'd find a way to tie the Navy to any good story." They sat together, sipped their coffees, and waited. About half an hour later, they spotted Jason leaving his townhouse and stayed low in their SUV so they wouldn't stand out. Now they knew his address as well.

Arriving back at the apartment, Morgan gave Sandy the package from Amazon. They tested out the tiny camera, and it worked as expected. Easy to conceal in a jacket pocket but providing crystal clear audio and video.

While at the apartment, they dove into the property records as well as the reverse telephone directory and were able to get the names they needed. The black Escalade driver was Leon Davies. Digging further, they discovered he was a former DC cop. It turned out that Jason was Jason Roberts and, based on his LinkedIn account, now worked for OI Research in Tysons, which lined up with Karen Young's car registration. Jason was a former salesperson for a flooring company. Reversing their look at OI Research, they found half a dozen people with LinkedIn accounts, including Harriet Campos, who listed herself as CEO. They spent the rest of the day gathering intel via Google, Facebook, and others and learned a lot about the individuals working at the company. They even had Campos's home address in McLean.

As soon as Vicky arrived home from work, they ate an early dinner. Jackson's shrimp on the barbie was awesome with a sweet Asian sauce with a touch of cayenne, providing an incredible flavor that added just the right amount of heat. Jackson showed them how using two skewers made it so much easier to flip a row of prawns.

After dinner, Sandy and Jackson headed out to kick the bee's nest. Fortunately, all of the people lived fairly close to each other. They thought about the order and decided it was best to go to the people that would react the least first. The first stop was Karen Young's house. It was pretty much dark by then, but at least it was not too cold. Sandy walked the half-block back to the house, up to her door, and knocked. Karen's husband answered the door, "Can I help you?"

Sandy asked to see Karen. A moment later, Karen stood at the door, not inviting Sandy in. After a few seconds, she recognized him. "Hi, can I help you?"

"Good evening, sorry to bother you, Ms. Young. I just wanted to let you know I'm sick of you following me and resent the threats your company is making. Please stop now."

Karen paled. "I'm sorry. I don't know what you're talking about."

"Ms. Young, do you deny following me to Ithaca, NY several weeks ago? Do you deny parking outside the townhouse in Georgetown and so many other places we frequent? Do you deny this?"

"No, it's my job. You should take whatever they offered you, for whatever they want, and they'll go away. If you don't, I suspect it'll get much worse."

"Is that a threat?"

"No, just my experience. Good night." She closed the door, and he could hear the locks being engaged.

Back in the SUV, Sandy had a satisfied look on his face as he told Jackson, "That went well, not a threat but does go to the company being involved. She's scared now." And he glanced over at his friend, adding quizzically, as they pulled away from the curb, "Are you sure you can drive on the other side of the road?"

"Crikey mate, as long as I remember that I've got to be sitting in the middle of the road and you sitting on the shoulder, it works. Getting used to it. Glad you don't have a lot of roundabouts; that might be a bit dangerous. We're good."

Jason's townhouse was next, and again Jackson parked down the street. Sandy walked up to the front door, knocked, and was greeted by Jason. "Hi, what're you doing here?"

"I just wanted to say again that I'm not interested in your offer, and I'd like OI Research to leave me alone."

Jason's furrowed brows, reddening face, and clenched jaw signaled to Sandy, he had pissed him off - perfect. "Well, like I told you the other day, my client is very persistent and doesn't take no as an answer. Things are going to get really ugly for you if you don't change your mind – buddy. And I don't appreciate you coming to my house."

"Is that a threat?"

"In so many words, you should consider some really bad consequences to your decision."

"Ok, and as far as coming to your house, it doesn't seem to bother you guys in watching mine. Leave me alone and go away."

"Sorry, you're too stubborn to know what's good for you. You'll get what's coming to you. Watch out and stay away from me."

"You haven't seen the last of me." Sandy turned and walked away in the opposite direction of Jackson. After a few blocks, he called and told him where to meet him behind the Whole Foods store. Back in the SUV, he said, "We got a threat on tape. Now to Leon's house to really kick the bees."

Arriving in West Falls Church, Sandy rang Leon's doorbell. A minute or two later, he answered the door in casual clothes.

Without giving a hint that he recognized him, he said, "Can I help you?"

"Mr. Davies, I just wanted to confront you and ask you to leave us alone. We aren't interested in the offer, and I don't appreciate you following and threatening us. You need to go somewhere else."

"Listen, bud, you need to take whatever they offer and just go back to teaching school. If you don't take it, this will escalate and get very personal and dangerous to you and your family. Now go away and rethink your decision." Leon slammed the door in Sandy's face.

Back in the SUV, Sandy grinned. "We got them. Let's go see what their boss says."

Harriet Campos couldn't believe someone was knocking on her door at nine o'clock at night. She opened the door of her beautiful, clearly expensive, home in McLean and was shocked to see Sandy Powell standing on the front porch.

"Ms. Campos, I'm Sandy Powell, which I suspect you already know. I want to inform you that I'm sick of your company harassing and threatening me, and I'm here to ask you to just leave us alone."

"Mr. Powell, I can tell you that if you don't accept the offer from our client, that things will get really bad for you and perhaps your family. Our client is even more stubborn than you are, and they really don't care what happens to people that say no. So just go home, make a smart decision, and all of this goes away."

"I'm not changing my mind and you need to stop the harassment."

"Mr. Powell, your life as you know it's about to take a sharp turn down a dark road. Remember this; you're the one that's causing all the harm you're about to face. Good night." She swiftly closed the door, and again he could hear the locks engaged.

Back in the SUV, Sandy said, "Well, we got what we need, and the bees are going to be flying tonight. Let's head back and see what time they all get together at the office. Bet it's early."

Safely back in Alexandria, they turned in with a plan to rise early and watch the office.

Charles Caserta made an appointment to see the President at the White House in the situation room.

At two o'clock sharp, the President entered the situation room. He was tall, thin-framed, with graying hair and piercing gray eyes. He had the look and feel of someone you could instinctively trust. At the same time, he commanded attention as a natural leader. He found Charles Caserta, the Attorney General; Rod Holloway, Assistant Deputy Attorney General; Meredith Drake, Director of the FBI; and Lester Hodges, Deputy Director of the FBI, starting to stand. "Please sit. Charlie, what's up? Clearly, this is important enough to bring Rod, Meredith, and Lester along."

"Yes sir, it is. We've got uncovered a conspiracy involving our three largest oil companies' executives that goes back years that involves murder, price-fixing, bribery, and more on a global basis. Lester has led the effort to pull this case together, and I would like him to brief you."

"Mr. President, almost by chance, we uncovered a plot in Nigeria where the CEOs of Texas Oil, Sunco, and American Petroleum ordered the assassination of the Minister for Oil and Gas, Ali Mohammed. As we drilled into things, we discovered they were working together with a company named Paragon based in New York City to disrupt competitors around the globe. We recorded a meeting they held with the CEO of Paragon in Miami, where they confirmed what we learned in Nigeria and discussed price-fixing. We now have two FBI agents working inside Paragon and have copied all of their data. Going back years, we can prove that they've worked closely to disrupt things around the world. In addition, we know they've collected dirt on politicians both here and globally that puts them in a unique position to pressure people on both sides of the aisle."

Charlie edged forward in his seat. "Mr. President, first we wanted to give you a heads up that we're in a position to arrest Bryce Carrington, Reginald Clark, and Harold Watson. We also will be arresting Jacob Holden, the former CEO of Texas Oil. We know you've met with these people and wanted you to be briefed before we take action."

"Wow, this is stunning, and I know each of you wouldn't be bringing this to me if it wasn't solid as a piece of granite. Ok, next steps?"

"Mr. President, we could use your help. There are multiple numbered accounts in the Caymans, and we need access to their transaction history to complete putting this all together. We've reached out to the highest levels we can in the UK to get this information to no avail. Would you be kind enough to make a brief phone call to Number Ten and request his support?" Charlie slid him a piece of paper with the name of the bank and a list of the accounts they needed access to.

"If you've tried all your resources without success, and I'm very confident you have, of course, I will. I'll give him a call as soon as we finish this meeting. Anything else?"

"No sir, that's it on this matter."

The President nodded. "I'll relay my results to you later today. Thanks, and keep me in the loop. This is going to be huge and will impact all of us. Please give me a detailed written briefing prior to making the arrests. It's sure to be front-page news when it happens." Everyone stood, and he said, "I'll let you know once we've got word on access to the bank records," then he turned and left the room.

****

The President called the Prime Minister and gave him a very brief account without details and requested access to the transaction history for the specific accounts at the bank in Grand Cayman. The Prime Minister, now a close friend, was happy to oblige.

****

Nigel Williams, President of First National of Caymen, was almost ready to leave for the day when his secretary came into his office with a startled look on her face. "You have a call from the Prime Minister's office," she said.

Nigel Williams's eyes grew big as he reached out for the receiver.

"Mr. Williams, this is the Prime Minister's office. Please hold for Sir Robinson."

"Hello Mr. Williams, I'm making an official request that you release all the details for a number of accounts at your establishment to the US FBI immediately. This is a matter of international importance. Do you understand?"

"Yes, Mr. Prime Minister, but our bank secrecy laws!"

"Stop right there. You know we have anti-money laundering legislation. You will provide full access and support to the FBI immediately. Am I clear?"

"Yes, Mr. Prime Minister, we will help them in every way possible. Thank you, sir."

Within the hour, three FBI agents were in Nigel Williams's office with the list of the accounts and advised him there may be more accounts once they began their investigation. Williams was still in disbelief that he'd spoken with the Prime Minister. Williams instructed one of his technical people to download all the data, including ownership of the accounts, to the FBI's computers. The information was transmitted within hours to FBI headquarters in Washington, and a team of five financial experts dove into the records.

After working all night, they met with Lester the next day. One of the analysts looked like he had tripped on coffee for 24 hours and was sans tie. "Sorry, sir, I didn't have time to run home for a suit."

"No worries, son, I'm much more interested in what you learned than what you look like. My suggestion is you should keep a spare suit on the back of your office door."

"Sorry, I don't have a spot to hang a suit in my cube."

"Good point. I'll have to work on lockers for you guys. So, what've you discovered?"

The team put up a diagram on the screen showing the companies and how they all related to one core company. "As you can see, sir, this company, Pinnacle Limited in the Caymans, sends money into this one account owned by Globex Limited, also in the Caymans. The money in Globex then flows out to corporate accounts of companies all over the world."

"Do you have a company located in Nigeria?"

"Yes sir, right here," he said as he pointed to it on the screen.

"Great. Ok, what about New York?"

"Yes sir, and they have the largest flow of funds, nearly $15 million per year. There are other accounts in the US in Washington, Los Angles, and Houston. The company name in New York is Paragon Research," said Anna Knight, the lead financial analyst on the data.

"Anna, what do you know about the money coming into Pinnacle Limited?"

"Sir, almost all the money comes from three companies in even amounts every quarter. The companies are Jethro, EllyMay, and Clampett. We don't know anything about these companies."

Lester stood up. "Ok, thank you, Anna and team, great job in a few hours. I'm ordering you all to get some breakfast. Send me the expense report, take an hour's break, and then write a clean, brief summary with all the company names, addresses, and money flow. I want it on my desk by three this afternoon. I don't need to remind you this is classified top secret, need to know. Again, great job, and you can expect a call from Nina Craig in an hour, who'll dig into the three companies feeding the money into Pinnacle Limited. Thanks."

Back in his office, Lester's admin had Nina Craig on the line. "Nina, I need you to call Anna Knight in an hour and get what information she has on the three companies funneling money into Paragon Limited. I need by tomorrow morning all the details you can muster on these companies, financials, and most importantly who owns them. They could be shells, so it could take some digging. Assemble your team and order pizza or Chinese for tonight - it could be a late one. I will have Suzie clear my calendar at 10 for your briefing."

Later that afternoon, Lester had the brief from Anna. The scope was truly global, with companies primarily in oil-producing areas around the world, including Russia and China. The next morning, he sat with Nina and received her brief.

"You were right. They were all shells. Piercing the corporate veil was not difficult. Each company is ultimately owned by Texas Oil and Gas, Sunco, and American Petroleum, respectively. They push money into Pinnacle every quarter and have been doing so as far back as we have records. It amounts to tens of millions per year."

"Excellent work, thank your team. Ok, take your time but assemble a thoughtful report and be prepared to present this to a grand jury at some time in the next few weeks.

Lester assembled a conference call with the executives at DOJ and FBI and shared his thoughts on the next steps. Charlie agreed to brief the President.

About 7 a.m., Sandy and Jackson watched on the tracking software the OI staff cars leave their homes and head for the office. Then they began watching the view from the camera in the hallway. At 7:15, the OI Research bees were assembling in the office. "Yup, just like we thought. We gave them an early start to their day."

Sandy let Morgan enjoy her coffee and watch a bit of the morning news. Still in her PJs and a robe, she watched the recording from last night's encounters with OI people. "This is great and is clear enough to go to court and request at a minimum a restraining order and possible arrest on grounds of the threats they made. I'll call a friend from college that deals with divorce cases with a lot of experience in getting restraining orders against unruly spouses and confirm my thoughts."

About lunchtime, Morgan was all dressed, wearing a nice pantsuit. "I'm going to meet Marlene Pope for lunch and review the videos with her from last night. You guys have a fun afternoon, and I'll see you later."

Sandy smiled. "Sounds good. We'll come up with an idea for dinner, so we may be out shopping when you get back. Have fun, love you."

Morgan called for a cab and was off to meet Marlene

at Georgia Brown's for lunch. It was an institution in DC on 15th Street near the VA headquarters. A bit pricy, but oh so good. Their Low-Country cuisine was to be savored, and she knew Marlene loved the place. "Mar, so good to see you. It's been forever. How are you?"

"Great, and I see you're doing well, striking out on your own. And I hear you're very busy."

Morgan grinned. "Yes, tons of work, and I've finally found my guy. So, I'm the happiest gal on the planet. And how are you and Mark doing?"

"We're great! The kids are now three and five. Oh my word, they're a handful. They're like bottled energy."

They sat and ordered. Morgan chose she-crab soup, and Marlene settled on the shrimp and grits. They also ordered a plate of fried green tomatoes to share. Morgan shared the video with Marlene, and they agreed they had enough to go to court for a restraining order against the individuals and the company. In addition, they could meet with the Fairfax police regarding having people arrested. The lunch was awesome, and Marlene said she would take the case forward with Morgan. She would try to get on a judge's docket this week.

When they left Morgan's townhouse to stay at Vicky's, Morgan had forgotten a file for one of her most important clients. Since she was already downtown, she thought she'd run into her house and grab it before heading back to Vicky's place. It'd only take a few minutes, and she'd be in and out. She hailed a cab and was off to her townhouse.

She didn't even try to have the cab wait knowing they'd be gone anyway. She unlocked the front door, disabled the alarm, and headed for the stairs to her office.

Leon was in his Escalade behind the townhouse when the alarm on his cell phone went off, indicating that someone had tripped the motion detector on the front door. He pulled up the video and saw that Sandy's girlfriend had just entered the house. This was his lucky day. He quickly jumped out of the car and ran to the back gate. In one minute, he had unlocked both backdoor locks and was inside. He knew the alarm would be disabled with her inside. He carefully sneaked into the kitchen and could hear her upstairs. He moved over near the staircase and waited. After about five minutes, he could hear her moving again.

Morgan had the file she needed and headed downstairs. When she was almost to the first floor, someone tripped her! She hit the floor hard. A large man grabbed her around the waist with one gloved hand and covered her mouth with another. She could barely breathe. The file went flying. She jerked her mouth open and bit down hard on some fingers. He cursed her but didn't let go. The next thing she knew, she was sprawled face down on the floor with her arms wrenched behind her back. She felt plastic wrap her wrists and heard zip ties pull tight. She screamed, "Let me go!"

"Listen, lady. You aren't going anywhere. So, shut up, and you won't get hurt." He examined his fingers where she'd drawn blood.

The next thing she knew, ties were zipped around her feet, slamming her ankle bones together. The man chuckled. "Stay put. I'll be right back. Not like you're going anywhere." He headed upstairs and was back almost immediately. He stuffed a washcloth in her mouth, put a pillowcase over her head, and rolled her up in a sheet. He picked her up in both arms and carried her out the backdoor. No one was around, walking the short distance to his Escalade car. He roughly tossed her in the back seat and rolled her onto the floor.

★★★★

Charles Caserta had advised the President that the operation would begin tomorrow afternoon. Being global, it would roll out across the planet and take nearly 24 hours from start to finish.

Lester Hodges assembled a small operations team. They'd spent the last two days carefully planning the global arrests. Since the international portion of the plan required coordination with local or national police, it had to be carefully orchestrated. A major concern was a leak that the arrests were coming. So, on the international front, they only advised their partners it was a global conspiracy and provided no details.

Morgan couldn't believe what was going on. It was clear she was being abducted but had no idea by whom. She suspected it had to be one of the people from the company trying to pressure Sandy to sign over the patent. She slowly worked the washcloth out of her mouth. "Mister, let me go, and I won't press charges."

"Lady, like I said, shut your mouth. If all goes well, you can go home to your boyfriend tonight. No harm, no foul. So, just be quiet."

She felt the car moving but had no idea going where. Disoriented from the pillowcase blocking her view, she was beginning to feel carsick.

Leon called the office. "Harriet, you won't believe it. I caught Powell's girlfriend. I have her in the back of the car. I'm headed to a safe place to make an exchange for him signing over the patent. I'll text you the address in a few minutes. You better send two guys to back me up. You may want to come to witness the signing."

Harriet replied, "Be careful. She's a well-respected attorney. Don't harm her!"

After ten minutes, Morgan felt the car pull over and

stop. She imagined he was sending the text.

After nearly an hour of fast, slow, and start and stop driving, she could hear the crunch of the tires on gravel. She was amazed she hadn't tossed her lunch. After a bit more driving on rough roads, they finally came to a stop. She heard and felt her car door open. He lifted her out of the well in front of the rear seat, carried her up some stairs, and set her down. She heard him jingle some keys and unlock a door. Then he picked her up again and laid her on what she imagined was a couch. Even thru the sheet, she felt the cold from the room.

"Where's your cell phone?"

"What?"

"I need to call your boyfriend to come pick you up, blondie."

"It's in my purse. I hope you brought it."

"Yup, it's in the back of the car. Be right back."

A few minutes later, he was back. "What's the number to unlock the phone?"

"1 1 1 1"

"That's creative. Well, lucky me, his number is the only one stored in your contacts." She heard him dial. "Mister Powell, this is Leon. Remember we met last night. Well, it seems I've got your blonde girlfriend here, and if you want her back in one piece, you better come pen in hand. Drive to Poolesville, Maryland, and call this phone when you get there. Come alone, and don't involve the police if you want a good outcome." He hung up the phone and turned on the heat in the cabin.

When Marsha Cohen took her lunch break, she met with the team preparing to raid the Paragon office in New York. They attached a throat microphone under the neck of her beige turtleneck and a tiny wireless earpiece. She added her standard-issue shoulder holster, handcuffs and had her FBI badge tucked in an inside pocket of her navy-blue jacket.

Back at her desk, she worked on her assigned project for the afternoon. At 2:57, she whispered into her microphone, "I'm a go for Peterson's office." She stood up and walked back to Todd's office.

His admin looked up and said, "Can I help you?"

At the same time, the FBI technician in the basement was cutting the data feed to the Paragon office.

"No, I'm good. I need to see Mr. Peterson about a matter of importance." She opened his door before the admin could react and walked into his office. Pulling her gun and badge at the same time from under her jacket, she said, "Mr. Todd Peterson, I'm with the FBI, and you're under arrest. Raise your hands and don't touch anything." Peterson stood and stepped back from his desk, leaving his laptop on.

The team of six FBI agents was waiting in the

elevator one floor below the office. Hearing her say "Mr. Peterson," they hit the control to go up to the Paragon office lobby. At the same time, another team of six entered the back of the office through the emergency exit. The team leader with a bullhorn announced to the entire office. "We're with the FBI, and you'll put your hands on your head, interlace your fingers, and remain at your desk until further notice." The agents moved swiftly through the office to secure the premises.

****

At 3 p.m. Eastern time, raids were simultaneously launched in the Cayman Islands, New York City, Westchester, Houston, Los Angles, and Washington, DC. Hodges knew the key was to get Paragon's home office in New York City and, more specifically, Todd Peterson on time.

Lester had decided, and Meredith and Charlie concurred that they wouldn't arrest the CEOs in one of those classic FBI pre-dawn raids with a SWAT team entering their homes.

In Westchester, New York, at 3 p.m., three FBI agents dressed in business suits went to the top floor of Texas Oil and Gas and walked into Harold Watson's executive suite. They pulled their badges out of their suit jackets and told HW's secretary they were from the FBI and asked her to roll back from her desk and not to touch anything. They opened HW's office door, and while one watched the admin, the other two confronted HW at his desk. They told him he was under arrest. "We don't want to make a scene, so please stand and walk with us. We won't handcuff you now."

They escorted him down to the basement parking garage to the awaiting FBI SUVs. Both HW and his admin were placed in separate cars. One agent remained in the office to make sure nothing was touched.

A similar scene occurred at 2 p.m. central time at the American Petroleum office of Bryce Carrington. In Los Angeles, the FBI detained Reginald Clark while he was holding an early lunch meeting high above the LA skyline in a very swanky restaurant. Jacob Holden, the Chairman of TXO, was arrested in his mansion in Scarsdale that backed onto the beautiful Fenway Golf Course and a small lake.

Raids occurred at the Globex office and Pinnacle Limited in the Caymans and the Jethro, EllyMay, and Clampett offices, all of which were located in various cities in the United States. Paragon subsidiary offices from Abu Dhabi to Jakarta were each raided shortly after opening their office for the day in their local time zones. As in New York, communications lines were cut just before each raid so they couldn't inform other locations of what was happening.

****

Sandy was shocked. He couldn't believe they'd captured Morgan. It was his worst nightmare. He almost crushed the phone in his fist, and just glared at it.

Jackson put his hand on Sandy's shoulder, "What's up, mate?"

"Leon, the guy with the Escalade, has taken Morgan hostage."

"Shit! Do we know where?"

"He said to go to Poolesville, Maryland, and call him when I get there. Of course, he also said not to call the police and come alone."

"Well, that's not going to happen."

Sandy almost instantly switched from pissed off boyfriend to SEAL commander. "Ok, let's get changed into our tactical gear and rollout in 10 minutes."

"Roger that."

Sandy rushed upstairs and changed into black tactical pants and a black turtleneck. He was thinking how could he have captured Morgan? God, he hoped she was ok, or they would find corpses when he finished with them. His gear was in the back of the SUV. He would have to assemble it when they got there. In a few minutes, he was back downstairs as Jackson was also ready to go. They climbed into the Tahoe. "Jackson, why don't you jump in the back seat. All the gear is in the back. You can assemble things while I drive."

In the back, Jackson turned on the GPS app and he could see that the Escalade was parked a few miles south of Poolesville.

****

Harriet Campos had received the call from Leon Davies that he had secured Dutton and received the text from him on the location for the meeting with Powell. She called Ivan Hammond and Karen Young and told them where to meet Leon outside Poolesville. She was starting to assemble the agreement for Powell to execute when the FBI entered the office. She was arrested, and her staff was told to remain in their seats. Campos was handcuffed, and led out of the building, and driven downtown. The notorious DC traffic was full on by 3:15, and they crawled down 66 toward the city.

Sitting with her hands uncomfortably handcuffed behind her back, Campos was plotting her next move thinking. I've got to give them something to get out of this mess. She decided the best course of action would be to throw Davies under the bus. While he did a good job, the arrogant former DC detective was not her favorite. They arrived at the FBI headquarters building and parked underground. She was led to the elevators and then to a small interview room upstairs. Finally, two agents entered the room. They removed the handcuffs and then re-cuffed her to a ring on the table.

"Ms. Campos, you're under arrest for several charges related to your operation of OI research, a subsidiary of Paragon Research in New York. That office has been closed, and Todd Peterson is also under arrest. We suggest that you cooperate fully, and this may assist you in your case."

Campos sat as dignified as possible and looked at the agents. "Happy to help clear up any misunderstandings. I want to let you know that one of my staff, against my orders, has kidnapped a person we were observing and is now holding her as a hostage, at this moment, in Maryland."

One of the agents stood and exited the room. Outside he called Lester Hodges's office. He advised

Suzie of what he had just learned and suggested that Mr. Hodges might want to take a minute to meet with Campos.

A few minutes later, Lester entered the interview room. "Ms. Campos, my name is Lester Hodges, and I'm the Deputy Director of the FBI. I understand you're alleging that one of your staff is holding a person as a hostage. Is that correct?"

"Yes sir, it is." Campos looked up at him standing in the doorway. "I'm happy to provide the details that I've got so you may resolve this situation. If you would give me my phone, I can provide you with the address where I believe he is holding her."

One of the agents removed her phone from her purse, "Give me the PIN code, and I will check your messages."

"1955."

With the phone unlocked, he went to her messages and saw the directions.

In Poolesville take Budd Rd South to the end, continue south on Hughes Rd to the end turn left on Hunting Quarter Rd to the first driveway on right – south to the end by the river – my cabin

Lester said, "Thank you, any other details you would like to add?"

"Yes, his name is Leon Davies, and two other people will be joining him. Ivan Hammond and Karen Young."

Lester left the room and went back to his office and contacted the elite Hostage Rescue Team (HRT) stationed at Quantico, Virginia. The team of six on standby was suited up and assembled in the ready room. They were briefed, and the decision was made that they'd take the Bell 407 chopper, quietest they had, and fly to Maryland. The straight-line distance was only 45 miles, and they should be on the ground in about 30 minutes.

Chapter 49 Alexandria, VA

They were a bit ahead of rush hour and rolled up Route 1 Sandy thought it was not that long ago that he and Morgan were headed this same way driving up to Ithaca. On the other hand, it seemed a lifetime ago.

In Rockville, they exited 270 and took Route 28 west towards Poolesville. Forty-five minutes later, they were in the middle of Poolesville. Sandy pulled off on a side street near a vacant park and jumped out of the SUV.

Opening the tailgate, he removed his coat and put on a black tactical vest. Then he began loading his pants and vest with needed supplies. He put one gun in his holster on his right hip and the other 9mm Glock in his pants behind his vest. Jackson told him both were loaded with a shell in the chamber, safety on. Next, he strapped a Beretta Nano to his right ankle. He tucked spare clips for the Glock in his vest pockets. I hope I don't have to use these, but better safe than sorry. Jackson was also loaded up.

They both had tiny earpieces and throat mikes which they tested to make sure they were working. It was dusk but not yet dark. As they stood outside the Tahoe, Jackson remarked what Sandy was also thinking, "We need to wait a little bit till it's dark to make the call. We'll need the element of surprise with this guy and who knows how many others."

"Totally agree, let's give it half an hour. How about we roll over to the McDonald's and grab a coffee in the drive-thru while we wait?" Jackson opened the app on his phone. "Looks like Ms. Young is also at the same location as Davies. We may have more company we can't see. I'm sure glad you have those night vision goggles. We'll likely need them."

Half an hour later, parked in the McDonald's lot, Sandy called Davies. "Hi, I'm in Poolesville. What's next?"

"Took you long enough. Ok, I'm going to send you a text with directions. You should be here in 10 or 15 minutes. Drive safe. There are lots of deer."

Sandy's phone pinged, indicating he had the text. He looked at the instructions. "Ok, got the text. I'll be there in a few."

****

The FBI helicopter flew northwest to Leesburg, Virginia and crossed the Potomac near White's Ferry, and then flew south low over the Potomac. With the wind out of the east, it helped mask the noise of the chopper. The FBI Hostage Rescue Team landed about a mile north of the location based on the directions in the text. Fortunately, this area near the Potomac River had several sod farms, so they had a flat open landing area.

All the agents were equipped with night vision goggles, wireless earpieces, and microphones. Each carried a Heckler & Koch HK416 – 5.56mm carbine and wore a Glock 22. The FBI team jumped out of the helicopter while the rotors began to spin down and began jogging in the direction of the cabin.

****

About a mile before the location of the cars, Sandy turned off the headlights. They'd checked at the McDonald's to make certain the inside lights wouldn't come on when they opened the doors. Half a mile before their destination, Sandy stopped, and Jackson jumped out and started jogging down the road. Sandy gave him a five-minute head start and then turned on the lights and rolled slowly down the road towards the cabin. As he neared the cabin, he could hear Jackson say, "Hold up, mate. I got one on the porch. Give me a moment to take him out."

Sandy heard Jackson shout out, "Excuse me, sir, I'm a bit lost and twisted my ankle. Can you help me?" Then he heard a bit of a scuffle over his earpiece. "Sandy, he's out of the picture. Roll on in. I'll go to the rear entrance."

"Roger that." Sandy pulled into the driveway and turned the Tahoe around, so it was pointed out in case he needed a quick getaway. He walked up the steps and knocked on the door, standing to the side in case someone shot at him through the door. Karen Young opened the door, and Sandy walked in with his Glock in his hand pointed down at his side.

He heard Jackson in his ear whisper, "I've got you covered through the window in the rear." Sandy nodded his head slightly.

"Ok, cowboy, put the gun down, and no one gets

hurt," Davies said.

"Morgan, are you ok?"

He heard her through the pillowcase, "Yup, just taking a nap."

Sandy looked at Young. "Cut her loose."

Karen reached into her large leather handbag, and Sandy saw the glint of a pistol handle start to emerge. He shot the pistol from her hand, and it went flying across the room. Out of the corner of his eye, he saw Davies reach inside his jacket. He yelled, "Davies gun!"

Morgan hearing the gun shot screamed! "Oh my God, Sandy!"

Jackson broke the window glass and shot Davies in the thigh just as Sandy was drawing a bead on him.

Davies screamed out as his gun emerged and shot wildly into the ceiling, then fell to the floor, writhing in pain. Sandy was about to move forward to kick the gun away when three FBI agents in assault gear burst through the front door behind him.

"Everyone stays put - don't move. Sir, drop the weapon." Sandy dropped the Glock as an agent moved forward and kicked Davies's gun away.

Sandy could hear Jackson over his earpiece say, "Yes, sir, my hands are empty and in the air."

Sandy said to the agent behind him, "Sir, I have another weapon on my back under my vest and another in my right ankle holster. My name is Sandy Powell. My girlfriend is the one who was kidnapped; she's on the couch. My friend Jackson Hawkins is outside in the rear."

"Turn around, please. Powell, you old water dog! Should've known you'd wash up in more trouble!" Spenser Graves was a former SEAL that went through training with Sandy.

"Spenser! Figures you'd become an FBI agent. I haven't seen you in years. Let's get this buttoned up."

The military training never far away, and recognizing Powell's senior rank, Spencer said, "Yes, Commander. Ok, we'll sort all this out in a minute." The agent then said over his throat mike, "Secure the outside, and I need a medic and transport for two injured civilians inside." Davies was very pale, breathing rapidly, but didn't have a lot of blood loss. One of the agents was wrapping gauze around Davies' leg. Sandy had seen much worse from a gunshot.

The other agent got a kitchen towel for the scratch on Young's wrist from having the pistol shot away.

Spencer pulled a multi-tool from a pocket in his pants, removed the pillowcase from Morgan's head, then cut the zip ties on her wrists and ankles. Spencer removed the additional guns from Sandy and placed them on the floor.

Morgan flexed her hands and shook her hair loose. Looking wide-eyed at Sandy, she said, "Am I glad to see you." She stood up, walked over, and gave him a huge hug and a long lingering kiss.

Graves smiled and said, "Well, I think we're sorting out who's who."

Jackson and Ivan Hammond walked in the front door, followed by two agents. "Sir, this is the individual who shot through the rear window just before we arrived. He says his name is Jackson

Hawkins. The other individual was tied up adjacent to the house."

"Thank you, that all checks out. Please go outside and put a flare by the driveway. We've got ambulances on the way for the two injured civilians. You two will stay with them until agents arrive to relieve you at the hospital. They're under arrest." Looking at Powell, Spencer concluded, "Looks like you had things kind of under control when we arrived. Sorry, we weren't here quicker."

"No worries, very glad you're here. Can we go now, or do you need us for a debrief?"

"I want you to drive to headquarters in DC with Agent Cohen and your two companions. You can debrief the team there."

"Thank you again, and very happy to help. Hey, you need to make the get-together this spring, and we should do lunch one of these days to catch up."

Spencer smiled and nodded affirmatively. "I'll give you a call...through normal channels if that's all right?"

Sandy grinned a bit sheepishly. "I'd prefer it, and I look forward to that."

It was a little over an hour's drive back to DC, and they parked in the garage under the FBI headquarters. Morgan held Sandy's hand all the way, and the car was quiet on the way into the city. At headquarters, they were each placed in separate rooms while an agent interviewed them on the events over the past few weeks. After a few hours, they all were back together in a conference room.

****

"Hello, I'm Lester Hodges, and I'm the Deputy Director of the FBI. Please remain seated. I understand you've had a trying few weeks, and I want to personally thank you for all that you've been through. I can't go into details, but rest assured, the people that were causing your problems have been arrested. You should be safe now. We'll have an agent meet with you tomorrow to pick up your recordings, and we'll also send a technician out to make certain there are no viruses on your phones and computers. We'll reach out to you at some point in the future if we need you to testify to the grand jury or in a trial. If you've got any concerns whatsoever, please feel free to contact me directly. Have a good evening." He placed his business card on the table in front of Sandy.

HW had fully cooperated with the FBI. After the initial set of charges which included conspiracy to commit murder in Nigeria, was explained to him, he held nothing back. He was released on bail and returned to his office the next day. He decided he had millions of dollars saved over the years in his retirement plan and was now sick of the corporate world and would retire. He went into his office to pack up his personal things. He emerged from his office with two large FedEx boxes. "Leslie, please send these by bonded courier to Sandy Powell. His address is on the Post-it." A short time later, Watson walked out of Texas Oil, a company he had been with for decades, and walked into retirement. At least that was the plan.

****

Sandy, Morgan, Jackson, and Vicky were all back together at Vicky's condo in Alexandria. Copper was excited that everyone was back and circled around and around Morgan's legs. Since it was late, they ordered Chinese and told stories about the crazy day.

Jackson thought for a moment. "I've got a great idea. Why don't you all come to Sydney for New Year's Eve? It's an awesome time, middle of summer, so you won't need anything but shorts, a top, swimmers, and thongs. Come for a week or a fortnight, and I can show you about."

Sandy's eyes rolled. "Thong! Sorry buddy, the girls may wear a thong, but it won't work for me."

"Ahhh, what do you call them? Oh, yeah flip flops."

"Gotcha, ok, great idea! Morgan, Vicky?"

"My noble knight, this is really simple. I'm not leaving your side. I'm stuck to you like glue, and I think we should go," Morgan replied.

Vicky said, "I will check with my boss in the morning, but I'm all in."

Sandy grinned. "No worries, I will cover the cost of the trip for all of us."

As they were getting ready to turn in, Vicky whispered in Jackson's ear, and then Vicky was leading Jackson upstairs.

Morgan's eyes twinkled. "Surprised they lasted this long, bet they sleep in tomorrow." She turned and looked up into Sandy's eyes. "Off to bed, Sir Knight, I need some personal comforting..."

Copper, already at the top of the stairs, said a quiet woof, like hurry up, it's time for bed. Sandy just grinned and let Morgan take the lead up the stairs.

Available on Amazon

The Oligarch

Book 2 in the Sandy Powell Trilogy

A Russian oil oligarch uncovers Sandy's invention to create cheap hydrogen and transform the world. What's his play? Meanwhile, an American oil tycoon is still trying to stop the discovery in this impactful sequel to "The Pinnacle Club." Sandy Powell must make life-or-death decisions as he transforms his grandfather's discovery from theory into a business.

As Sandy and his girlfriend, Morgan, begin to build a new industry with the help of an unexpected ally. Their dream is in constant danger as the oil industry will not give up billions of dollars and their political power without a fight. One industrialist, with nothing to lose, personally targets Sandy, Morgan, and their process to create cheap hydrogen. Even their heroic Golden Retriever is in the crosshairs.

Who wins? Who loses? Does Sandy make the right decision regarding the Russian oligarch?

Sign up for news at

https://www.drewthorn.com

THORNEBROOK
LLC

To sign up for the Drew Thorn news, discounts and
to learn more about Drew and upcoming books go to

https://www.drewthorn.com

Facebook: drew.thorn.9615

Twitter: @DrewThorn55

LinkedIn: drew-thorn

You can email me at   drew@drewthorn.com

Drew Thorn

Drew Thorn is proud and very lucky to grow up on a dairy farm in upstate New York, a few miles from Vermont. The hard work and play helped shape his character. He attended Tamarac High School, which was small enough that everyone knew each other and remain close, even to this day. He went on to join Alpha Gamma Rho and graduated from Cornell University.

His professional life is marked by transformation. He began in the farm equipment business and migrated in the early 80s to the nascent personal computer industry. Next, he learned about smart cards, a credit card-sized plastic card with a computer chip to store information. He transitioned this expertise to manage the global migration from magnetic stripe to smart card technology at MasterCard.

He has been fortunate to have traveled across the globe visiting six continents and having lived in multiple cities in the US and Australia. Beyond his passion to write, Drew enjoys gardening, cows, woodworking and used to love travel – today it's just hard.

He is very proud of his family. Judy is a college professor, son John, a commercial truck driver, and daughter Lizzy is a Captain in the Army currently stationed in Vicenza, Italy. All doing incredible things.

Transitioning again, today he is loving the freedom of writing novels where the only limits are what you can imagine. He lives with his family in the Ozarks of Missouri, enjoying the calm of Midwest life.

https://www.drewthorn.com

About the 2nd Edition

You may be wondering why a new release. Over the past year since first releasing The Pinnacle Club, I've learned so much about writing a novel. I felt a revision would improve the book. Some of the things I've learned:

My writing in the past had been primarily technical. When writing standards, proposals, or white papers on very technical things, it's important to be accurate and present the entire information in a very organized manner. As a friend summarized the style: beginning, middle, end, and sometimes repeat. However, in a novel, if you break a scene and move part of the scene to another section, it can create tension or suspense.

The concept of point of view took me a long time to understand. Basically, a hard rule in a novel is that a scene can only be from one character's point of view. So, for example, if Sandy is thinking about another person or situation, Morgan can't have her thoughts in the same scene. She can have a conversation providing her thoughts as speech.

Showing not Telling: telling the reader about an event isn't as effective as showing. It's better to create a dialog to show the event through someone's eyes and senses.

There's a whole long list of words you should avoid or use sparingly; that, thing, was, really, very... In general, they tend to be fillers and not move the story forward.

Cover – I liked the first cover, but it seemed a bit simple. My good friend Steve Bassett worked with me to design a new, more exciting cover. He is also an amazing author – you should check out his books under his penname Eli Pope. His books are dark and an emotional roller coaster.

Favorite Authors

There are so many authors that I enjoy. Their command of the craft inspires me to do even better. Here are just a few from over the years.

Jim Kjelgaard wrote 'Big Red' and many others, is the first author I remember from grade school. He mentioned a "Tarbox" in one of his novels. I wrote to him and asked about it. He had passed but his wife wrote a wonderful letter back that I will always remember and set me on this path.

Some well-known favorite authors

David Baldacci	Steve Berry	Dan Brown
Tom Clancy	James Clavell	Cleo Coyle
Clive Cussler	John Grisham	Louis L'Amour
James Michener	Robert Frost	Rachael Treasure

Authors I know and work with every week

Every other week a sub-group of the Springfield Writers Guild gets together to critique and support each other's work. These folks have helped me so much over the past year, words aren't enough. The following are published authors and playwrights. I love all of their works. For a full list of the thriller group see the credits at the beginning of the book.

J.C Fields	www.jcfieldsbooks.com
Eli Pope	www.elipope.com
Antim Straus	www.antimstraus.com
Malcolm Tanner	www.malcolmtanner.com
Ann Stang	Find her on Amazon

Made in the USA
Middletown, DE
20 September 2024

61198937R00182